SACRED TIES

LAYLA GRIM

Published by Layla Grim

Second Edition

ISBN: 979-8-9905953-0-9

Cover Design and Interior Formatting by ANKBookDesigns

BAD BITCH CLUB

The QR code has all of my socials.

It also has a Spotify playlist for the boys mentioned in this book.

I've got a lot of people to thank and I will definitely miss half the people I need to thank for this story. I thank Booby even though you will never read this (do not read this). I also thank Koyena; I am terrible at expressing myself but I truly thank you so much. I thank every person from the fandom for supporting me with everything I published. A few of these include Abi, Aysha, Marta, Bella, Tooty Frooty, Em, Sam, Ann, Cecil, Marta, Evee, Taylor, Keziah, Kata, Ava, Mattie, Azariah, Kiara, Hailey, Cristy, Mara, Chloe, Kshitika, Cheyanne, Sileiny, Emma, Marysia, and Aditi. I've missed many, many of you bad bitches but I love you all and thank you!!

SERIES NOTICE

This story is apart of a series. It is the first book in the standalone series. Each book can be read separately, but it is best consumed if read in order. Each book will follow one of the boys. There are a few loose plot points toward the end of the book. This is on purpose; it will be explained in a different book.

CONTENTS

VERSE ONE

"How much longer are you going to be?" My phone was propped between my ear and shoulder as I tied the garbage bag shut. My dad's heavy breathing was on the other side of the phone.

He was somewhere in his office, finishing the last bit of outlining for Sunday's sermon. Wednesdays were always our nights. He would work in his office at church, while I cleaned up. Afterward, we would go to Gianno's and split a hefty cheese pizza.

Tonight, though, he was taking longer than usual. My stomach ached and growled with every step I took. I hadn't eaten all day, awaiting our large pizza tonight.

"Almost done, honey." Dad let out a grunt before continuing. "My head is killing me."

"Probably because you're hungry." My stomach growled. "Can you please just hurry up?"

I tossed the trash bag over my shoulder, my back aching from the weight. Tonight, I went through the old hymn books that were too destroyed to donate or sell. Unfortunately, the garbage was where they were going to reside.

"Ten minutes. Promise."

I hummed in response before clicking the red button on my phone. I shoved it into the back pocket of my skinny jeans.

Thump. Thump. Thump.

Rain pattered down on the roof, intensifying by the second. I scowled, reaching for the hood of my jacket. I pulled it over my hair.

I pushed open the back entrance with my spine, keeping my head tilted toward the ground to avoid my glasses getting wet.

I sucked in a breath before making a quick jog for the trash can. Thunder cracked in the sky, and lightning illuminated the dark alleyway behind the church. I never liked coming out here on Wednesday nights; it was eerily quiet.

Every sense was on alert when I reached the trash can. The storm made the alley extra creepy tonight. Our town didn't have many homeless, or crack addicts, but it didn't make it any less eerie. We had murderers and a nonexistent police force. I would prefer the crackheads over some of the creeps in this town.

My stomach fluttered with nerves as I threw the bag into the large green garbage container.

I wiped my hands together, before shutting the lid of the garbage can.

"You shouldn't be out here this late."

I shrieked, jerking my head in the direction of the voice. I was able to get a quick glance of who spoke before my glasses were clouded with rain and humidity. He was hidden on the other side of the garbage can. I couldn't see his face, but I could see worn black Vans, loose black jeans, and a flash of pale white skin where a rip was in his knee.

My heart pounded so hard in my chest that it made my head shake. I couldn't see much now, due to my soaked glasses, but I had definitely caught a glimpse of someone on the other side of the trashcan.

I jumped again. Lightning illuminated our surroundings and thunder cracked loudly in the sky.

The brief bit of light made me catch a glimpse of something moving toward my feet. The liquid that was seeping down the road, and toward my feet, originated from my stranger cowering on the other side of the trashcan.

Blood.

I shouldn't approach a stranger in the dark, especially if I didn't have a form of weapon on me. I wasn't stupid. But, he could be hurt. There was blood. He had to be injured.

I slowly made my way toward him, pushing my glasses to rest on top of my head.

My vision blurred without my glasses, but I was still able to discern the boy limp against the trash can. His black hair stuck to his face, his clothes completely drenched, his hands covered in blood, and his thin fingers wrapped around the bottle of some liquor bottle. His head was slumped down, blocking his face from my view.

If it weren't for the satanic jewelry hanging from his neck, I wouldn't be able to recognize him.

But, I did recognize him. Unfortunately.

Bishop.

"Bishop." My voice came after a second of staring at him. I debated running inside and calling the police. I doubted they would do anything.

My feet stayed locked to the pavement. I really, really wished it was a crackhead instead of Bishop.

Nonetheless, I continued. "Are you hurt?"

He slowly looked up the length of my body. His eyes were hooded, due to the alcohol, but I was able to catch sight of his pale green. My body tensed. It felt sinful for him to be looking at me. Especially in the way he currently was. If Dad were to walk out here, he would never forgive me for even looking Bishop's way.

His eyes only held my own for a second, before they slid down to my neck. Goosebumps spread across my collarbones. It felt like his fingers were there, lingering against my skin. He looked to my heaving chest, then to my stomach, and down toward my thighs. Every place he touched resulted in my heart rate picking up, and the phantom linger of him sliding down over me.

My body was decently covered. I wore jeans, a white tank top, and a red cardigan. He was looking at me like I was completely naked.

I looked at his hands. There was blood. A lot of it.

Crimson was dried beneath his nails, on the palm of his hands, and seeping into the puddle of water collecting beneath him. But, there was no sign of a wound anywhere, unless it was on his palms.

"No one hurts me," Bishop slurred.

I could smell the alcohol from here. I could smell his scent; cigarettes, alcohol, and occasionally laced with the reek of marijuana. The scent of a boy trying to numb whatever was going on between his eyes.

"Bishop, you can't be here." I lowered my voice. I looked up toward the window where I knew my dad was working. If he saw Bishop, he would perform an entire exorcism in this alleyway.

Bishop didn't just praise Satan like I praised God; Bishop was the Devil. To this church, at least.

He looked down at his hands and then at the bottle between his legs. A weight lifted from my shoulders when his eyes left my body; it felt like he was pinning me to the ground, committing vile acts, with just his eyes. But, when he was looking at his hands, I was free.

No one hurts me. He lied. Something, or someone, definitely could hurt him. Even if it was himself. He was hurting himself now, poisoning himself with the alcohol and cigarettes he consumed. The blood on his hands didn't help his case. Something was hurting him. Bad.

His lips moved deeper into a frown, before taking another shot of the alcohol. Half the bottle was gone already.

It was strange seeing him like this; the boy who terrorized my dad's church. He was a vile, cruel man who brought nothing but pain to this town. Specifically, to the building we currently stood beside. But, apparently, even the Devil could ache.

I looked up to the sky, praying to God that this not be my time. I took in a lungful of air before approaching him. "Come on," I muttered, crouching down in front of him.

I wrapped my fingers around the neck of the bottle. To my surprise, he did not retaliate. I was taking his comfort, the elixir that was helping him through whatever was upsetting him on this Wednesday night. I rolled it down the alleyway, watching as the rest of its contents diffused with the rainwater on the street.

He muttered a few cruel words beneath his breath, like "fucking prude" or "stupid bitch." I ignored him, knowing it was just the alcohol forcing the words out of his mouth.

The tension returned to my chest when he moved his gaze back to my body. My breath caught. I looked down at his hands, not wanting to meet his eyes. Even without looking at him, I could feel every part of my body he was staring at. Again, it moved from my chest to my legs, and then back to my chest.

There was a small bit of space between his legs, where the bottle once was. I moved from my crouching position to a kneeling position between his knees. Thankfully, nothing of his legs touched my thighs. That in itself would cause me to shriek loud enough for Dad to come running down to see such an atrocious sight.

I stared down at his hands, forgetting what I was even planning on doing. There was a small inch of space separating his knees from touching my thighs; I could feel the electricity of his aura seeping into my skin. I wanted to move, just a little, to feel what it would feel like. For his knees to be touching such an intimate part of my body.

I didn't.

I blinked a few times before reaching for his left hand. My hands were trembling when I grabbed the back of his hand, facing his palms upward. It was where most of the blood was coming from. My fingers rubbed against his palm, letting the rainwater wash away the blood.

There was no wound.

I'd rather a wound than someone's blood be on his hands.

I reached for the other hand, repeating the process. As before, there was no wound, only confirming my suspicions.

This was not his blood.

Bishop was boring a hole into my face; it caused my hands to tremble more. It felt like he was analyzing me. Every movement. Every mannerism. He was memorizing me.

That terrified me, more than the blood.

I pulled my hands away from his. My throat dried. Bishop felt so intense, everything about him. Even if he was not uttering a word. The last time I saw him was in this alley, about a month or two ago. He had a bottle of black spray paint in one hand, and a carton of pig's blood in the other.

I was the one who ended up cleaning the words "God is a fucking joke" and "Christians will rot" from the side of my dad's church. I also scrubbed the pig's blood off the walls for hours, before my dad was able to see any of the vandalism. It would hurt him. Bishop wanted to hurt him.

I pushed myself back onto the heels on my feet, but I remained kneeling in between his legs.

Something was wrong with him. I could see it in his eyes. There was something going on behind the green; something only his alcohol could reach.

"Did you drive?" I asked, looking toward the end of the alleyway. There was no sign of a car.

He tensed before shaking his head. His gaze moved down toward the silver cross sitting against my pale flesh. Bishop scrunched his nose, judging it the same way I judged his sigils. We were both hypocrites for that.

With a grunt, I pushed myself away from him, collapsing against the small space beside him. The church wall was to my left, the garbage can to my back, and Bishop to my right. I was completely encased.

I should have stayed kneeling.

His thigh was pressed firmly against my own, denim on denim. I felt the heat radiating through his loose black jeans, and seeping into my tight blue ones. His bony hip pushed against my soft hip, and our shoulders were so tight together it was as if we were combined at the joint.

Shit, why didn't I sit on the other side. I had a little bit of roof protecting me from the rain on this side, but I was practically on top of him.

His head tilted to face me. I kept my eyes down on my knees, feeling his hot breath against the side of my face. Again, I could feel where his eyes traveled. Goosebumps rose and trailed behind his gaze, warning me of his intention.

His eyes were glued to my chest; the cross necklace I wore was his peak interest right now.

I didn't know why he hated my religion so much. My God. I didn't like him, but I didn't hate what he believed in. I didn't go out of my way to ridicule him for it; something was implanted deep into his soul at birth. Hatred. For God, specifically.

My heart sped up, ramming dangerously fast against my ribcage. He reached up for the cross necklace, fiddling it between his fingers.

I reached for his wandering hand, pulling it away and dropping it at his thigh. If he were sober, he would have ripped it straight from my chest. Bishop Black had graduated before I attended Northside High School, but I had heard some of the stories regarding him. Girls from church told me about how terrible and blasphemous he had been; he would rip their cross necklaces from their necks.

There were five of them in high school. Now, there were four. Cain, the lone man of the group, had disappeared a year ago. Fled from this town. I didn't blame him. This town was cursed. But, it was cursed because of Cain.

The five of them were spoiled little brats, putting it lightly. Cain, Coen, and Bishop attended Northside before I entered school. Solomon was a grade above me, and Baylen, the youngest, attended Southside High School.

Cain, Solomon, Bishop, Coen, and Baylen; the reason this town was cursed. They believed they were above the law, and with Cain, they were. But, Cain was gone. Their protection was gone. Now, they were the same as I was.

Solomon was the only one I spoke with, once. I needed help with an AP Calculus assignment, and he just happened to be the smartest person in this town.

I reached for my phone, clicked on Solomon's contact, and rang his line. My heart pounded in my chest. I was all too aware of his eyes glued to my chest. He was probably imagining how he was going to rip it from my neck and terrorize me. Dad always warned me to stay away from him, yet here I was.

"Who is this?"

I jumped hearing Solomon's voice rip through the phone.

I looked at Bishop, our faces so close I had to back my head against the wall to avoid grazing our lips together. He was asleep. Or awake. I didn't know, I couldn't tell anymore.

"Um. Hi. I'm Ethel." I hesitated, watching Bishop's eyes open in the slightest. His gaze moved to my lips. He fixated on them as if they were the most peculiar thing he'd ever seen. "I don't know if you remember me, but your friend Bishop is plastered outside of my dad's church right now. Can you come get him?"

I stared up at the rain, trying to calm my shaky breath. My phone was most likely ruined now due to how wet it was getting, but the idea of going inside and leaving him out here felt wrong. Like I was leaving a ticking bomb to explode.

"Yeah. Be there in ten," Solomon replied. I opened my mouth to say thank you, but he hung up the phone before I was able to properly respond. Jerk.

My breath hitched feeling cold, wet fingers. His digits brushed against the cross necklace. I didn't push them away this time. I only watched his fingers curiously. They were pale, like the rest of him, and his nails were painted a chipped, black hue.

His fingers slid down, away from the cross, and fell lower. And lower. I stopped breathing and every muscle in my body went stiff. My chest stopped heaving, watching his wandering fingers nervously.

I didn't even realize how exposed I looked in the white tank top. I wasn't wearing a bra, and due to the rain, Bishop was able to see everything. My nipples were tight, cutting through the thin fabric, jotting outward for his viewing pleasure. If he looked hard enough, he could even see a pink hue.

Shit.

Upon realizing this, it wasn't just goosebumps beneath his touch; it was pure fire. Like, electricity was pulsing out of his fingers and into my skin, wherever he touched. If I was able to breathe, I'm sure I would be gasping at how strange it felt with his skin against my own.

Bishop moved his fingers over my tank top, grabbing my right nipple between his thumb and index finger.

The drunk little shit pinched my nipple.

I gasped, slapping his hand away. He grinned, letting his head fall against the garbage can behind him. He stared up at the sky like he had not just squeezed my nipple. It was harder than it was before. So hard that it was hurting against the fabric of my tank top.

"You look good when you're wet," he mumbled, his hands falling back into his lap. His lips were ajar, head limp against the trash can. His breathing began to slow as he slipped in and out of unconsciousness.

I really really hoped he was blacked out right now. It was terrible for me to wish upon someone, but he had certainly just seen my entire breast through the thin, wet, white tank top I was wearing.

My cheeks grew hot. Bishop was the first man to ever see me like this. He was also the first man to ever pinch my nipple. That was not a good thing. This entire situation was terrible. Shit, I hoped Solomon would be here soon.

I pulled my jacket tight against my body; I was now hyper-aware of just how bad white tank tops and water mixed. He wouldn't remember it in the morning. He wasn't able to stay awake for more than ten seconds, which had to be a sign of being blackout drunk.

We sat in silence for the next few minutes. Occasionally, he would wake up, and look at me, before falling back asleep. It was like he was checking to see if I was there. Hopefully in the morning, he would think I was just a drunk hallucination.

A few minutes later, Solomon arrived in the alleyway. It was like an instant break through the tension; I could finally breathe again, knowing someone else was here to soak in the thick air between us. To buffer through the feeling floating around our air, of what could have happened.

"Shit," Solomon muttered, stepping out of his Mustang. Compared to the rest of them, Solomon's car was trash. Cain had bought them all fancy, expensive cars, from various foreign countries. Solomon's black Mustang was nothing compared to the cars sitting in their driveway.

I shifted, weaseling my way out of the confined space. Solomon looked down at his inebriated friend for a second, his gaze softening, before reaching down for him.

Bishop looked different when he slept. He looked peaceful. Like he wasn't on the verge of punching everyone in this town, for shits and giggles.

I reached down for Bishop, grabbing his right arm, whereas Solomon grabbed his left. We hoisted the tall man to his feet, pushing him toward the Mustang. He was the tallest of all of them, though he was also the thinnest. He was around six foot four, but his weight was concerning. He was nothing but skin and bones, as of recently.

He was spiraling. Even an outsider, like me, could determine that.

His hand reached up for my face, before slowly sliding down my front side, and falling limp to his side. Was that a reflex? He was asleep, it had to be a reflex. His face rested against my shoulder; his breath, and lips, were rubbing against the small bit of skin between my neck and shoulder.

Everything was so, so sensitive. I could feel every breath he took, every movement, every heartbeat.

Solomon let go of him, forcing me to hold onto all of his weight as he opened the back door.

The lips on my neck slowly slid into a curve, his teeth now grazing the flesh that he was once sleeping against. Scratch that, he was definitely awake. I gasped as his teeth gently sunk into my skin, and he sucked on the flesh in between his teeth.

"Bishop," I warned, pushing him off of me and into the backseat. His body fell unconscious into the backseat, but I knew he was awake. I reached up for the skin, feeling the bruise already forming.

Bishop was now the first boy to see my nipple, pinch my nipple, and give me a hickey. All in one night.

"Thank you," Solomon muttered, ignoring that I was clamping my hand down on my neck. He didn't look up at me once. He pushed Bishop's legs into the car and slammed the door shut behind him. He moved toward the driver's seat, starting the car, and leaving me in the alleyway like nothing had happened.

Strange. Every last one of them was strange. Terribly, horrifyingly strange.

I rubbed at the sore patch of skin on my neck, making my way back toward the church. I shivered, slamming the back door shut behind me. I leaned my head against the door, welcoming the warmth of the church like it was a blanket.

It was going to be hard to explain to Dad why I was soaking wet, and out there so long. Maybe I locked myself out? That would be a good excuse. If I told him that I just helped the bane of his existence find safety, I would be an absolute shame to him.

Shit. I just helped the bane of his existence, and he gave me a hickey. Not to mention the nipple pinch.

I reached for the cross necklace to fiddle with it.

It was gone.

VERSE TWO

"**G**randma!" I squealed, wrapping my arms around her neck. I stood up on my tiptoes to reach her height.

I hadn't seen her in over five years. The last time I saw Grandma and Grandpa, was at my mom's funeral. All of my family lived in Florida, making it too far to drive to them and visit.

"What are you feeding her?" Grandma asked, squeezing me harder against her. The last time she saw me was when I was thirteen years old. I had grown since then, seeing as I was eighteen now. "She's gotten so big."

Guilt crept up my stomach. We could have at least tried to visit them. We lived over eight hours away, but it was worth the drive to see her.

Something happened at the funeral, though. Dad and Grandma got into an argument, and since then we haven't spoken. I never asked what happened, but from the way Dad acted after, I knew it was bad. He refused to speak about his own mother, and when he did, it was a seethe.

Grandpa walked in shortly after, joining in on the hug. I smiled, looking up toward Dad. He stood in the corner of the room, watching the scene unfold before him. His arms were crossed over his chest, his lips settled in a deep frown, and his eyebrows furrowed.

He wasn't happy.

"We are late. We should get going," Dad huffed. He grabbed my bicep, pulling me away from them.

Silence and tension swarmed around the room as we broke our hug. Grandma and Grandpa were staying at a hotel, despite us having a guest bedroom. Again, I did not question what happened, but the tension from five years ago was still here. My high school graduation was a few months ago, that was the only reason Dad let them fly up to visit.

Tension aside, it did not matter. They were here.

"Ethel," Grandma began, her lips deepening into the same frown Dad wore. "Why don't you ride in the car with Grandpa and me?"

"No," Dad snapped. He grabbed his coat from the rack beside the door. "We can all ride together."

His service started in an hour. But, he always liked to get there early to review the sermon. Occasionally, members of the congregation would come early to be prayed upon by him. We were certainly running late compared to our usual Sunday routine.

I smiled at Grandma, ignoring the feeling in the room. Our families never got along. Never. Mom's side of the family fought with Dad's. Grandma always fought with Dad. Aunt's always fought with uncles. Truly, it was a curse upon our family.

I just trusted Dad.

We hopped into Dad's minivan and drove toward the church. I wore a black sweater, a pair of black leggings, and some black sandals to match.

It was getting cold. Fast. Winter was going to be bad this year. It was only September, and the town was nearly frozen over.

Dad's church was more casual compared to other churches outside of our town. It was the only church in town, so dress attire usually didn't matter to Dad. Fishnets, short skirts, and any extreme graphic tees were usually frowned upon, but at the end of the day, he didn't care. Just as long as they were there.

He was a good preacher for that. A good man.

There was only one person in this town that he had forbidden from ever stepping foot in his church. He just so happened to have given me a hickey a few nights ago.

Once we reached the church, Grandma and Grandpa took their seats in the front row. They left me a seat in between them, while I made my way outside. Dad went into his office, like he did every Sunday, and reviewed the sermon one last time.

I stood at the front door of the church with an armful of welcome brochures in my hand. It usually had the outline of the sermon, a few quotes, and the highlights of the church's community. This week's main highlight was Mrs. Davis; she announced her fifth pregnancy.

I smiled and nodded at everyone entering the church. I muttered a welcome under my breath with every guest and passed out the brochures.

I wasn't a social person. At all. Church was the only place I was semi-social, but even here, I was still anxious.

I reached up for my *new* cross necklace, fiddling with it between my fingers.

I leaned against the door and took a deep breath as another break came. The church crowd usually came in flocks. There would be a large group, and then a break for about ten minutes.

A pair of footsteps came from up ahead. I grabbed a hold of a brochure, ready to greet whoever was approaching.

My smile fell when a *sober* Bishop came into view.

There was a joint between his lips and smoke was seeping out of his nose. The smell was strong. So strong. I did not doubt that the people in the back pews were able to smell the marijuana.

"What are you doing here?" I seethed. I shut the church door behind me, stepping outside to block him from entering the church. He had a terrible history with churches. This church. He had an awful history to do with Christianity in general; he hated anyone who dared wear a cross around their neck.

The only time he ever came to church was to ruin the service, yell some vulgar obscenity, or vandalize the property. As of recently, he had been preferring vandalization over everything. Unfortunately, I was the one who cleaned it up.

"That's not very inviting of you, now is it? *Church girl.*" He kept walking toward me, into the little space left between us. My back was pressed hard against the door, unmoving. I would stand here all service if it meant him not going in there. This was the first service Grandma and Grandpa had seen in over five years.

Bishop's eyes moved down toward my chest. I recalled the last time he saw me, and how exposed I was to him. "Isn't the 'House of God' supposed to be inviting for everyone?" He said 'House of God' like it was something bitter on his tongue.

"Bishop," I warned. My voice was shaky; he was still slowly walking toward me. My back was pressed so hard against the wood I was on the verge of seeping into the door.

He smiled, flashing his ridiculously perfect teeth in my direction. I thought that they would be rotten, or falling apart, given how much he smoked and drank. Every time he entered the church to vandalize, he had his friends with him; a drink, and a cigarette.

The sight of him smiling was an anomaly in itself; it felt like he was going to burn down the church if I made one wrong move.

"What do you want?" I repeated. My glasses slid backward due to having to look up at his towering figure. He had to be almost a foot taller than me. I gulped, tilting my head further upward to reach him.

My breath was lodged in my throat somewhere. He leaned forward, brushing his three middle fingers directly above where my pulse was hammering embarrassingly fast against my skin. My lips parted; I had forgotten what his skin felt like against my own. I stifled the quiet gasp I wanted to make.

This was not normal.

I looked up at him, watching him with rounded eyes. He took a final step toward me, pinning my body hard to the door. Every brochure in my hands fell to the ground; that was another first. Bishop was the first boy to ever put his hips against my own.

"Bishop," I gasped. This time I couldn't conceal it.

If Dad, Grandma, or Grandpa came out right now, I don't think I would ever hear the end of it. I would be sent to a different state for so much as being in a presence as sinful as his.

"A gift." I flinched when he spoke. He sounded different when he wasn't drunk. His voice was deep, and raspy, like he hadn't slept in days. "For helping me."

I furrowed my eyebrows together, my gaze unmoving from his. His fingers gently traced the pulse point, before dropping down toward my hand. He pried my fist open and dropped a small cloth bag into my hand.

I couldn't speak or move. I clenched my hand around the bag and slowly nodded my head. It didn't feel like there was a finger in the bag, or some other vile object. But, I refused to open it in front of him; I didn't want him to have the satisfaction of seeing my face whenever I saw whatever cruel *thing* was in there.

A car door slammed shut, and a large group of guests made their way toward the church. I placed my hands on Bishop's chest, pushing him off of my body. Thankfully, he bulged. However, he did make sure to step on every last brochure in the process. He twisted his foot, destroying them all with the bottom of his shoe.

"I will see you soon, church girl." I did not doubt that. The way he said *church girl* was like he was promising something I wanted nothing to do with. My thighs tightened, and I shook my head. I couldn't speak. I was stunned.

His eyes moved down toward my thighs, and then back up toward my face. I wondered if he could see how he was impacting me. Every limb his eyes touched pinned me harder to the door, even though there was a foot of space between us now.

I didn't have time to protest. He was already gone by the time I regained my composure.

"You okay?" I looked up at the woman standing in front of me; she looked toward the brochures at my feet. I nodded, opened the door, and disappeared inside. It was close to the service anyway. They could pick up their own damn brochures.

I leaned against a pillar, slowly opening the bag to see what was inside. A necklace slid out and pooled into my shaky palm. I pulled it upward by the clasp; there was a name written in silver script.

Bishop.

I scoffed, shaking my head. Did he actually want me to wear his name around my neck? Did he think I would? Like some sort of dog?

Another item fell from the bag. I grabbed the folded piece of paper and slowly opened it up.

A replacement, the paper read.

I reached up for my neck, but once again, the cross necklace was gone.

VERSE THREE

Routines were good. I liked routines.

Ever since I graduated from Northside, my week had become routine. On Sunday I would help Dad with church and go to dinner after. Wednesday, I would wait for him to work in the office, while I cleaned the church and organized various cabinets.

For the rest of the week, I read and wrote; my goal was to write a novel by the end of the year. But, given how fast the holidays were approaching, I doubted I was going to make it through my first manuscript.

I slid in my AirPods, grabbing a hold of the trash bag. As usual, I started my Wednesday cleaning with the trash. My plan today was to deep clean the church; this usually consisted of taking out the trash, wiping down all surfaces, vacuuming, and moping. I never really knew; I just opened the cleaning supply closet and saw what looked interesting.

My spine hit the backdoor, pushing it open. I squinted up toward the sky, examining the setting sun. Unlike last week, it wasn't raining today. Thankfully.

I threw the trash bag into the trash can and shut the lid. My eyes lingered on the spot Bishop and I had been sitting a week ago when he drank his entire weight in alcohol. My stomach twisted at the memory, but I ignored it.

I reached for the door handle, attempting to pull it open, but a foot stopped it from swinging open. I looked down toward the foot first; a black shoe was pressed against the bottom of the door. Attached to said shoe was a long leg, and familiar black jeans.

I didn't even need to turn around to know Bishop was behind me.

"You can't be here," I informed, my back still toward him. I jerked one of my AirPods out, listening to his breathing behind me. How did I not see him when I walked out here?

My hand rested on the door handle; the second his foot moved, I was going to dart inside and lock myself in. He didn't smell of alcohol, nor was he stranded in the pouring rain. I did not feel bad if I was to leave him out there.

"So you keep saying," he replied.

His fingers brushed against my jugular; his touch was so light, it was almost cruel. I jerked my head away from his digits, before turning to face him.

I didn't realize how close we were standing until my hips brushed against his. I looked at his hips first, then back up to his face. "What are you doing here?" I asked. My breath was embarrassingly shaky; even a blind man could tell I was nervous.

He smiled, taking a step forward. Into me. Every part of his body was flush against me; breasts against chest, hips against hips, breath against breath. I tried to back further into the door, but I was going to break the wood if I pushed myself into it anymore. "Waiting for you."

My body shuddered as his eyes left my face, touching everywhere but my eyes.

I laughed. Hard.

The alcohol must have destroyed every last bit of sanity he had left. And judgment. "No," I began, shaking my head. I was looking up at him, but his gaze was still elsewhere on my body. "No. No. This is not happening."

I wasn't sure what exactly this was, but it wasn't going to be happening. Showing up Sunday was beyond crossing the line; at this point, Bishop was drawing a completely separate line miles away from the first.

I placed my hand on his chest, attempting to push him away. It didn't work. He took a step closer, and my palms became too aware of his bone and heat beneath my touch.

I choked. His body wasn't just against mine now. It was hard against me. Every possible inch of flesh was pressed hard against my own; the only thing not touching me was his face. And, from the way he was looking at me, I prepared myself for that too.

"Yo-you have a thing about pushing me against doors," I stuttered, looking down at my hands. They were still pressed against his chest, though I wasn't trying to push him away anymore.

God forgive me for how my body is reacting to this.

"You have a thing about standing in front of doors."

I found the courage to look back up toward him. I prayed to God he was oblivious; that he couldn't feel how quickly my chest was rising against him. He was fixed on my breasts. He had to have seen how fast they were rising and falling.

Bishop was not a good person. He never had been. Of his little friend group, whenever violent bidding needed to be done, it was Bishop or Baylen they called to finish the job. It explained why there was so much blood on his hands last week.

But, there were worse people in this world; Baylen was one of them. Even an all-forgiving God would turn his back on Baylen.

A rough tongue grazed over my neck. I trembled, attempting to push him off of me. His mouth was hovering over the patch of skin that was faintly bruised from last week; he clamped his teeth down, making the pink bruise turn red. "Bishop," I hissed, pushing harder at his chest.

He obliged, lifting his face in front of mine. I narrowed my eyes at him, gritting my teeth. He was completely sober, yet he was still acting as he did when blackout drunk. Was this just how he was? Invasive?

"I don't like this," Bishop admitted, trailing his fingers down toward the third cross necklace. I grabbed a hold of the crucifix before he was able to wrap his sticky fingers around it; I'd be damned if he stole another necklace from me.

"Good for you. Personal space."

He didn't move. He tilted his head, looking at me like I said something worth pondering about. He reached up for my hair, examining the blonde strand he was wrapping around his fingers. He looked at it like it was the most peculiar thing he had ever seen in his life.

I feared my legs were going to give out.

His eyes dropped down toward my cleavage, then to my hands holding onto his shirt. I didn't even realize I had adjusted my fingers to dig into his shirt.

I never understood sex. It felt good to rub one out every once in a while, but I never understood how primal it made people. How natural it came to people in the books I read; how responsive it was.

Until now. My body was reacting to him, and I was restraining myself from indulging in how good his body felt against mine. God forgive me. It was a responsive feeling, one I never thought I would feel in my life.

Another first.

"You can have your necklace back. I'd die before I'm seen wearing your name around my neck," I snapped, narrowing my gaze into slits.

He tugged his lips between his teeth, and for a second I wondered how they would feel between my own. "You will one day. You will wear my name," he began. My breathing became heavy as his fingers moved away from my chest and toward my throat. His touch was lighter than anything I had ever felt; it was so gentle, so merciful.

It didn't feel like Bishop.

His hand moved toward my throat, whispering against the skin. "My hands."

"You're bold," I said, swatting his hand away. His eyes lit up for a second until I reiterated. "In a creepy way."

"You're nervous."

Bishop took a step away from me, my front side instantly feeling empty without the feeling of skin on it. I thought he was leaving, but he grabbed my hip instead, spinning me around to face the door.

The sudden motion, and the press of the door against my chest, made me grunt. My hands flew up to the door and I planted my palms against either side of my head to steady myself. His chest returned to my body, this time resting against my back. He was so tall that the back of my head only reached his chest.

"I like you, church girl," Bishop admitted, leaning in toward my ear. I knitted my eyebrows together, listening to his words. "I'm going to have you."

A bitter laugh left my lips. "No, you are not."

"Yes, I am."

"No.

"Yes."

My chest was hitting the door with every breath. I could feel his breath sliding down the back of my neck. I felt his eyes slip to the nonexistent space between my ass and his groin. It was all I could focus on. I could feel it.

"Get a life," I snapped.

"Tell me about yours," Bishop responded quickly. It felt like he was born to be in this type of situation; like he was born to flirt. He could make a wall blush if he tried hard enough. He was making me blush, even though I wanted nothing to do with him. That was pure talent.

I smiled, pulling my bottom lip between my teeth. "No."

My smile fell soon after. His wet lips clamped down on the hickey again, sucking it between his teeth. He wasn't drunk anymore; he had no excuse as to why he was putting his mouth on my neck. But, God, he sure knew what he was doing with his mouth. Every goosebump, sensation, and rush of heat went straight between my legs.

"Bishop," I warned, though my head still fell backward against his chest. It was giving him better access to my neck; that should be a reason in itself to pull away from him. But, I didn't. I stayed still, allowing him to work with the flesh between his teeth.

His hand slid up, wrapping his fingers around my neck like the necklace he promised moments ago.

Why wasn't I moving?

"Go to dinner with me," Bishop hummed against my neck. He moved his lips to the other side of my neck, planting an open-mouthed kiss on the skin. He flawlessly found the part of my neck that made my eyes flutter.

"No." He responded by placing a kiss on the back of my neck. My body was tense, fighting the deep ache in my belly, and the logical side of my mind. No side was winning; I stood still, trying to figure out exactly what I was feeling.

I wanted to leave him in this alley, just like I should have left him a week ago. But, that didn't feel right.

I also wanted to turn around and replace my neck with lips. Just to taste him; to feel what it felt like to kiss a boy. But, that also didn't feel right.

Nothing felt right, but that did not mean it didn't feel good. His lips felt very good.

"But, you go to Gianno's with your father every Wednesday night. Not me?" His lips perked up against my skin. Every drop of blood in my body went cold, and my muscles tense against him. How did he know that? Was he going to kill me for witnessing the blood on his hands?

"You are stalking me," I panted. My face was an unnatural shade of red. I panted. Actually panted. He just admitted to stalking me in some form, or another, and I panted? Something was wrong with me.

"Solomon just needs a name."

Of course. Solomon. The boy genius that lived in this town. If you wanted information, it was Solomon you went to. He could find everything about your life with a simple name, as Bishop said. Every streetlight you have ever passed. Every class you have taken. Apparently what restaurants you eat at.

His fingers moved away from my throat, trailing toward the necklace I wore. Before I was able to stop him, he wrapped his hand around the cross and yanked it straight from my neck.

I scowled, pushing him off of my back.

He let me.

"Give it back." I narrowed my eyes, turning to face him. He opened his palms, showing me that he was not holding onto the necklace. I looked down toward the ground, around us, and even in his front pocket. The necklace was nowhere to be seen.

"Guess you will have to pat me down for it."

I rolled my eyes, crossing my arms over my chest. "I would buy a new one before I touch you."

I watched a muscle in his face twitch, and his lips curve into a grin. "You didn't seem to mind a few seconds ago."

"What do you want, Bishop?" I regretted coming out of the door behind me last week and I regretted coming out of it today.

I'd heard too much about him from his years at Northside. He had graduated a little over four years ago, but I believed him to be the same person. Especially after how he had been treating my dad over the years. He was a lonely boy, besides Cain, Baylen, Solomon, and Coen. Bishop didn't cross many people's paths; if he did, purposely, it was not with good intentions. But, for some reason, he was forcing himself into my path.

The thought made me shake.

"You knew that blood was not mine. You saw blood on a man who terrorized your father for years. I was drunk and vulnerable, and you still helped me. I'm going to have you for that." Bishop looked down at me like I was a meal he was literally about to eat. His eyes were constantly flickering from my feet to my face. I hoped he couldn't see how wobbly my balance was becoming, due to his words.

"On your hands, knees, back, and stomach, I will have you, Ethel," Bishop promised.

I shook my head, staring up at him with wide eyes. I believed every word that he had spoken. That terrified me. I couldn't even speak; if I did, it would come out as a croak, and I didn't want to give him that satisfaction.

My fingers trembled around the door handle behind me, but I was able to twist it open and slip inside. I shut the door, leaning my back against the wood. A door separated us, but I could still feel his presence on the other side. It was suffocating me.

He was right. He terrorized my father, and his church, for years. He used the only church in town to take out all of his pent-up anger. Graffiti, interrupting the service, letting snakes loose during the sermon, and once even setting a bible on fire mid-service.

He was a terrible, awful soul.

I leaned my cheek against the door, steadying my breath. I don't know what was worse; the fact that he wanted me, or that my stomach was aching just as badly. The area between my legs felt raw. It felt like he had just gotten done doing all the heinous acts he had running around in his head.

God, what did I get myself into?

VERSE FOUR

I t was three in the morning when I realized that I was not going to be able to get a wink of sleep. I tried. Occasionally, I would slip off into a dream, but I was awoken by the feeling of goosebumps trailing across my body. Fingers whispering against my skin. Lips clamping down on my neck, like he owned it.

I still felt him.

I could feel his hands lingering on my skin, so gently it felt as though he was afraid to break me. I could still see his eyes, telling a different story than his fingers. When I closed my eyes, I recalled how he looked down at me, like he wanted nothing more than to break me.

I sucked in a breath, reaching up for my neck. My fingers gently massaged the spot his lips had clamped down on earlier, sucking until a dark bruise had formed. He had marked me, branded me as his own; the thought of that made heat brew deep in my stomach.

My bed made a quiet squeak when I rolled over onto my back. I adjusted my legs, rubbing my thighs together to ease what was happening between them. Ache. Pure ache and need pulsated between my legs; it was painful how badly my core was reacting to him.

How could one person be so sinful, but feel so good?

I was embarrassed. I imagined him, standing in front of me, laughing at how worked up he was making me. Little church girl can't keep her legs closed after a few neck kisses, and some gentle touches.

There was a feeling about him. About his touch. It was like his hands, lips, and skin were made to be against mine. As if we were made to be touching each other. I wanted to find some other boy and ask him to touch me in the way Bishop had. To see if it felt the same with every other boy, not just Bishop.

I doubted it did.

My hands slid away from my neck and toward my cleavage. My breathing became staggered as I recalled the first night outside of the church; I was covered in rainwater, indecent to him.

I looked down at my nipples; they peeked through my cotton dress. I rubbed my thumb softly against the tightening bud, but it didn't feel the same. Nothing felt the same compared to Bishop. Why did he feel so good? Not just his touch, but also his presence. In the three times I have seen him, it felt like nothing but euphoria.

That terrified me.

My hands were beginning to work on auto-pilot, moving down my body before my brain was able to stop it. They slid down my stomach and landed in the heat between my legs.

But, it wasn't my hands moving; it was Bishop's. In my imagination, Bishop was sitting right above me, trailing his fingers gently down my torso. He would be looking down at me, at my shuddering body, with one thought in mind.

To break me.

I trembled, letting out another shaky breath. I slid my panties to the side, sliding my middle finger through my slick folds. I pulled the finger back up toward my face, examining the tip of it. I was soaked.

I hummed, returning my finger between my legs.

Bishop was going to be a first for a lot of things. First boy to give me a hickey. First to push me against a door.

First to make me wet.

With my pinky and thumb, I spread my lips further apart. I pressed the remaining three fingers down against my clit. My back arched upward to roll my hips harder against my fingers. I had to bite my lip to avoid a noise slipping out.

My clit was so sensitive. I had rubbed myself many times, but it had never been this sensitive before. Then again, I had never thought of Bishop in such a way before.

"Ah," I groaned beneath my breath. I started to rub slow circles against my clit, applying the perfect amount of pressure. I moved my head to the side, clamping my teeth down on my pillow, to avoid waking up the entire house.

In my mind, it wasn't the pillow I was biting into. It was Bishop's skin. I imagined his neck, sweaty from the acts we would be doing, muffling every noise that he forced out of me.

My breath was coming from my stomach now. My navel was rising and falling as fast as my breasts were.

I applied more pressure to my clit and sped up the circles around my pulsating bundle of nerves. My lips were ajar, and quiet pants were slipping out of my mouth. Shit, this felt way too good. Would it feel this good if it were Bishop's fingers?

My eyes moved upward, away from the pillow, and toward the lamp. I locked my gaze on the silver necklace engraved with Bishop's name. It hung from my lamp, glinting in the dim lighting. I refused to put it on, but I hadn't thrown it away.

A noise came from my chest and slid out of my throat without warning. It was a noise straight out of porn. I've never watched porn, but that was definitely what kind of noises they made.

It was carnal.

I clamped my eyes shut as my orgasm approached. Even the most faithful man on this planet could not deny how good an orgasm felt. But, imagining it was Bishop's hand on my clit? It made the orgasm otherworldly.

Quiet pants continued to come from my lips, and my fingers were starting to shake against my clit. I was rubbing so roughly it was beginning to strain my hand, but I didn't stop. It felt too good.

I wondered if Bishop would be gentle.

I tugged my lips between my teeth, gnawing so hard my lips bled. My mind went back to him, imagining it was him driving me to this orgasm. In my head, he would start gently, but from his eyes, I could see just how rough he liked it. He would hurt me; God forgive me, the thought of being hurt by Bishop made my pussy tighten and convulse.

I sucked in one last sharp breath, and my core clenched hard as release flooded my body. My fingers shook, unable to even move during the aftershocks of my orgasm. I could feel my entrance throbbing, convulsing, even though it was my clit I played with. My ears were ringing, and my vision was flooded with stars for a very short second.

Even my nipples were reacting to the orgasm. They had tightened so hard it hurt. I wanted his palms to cover my bare breasts and soothe how painful he was making my nipples.

"Shit," I cursed. I pulled my hand away, shame sliding up my body as the orgasm wore off. I wasn't ashamed of what I had just done; I was concerned by how ungodly it felt.

Another first. Bishop just made me come harder than I ever have, and he wasn't even here.

VERSE FIVE

For the past five hours, Gwen and I had been straddling this park bench, a set of papers between us. She would sloppily write down any ideas we came up with for raising money for the church, and other fundraising opportunities. Five hours later, we concluded that a bake sale would be the best approach for raising money.

Well, Gwen did. I just listened, staring at a paint chip a few inches from my thigh. I have been distracted all morning, thinking about a certain boy that I had come hard to the night before.

Gwen and I were usually the opposite; I would speak, and she would nod while zoning out at some spec on the floor. Now, the roles had reversed. She was saying something; I'm sure if I just listened for a second I would gather what we were supposed to be talking about right now.

I wondered why it felt so natural with Bishop. He acted like he knew me. If I'm being honest, it did feel that way; it felt like I knew him, without knowing him at all. I don't even remember his last name.

"Did you hear me?"

I jerked my head away from my paint chip, looking in her direction. She tucked a strand of her chestnut-colored hair behind her ear, looking down as a smile spread up on her face. She could tell I was not listening to a single word she was saying, and somehow it was amusing to her.

"Distracted?" Gwen asked, looking back up to me.

Gwen was a beautiful disaster. She was a bundle of chaos, trapped in skin, trying so hard to be graceful. She couldn't walk into a room without bumping into someone or knocking something over. Her hair was always pulled into a messy bun, with bumps and flyaways. She wore her previous night's sleep on her every day; dark circles beneath her large eyes, frizzy hair, and bloodshot eyes. She was wearing her black and white checkered pajama pants and a baggy black tee shirt.

"Sorry." I let out a sigh, pushing my glasses up my nose. "I got no sleep."

She laughed at this, pushing the sloppy piece of paper in my direction. I scanned it, seeing all the notes she had taken during our little "meeting" of sorts. Most of it was an outline of what she had been spewing, while I sat, lost in my thoughts. There were bullet points of simple things. Like how much we would make, and the price we should charge; she even doodled some ideas for cupcakes.

We said our goodbyes and agreed we would meet at my house whenever it came time to bake the food for our fundraiser. I hugged her, and we went our separate ways.

Gwen and I had been friends since I was little. She joined the church at a young age, with her older sister, and brother; however, it was just her there now. She admitted to me that she wasn't as religious as I was, and some days she questioned if God was even real. But, she was as active in the church as I was.

I think she used it as an escape, of sorts.

I never questioned it. She didn't want me to, so I didn't.

My house was only a few minutes from the park. I walked along the sidewalk, peering into a few of the stores as I passed by. Our town was small, so small; I loved it. We only had a few clothing stores, which I currently walked beside. We had one thrift store. One dress store. One bar. One shoe store.

Crimson was the only club in the town; it was the only source of real entertainment. Coen, Bishop's friend, was the owner of it. Given a literal nymphomaniac owned it, Crimson was a sex club of sorts.

And, of course, we had a single church in the center of the town. My dad's church.

My mouth dried as I passed the single bar we had in this town, besides the one in Crimson. The windows were tinted, so it was difficult to see inside, but there was no mistaking Bishop's lanky silhouette. Even if his back was to me, I would be able to spot his figure from a mile away.

He stared down at his cup on the bar top. His hands were balled up beneath his chin, holding his slumped head up. His elbows were lazily placed on the edge of the bar; at first glance, it almost looked like he was asleep.

He didn't see me.

I kept walking, keeping my gaze on the back of his head. My house was only three minutes away. I could walk home, be away from him, and act as if nothing had happened. My heart sank to my stomach; that was the boy who made me feel that way last night. His presence was enough to make my legs weak. Literally.

My legs grew heavy as I continued walking, ignoring him behind me.

It was noon. Why was he in the bar at noon? I don't know much about people's drinking habits, but noon was a little too early. I didn't even think bars were open this early to the public. Plus, he could have gone to Coen's club and drank half of his liquor supply for free. Why go here, and sit alone?

I stopped walking, scolding myself for what I was about to do. This is a bad idea. "Screw it," I muttered beneath my breath, turning back around to face the bar. I walked into the bar without a second thought in my mind.

VERSE SIX

The door chimed as I walked into the bar, but Bishop did not look up. He kept staring down at his cup, slumped in his seat. I watched his finger tap rapidly against the rim of his glass; that was the only indication I saw that he was awake.

A few other people were sitting at the bar, but most of them were munching on bar food. None of them sat alone, drinking, and sulking at noon. That was just Bishop, and whatever was happening behind his eyes.

I slid into the barstool beside him, my bare thighs grazing against the denim of his jeans. I was wearing a pair of running shorts and an oversized baby blue sweatshirt. I shifted in my seat when I realized how high the shorts were rising on my legs when I sat down.

He also noticed.

It was the first thing he noticed.

When he looked in my direction, his eyes landed on my bare legs first, and then my face. A trail of goosebumps spread wherever his eyes touched my body; my legs were covered in them. He wasn't trying to hide the fact that he was searching every square inch of my body.

I ignored him and how he was making my stomach burn inside. "Lonely?" I asked, looking up at the television above the bar. It was playing some sports game; I hated sports, but it was better than watching him stare at me.

I could feel his gaze on the side of my face now.

"You should show these more." I coughed when a hand unexpectedly came down on my thigh. His fingertips gently caressed the side of my thigh, moving up to my hip, and then to my knee. He pulled his hand away after feeling the smoothness of my legs, returning it to the bar top.

I refused to look away from the television. He would see how pink he made my face turn.

The touch caused everything from the previous evening to come back. The way he made me feel, without touching me at all. It was the heaviness of him, in my brain. It was completely, and utterly, haunting me. There was only one thing I could do to get rid of the thought of him.

Rub him out of me.

Literally.

And, even that wasn't working.

He was still there, living in my head, without paying a dime in rent.

"No," I bit. I slapped the hand that touched me, looking down at my legs. The left leg, which he touched, was now infested with goosebumps. The right one was smooth, untouched. How was my body so reactive to him? It felt like my legs were floating, even when sitting down.

It didn't feel like that when I was with Gwen. Bishop was the only person that made them feel like that.

He grunted, reaching for his drink. I smelled the whiskey from here. It was on his tongue; every time he spoke I could smell it, beneath the scent of cigarettes. When he came into my father's church, too many times, he smelled of it.

I reached for the drink before he was able to down the rest of it. I threw the liquid into the back of my throat, swallowing it before I was able to gag. I winced but was able to get it down. That had to be the strongest whiskey ever crafted.

"That was mine." He looked at me sideways. The right side of his lips perked upward. I was trying to hold back a cough. I wondered if that was what amused him.

"I was thirsty," I lied.

I lost my breath again. We stared at each other for a second too long. His gaze moved down to my lips, watching as I wiped a drop of whiskey away with my tongue. I didn't look away from him, though from my peripheral I could see how white his knuckles were becoming on top of his jeans.

I was going to need to pray after this.

"Why do you drink so much?" I asked, trying to break the thick air around us. Half of the reason I had come here was curiosity. Bishop was young, drinking at his age was one thing. Drinking in excess was another. But, drinking in excess, alone? That was a different beast entirely.

"What makes you say that I drink so much?" His head dipped down, looking at the bar top. This time, it was me staring at the side of his face. For the first time, since the evening in the alleyway, Bishop looked away from me.

Shame.

"Well, you are sitting here alone. Despite having four alcoholic friends—."

"Three," he interrupted. He pulled his chin up, staring at the television now. Shit. I forgot about Cain, and the groups falling out with him. "Continue."

"Sorry. Three alcoholic friends." I twisted myself in the barstool to face him. My knees pointed toward him, the bare smooth skin of my thighs rubbing against his rough denim. I shuddered at the feeling. "You don't want them to see you. Which means there is a reason."

I made a lot of observations and too many assumptions. It was what I hated most about myself. But, it was true. Coen, the owner of Crimson, had his own supply of alcohol. The four of them partied regularly; it was hard to ignore the loud thump coming from the house on top of the hill. Bishop easily could be with one of them, but he chose to be alone.

But, maybe I was wrong.

Every muscle in his jaw tensed and he had yet to look away from the television. I leaned my head against my palm, staring at him like he had his drink a few moments ago.

"Are you fed or something?" Bishop asked, letting out a huff. I was right. It was a weak spot for him, though, so I wouldn't pry on it anymore.

"Observant," I corrected.

"Maybe I just wanted to have a drink alone, church girl."

My spine straightened, a chill running down its entirety. The way he spat out "church girl" should be considered violent. It sounded as if he was going to turn in my direction and pounce on me for bringing up the sore subject.

I noted to myself to not bring that up again. I changed the subject, wanting to keep my throat intact.

"Will you walk me home?" I asked. It was a three-minute walk to my house. I was perfectly capable of walking home on my own. I did it every day. But, if he walked me home, he would close the tab.

He nodded. Once he closed the tab, he twisted to face me. The pulse in my throat quickened when he did. I looked down at our legs, seeing what the action did.

One of his long legs was now lodged between mine, and the other rested firmly on the other side of my thigh. Smooth against rough. I could feel the heat seeping from him. His body heat was a creature of its own. It crawled out of his body, into my pores, and resided happily inside of my own.

"Okay, let's go." My voice was embarrassingly shaky. I let out a nervous laugh, pushing myself off of the stool. I was sweating, despite it being the middle of fall.

I wiped my hands off, following him out of the bar.

He held the door for me, which I thought was kind until he was walking behind me. Then, his intentions were clear. "You have a nice ass."

"Bishop," I hissed, turning around to slap his bicep. A family was walking past, looking at the boy like he was insane for what he just said. Bishop grinned, staring down at me with his bottom lip between his teeth. "You're vulgar."

"You're beautiful."

A blush crept up my neck, spreading across my cheeks. I turned away from him so he wouldn't have the satisfaction of seeing how flustered he made me. How hot he was making me. God, forgive me, but how wet he was making me.

"You saw me for the first time like a week ago. You can't determine beauty that fast, I could have an ugly soul," I replied, once we were walking beside each other. His arms were brushing against mine, though it wasn't nearly as intimate as our thighs had been. My legs were still wobbly from that.

"No, I've definitely seen you before."

"Ah yes," I began, looking up at him. He was already looking down at me. I don't think he has looked away from me since we left the bar. "When you were vandalizing my dad's church?"

"Yeah." He grinned. He wore pride like a new set of skin. "I never vandalized you, though, did I? Church girl."

I looked down at our feet. My stomach fluttered so intensely that I was growing nauseous. Church girl. It was the way he said it. It was as if the two words were a vow; a promise of what was going to happen to me. My body. My soul.

"That's not the right word," I huffed.

"Would you prefer the word demolished?" Again, his words were laced with promise. Even if he didn't mean to do it. He was 'demolishing' my panties with every word that came out of his cruel mouth.

"Thank you for not 'demolishing' me," I said, air quoting the word. He was right. After everything he had done to the church, he never touched me. He never harmed me. He never even looked in my direction. He wanted to hurt my father for preaching what he believed, and I would have been the perfect way to do that.

But, he never took advantage of me.

"What were you doing last night?"

I choked on my saliva, jerking my gaze up at him. My face was on fire, and tingles spread to every inch of my body. I even stopped walking. How did he know?

"What?" I gasped, my eyes rounded.

Bishop's lip was between his teeth again. He smiled, looking down at me as if I was the funniest thing he had ever seen in his life. "At church. What do you do at church on Wednesday?"

"Clean." My voice came out as a croak.

"What did you think I meant?" I blinked, staring up at him. I was sweating even more than I had been in the bar. I was not a good liar. "Why does cleaning have you so flustered, Ethel?"

"It's hot," I lied, walking forward. I bumped his shoulder in the process. I kept my gaze on the ground, hoping my normal complexion would return soon. He laughed under his breath, continuing beside me. I could not have made it any more obvious.

A few seconds later, we stood at my front door. Dad wasn't home. It was noon, on a Thursday. Why wasn't Dad home? Usually, he was just out on Wednesday, Friday, and Sunday. He spent all Thursday at home to deep clean the house.

"What is your phone number?" Bishop asked, pulling me out of my thoughts. My back was to the door, again. But, he didn't press me against it. His eyes pinned me in place, instead.

"No."

"I will get it," he challenged. He took a step toward me. My back pressed harder into the door, but nothing of him touched me. It still felt like he was on top of me, though. His soul kept me in place against the flimsy wood.

"No, you won't," I countered.

"Wanna bet?"

I bent my neck upward, staring up at him. He wouldn't get my number. I rarely gave it out to people. Especially people like him. He would text me at two in the morning, for a late-night "booty call."

In his defense, I would have texted him last night if I had his number. Mid rubbing my clit.

"No invite to your bedroom." It was as if he was reading my thoughts. I shook my head fast, reaching for the door handle behind me.

"Never." I didn't go inside, but my fingers rested against the handle. I couldn't move. I couldn't look away from him. It felt good, his eyes scanning over my body like I was something he wanted to devour.

I only moved when my legs visibly began to tremble.

"I'm going to go inside now," I said. It felt like I was convincing myself, more than him. I hesitated a few more seconds, taking in his image one last time. God, I couldn't even open the door.

He didn't tell me goodbye, nor did I. I opened the door, shutting it fast behind me. I leaned against the wood, letting out a heavy breath I had been holding in.

I went into that bar to accompany him before he spiraled. But, as a result, I ended up spiraling.

VERSE SEVEN

I watched as my dad paced around the stage in front of me.

My cheeks were still slightly tear-stained from this morning. Me and Dad rarely fought, but when we did, it always ended with me in tears. This morning, the fight was regarding my career choice. He thought I was digging my own grave for wanting to be a writer when I grew up. It was what I was passionate about; however, he stated I would just "get knocked up. End up unemployed at home, cooking for my husband."

I loved my dad. I loved him with all of my heart. But, some days, it felt like he split. Like he was a different person over a single trigger.

Dad would go from a sweet man to a very angry man in a matter of seconds.

We were in the main sermon portion of the service. This usually took around thirty minutes of his preaching, and after this, we closed the service with a few hymns.

I always sat in the very front row. It was easiest for Dad to get to when the service was over. To my left was Grandma, and Grandpa on her left. There was an empty seat to my right, awaiting Dad once the hymns began.

I didn't even want to sit next to him right now. He expected me to get in the car, and move on, as if he hadn't proclaimed I would become a knocked-up stay-at-home whore. He acted like once the words were out, it was over with. That I was the one that needed to move on.

I looked down to my lap, where the hem of my dress had ridden up on my thighs. I shaved them this morning, just in case someone was to show up while I passed out brochures.

Since our little bar encounter, I had spent the days after thinking of Bishop. It felt like every second of the day was spent thinking of him, of whatever was brewing between us.

I deemed that there was definitely some sort of chemistry between us. As much as I wanted to deny it, it was there. God was strange in that way; putting those who you never expected on your path. I would have never expected Bishop, of all people, to be taking up some much time in my head.

I fiddled with the hem of my pale blue dress. Dad had made it his mission to never judge in the church, but when I walked out in the dress, he looked as if he were going to vomit. It was pushing it; I could see my cleavage, which I rarely showed.

I tried to wear my new cross necklace to distract away from the deep neckline, but it was still prominent.

Again, I could not help but think of a certain boy when pulling the dress on this morning.

My phone buzzed beside my thigh.

I looked down at the empty seat beside me, tapping on my phone screen. I rolled my lips together as I looked at the message.

UNKNOWN NUMBER: are you thinking of me?

My stomach fluttered when I read the words. How was he so flirty, without trying to be at all? I had no doubt this was my flirt texting me. I rarely socialized with people, let alone gave out my number.

ME: how did you get my number? creep.

I clicked a few buttons on my phone, trying to casually save his name as a contact. Everyone could see me if I was texting; I needed to make it as subtle as possible.

BITCHOP: all Solomon needs is a name, church girl.

I bit back a smile, looking at the contact name I had given him.

Solomon had my contact. But, even if he hadn't, he could get it. It was honestly scary how powerful Solomon was behind the computer. He could get anything if he merely had a name. Bishop would be able to know every detail about me if he wanted. Down to my bra size, and insurance company.

Solomon never spoke, but his skills with a computer were what made him terrifying.

I locked my phone again, looking back toward Dad.

My phone buzzed again.

BITCHOP: what r u thinking abt?

ME: not you.

BITCHOP: i'm thinking abt you.

A flush scattered across every inch of my face.

When I looked back up toward Dad, he was already looking at me as he paced the stage. He looked from me to the phone, and then back to the crowd.

That was disrespectful of me. I reminded myself to apologize to him later about being on my phone during his sermon. It was a sacred time, and here I was focused on someone who wanted between my legs.

God forgive me, he had unknowingly already been between them due to my tainted imagination.

My phone buzzed against my thigh. I almost scoffed, but I stopped myself.

BITCHOP: i like ur hair like that.

The hairs on my neck stood erect as I became aware of hot eyes focused on the back of my head. I slowly turned around, following the gaze that was burning a literal hole inside of me right now. I pretended to crack my back, making the motion as casual as possible.

Sure enough, my eyes locked with green.

He was sitting in the back row. He stuck out of the congregation, like a sore thumb. Everyone was dressed in colorful, playful floral clothing; their faces glowed listening to Dad preach.

Bishop, on the other hand, was wearing solid black. His face was deathly pale, like usual. He wore a few chains around his neck, though I noticed a few missing. He normally wore an upside-down cross and a sigil of sorts around his neck. But, today, he wasn't. This was the first time I'd seen him without it.

Was he being respectful of the sacred space?

He wasn't listening to the sermon. He looked like he was one second away from standing up and taking me in front of this entire congregation.

I turned back to face Dad. He hadn't noticed I was just staring at our vandalist in the back row. I reached for my hair, feeling the half up half down hairstyle, with two loose strands framing my face.

I blushed thinking about his words regarding my hair.

This was abnormal. He and I. Whatever was going on between us; this chemistry. It was wrong. He hurt my dad for years.

I reached for my phone, texting against the seat again.

ME: why are you here?

BITCHOP: listening to the word of god.

I crossed my arms over my stomach, looking away from my phone. Knowing he was here made this sermon agonizing. I could feel him staring at me now, every movement his eyes made against my skin. I hadn't noticed it before, but now?

It felt like his lips were on the back of my neck, fingers threaded through my hair. Occasionally, I could feel them move to the sensitive spot beneath my ear. It was as if he were touching me, despite sitting back there.

I adjusted in my seat, hoping it would aid some of the tension rolling down my spine, directly between my legs.

It didn't.

What is wrong with me?

Buzz.

BITCHOP: what am i doing to you in ur thoughts?

I blinked, staring down at the phone. Truly, it felt like he could read my mind. Maybe I had given it away somehow. Could he sense how tense I was becoming beneath his gaze, or how nervous my body language was?

BITCHOP: is it hard?

My breathing was growing so heavy that I was sure that Grandma could hear me. I ran a hand through my hair.

It would be rough.

I've determined that if anything did happen between us, it would end up rough. It would start slow, like we were soaking in the feeling of our auras intertwining together, but it would end up with hard, rough interactions.

When I thought of Bishop, sexually, a scene kept coming to mind. It's me, on my back, in my bed, with him hovering above me. My knees are pushed to my stomach, being pinned down by his body weight.

And he is pounding into me.

So hard, I'm crying from how good it feels. Begging him to give me mercy. Even if I don't know how sex feels, that is how I imagine it happening between us.

My throat dried. I had zoned out on the message he sent previously. During my dad's sermon. God, forgive me.

Whatever game, or thing, was going on between us, he was winning.

Another message rolled through as I was staring at the last.

BITCHOP: ur ears are red. it must be good.

I reached for the back of my head, itching my hair with my middle finger. Another first. Bishop was the first person I've ever flicked off, even discreetly. I hoped he saw it.

BITCHOP: flicking me off in church?

BITCHOP: naughty girl.

I had to wipe my hand down my face to control how red I had become. Following the naughty girl were three emojis. The first was the Devil emoji, the second was the peach, and the third was the palm of a hand.

There was no way he just insinuated spanking in the middle of church.

ME: i can't believe you haven't burst into flames yet.

BITCHOP: i can start a fire if u want.

A shudder ran through me. I slowly turned around to look at him. Again, I used the motion of cracking my back.

He was grinning ear to ear.

Bishop had not once, but twice started a fire in this church. Though, before he was not following me around like a dog in heat. But, such vile acts were in him; he had done it before.

My phone buzzed again.

BITCHOP: it was a joke, church girl.

ME: i'm turning my phone off.

BITCHOP: am i making you wet?

I turned off the phone, not responding to his last cruel message. Throughout the rest of the service, Bishop did not leave as I expected him to. Occasionally, I would turn around to see if he was still there.

He was staring at me the entire time.

VERSE EIGHT

Once the service was over, Grandma and Grandpa stayed seated, waiting for Dad to finish his conversation. Congregation members would come up to Dad, thanking him for the sermon; Janyce Williams, a seventy-three-year-old widow, was currently speaking with him.

She held a plate of cookies in her hand, giving it to my father. She always gave us cookies. Any chance she had, we were given cookies.

We wouldn't leave here for at least twenty minutes. Janyce could talk to a wall for hours. She didn't have many friends her age, just Dad. She adored him.

"I'm going to use the restroom," I whispered, leaning over Grandma's shoulder. They were mid-conversation. I didn't want to interrupt whatever Grandma and Grandpa were bickering about.

As soon as I broke away, I instantly searched for Bishop.

He was nowhere in sight.

I was tempted to turn on my phone and ask him if he was still lurking around the church somewhere. Maybe it was for the best. It was concerning that he even stepped foot in the building today; he hadn't been in this church without causing some sort of mayhem.

I stepped into the bathroom, positioning myself in front of the mirror. I pulled at the strands of my hair, making sure it was even atop my head. *I like your hair like that.*

I pursed my lips together, attempting to keep a grin from creeping up. He was a cheeky bastard, I would give him that. Beneath the hatred for my God and the violent acts he had committed in this town, he knew how to make a girl weak in the legs.

The door swung open so hard, it hit the wall behind the door. A black mass sauntered into the bathroom as if he owned it.

My eyes widened, locking with Bishop from the mirror. "Bishop," I gasped, turning around to face him.

I ducked down to check beneath the stalls. Thankfully, there was no one else in the bathroom. I don't know where I would even begin to start with explaining myself. *Yeah, Dad. Just having a little chat in the girl's bathroom with the boy that set your bible on fire. No big deal.*

"You can't be in here," I continued.

Bishop ignored me, taking a step toward me. I took one backward, hitting my ass on the edge of the sink. I tilted my chin upward to reach my gaze with his. There may be a foot of space between us right now, but it felt like he was currently holding me to this sink.

"Are you not accepting a sinner in the house of God?" He gasped. He acted like his own words were the most absurd thing he'd ever heard. "What a hypocrite you are."

He grinned, a shallow dimple on the left side of his cheek deepening.

"It's a bathroom. You're being a creep. Go." I gestured toward the door, but he did not move. Neither did I. I was unable to move an inch, truly. I was stunned. How was he so bold? And, why did he have such an interest in me? Something had to be wrong.

My stomach twisted at the thought of our current situation. We were alone, in an enclosed space. I could hear the handful of churchgoers walking about, just outside the door. Anything could have happened; anyone could have walked in.

I can't breathe.

"Do I make you nervous, Ethel?" Bishop took another step toward me. This time, there was half a foot of distance between us. His fingers reached up for the right side of my neck, gently skimming the skin beneath my earlobe.

His touch slipped down to my jugular, above the spot of skin my heart rate was slamming against.

My head tilted to the left, allowing him better access to the patch of skin he was stroking.

"Bishop." It was supposed to come out as a warning. But, to my horror, it came out as a gasp. A plea. A whimper. I sounded as if I was begging him to do whatever he was thinking of, to my body.

Bishop gnawed his bottom lip, staring down at me for a second too long. My lips were parted, staring up at him through my eyelashes. I could still hear everyone wandering around outside of the bathroom, chatting in the gathering area like nothing was happening a few feet away. They were so, so close.

The thought of being caught made this more rousing.

The bathroom had become dead silent. I would rather listen to him joke about setting the place on fire than listen to our heavy breathing.

Screw this. I wanted to feel it. For a second.

I took a step forward, closing the small gap we had left between us.

It only took a single step for all gentleness to dissipate.

Bishop wrapped his entire calloused hand around my throat, pulling me away from the sink, and into the closest stall. I had to grab hold of his wrists to avoid tripping over my own feet.

A whimper slipped out of me when my back hit the wall of the stall. He didn't bother to lock the stall door.

For a split second, I cracked. I had shown him that I wanted whatever this was, as much as he did. I wanted to feel it. Experience something. There was no going back now. He was going to do just that.

"Not here," I panted, staring up at him. His hand was still wrapped tightly around my throat, keeping me pinned in place against the stall wall. I shuddered from how cold his rings felt digging into my neck.

"Where?"

My lips were ajar, but no sound came from them. I stared up at him. His chest was rising and falling as fast as my own. He was looking down at me in such a different way. No boy had ever looked at me like this. I was starting to fear for my body.

His hips rolled forward, pushing my lower body to the small wall.

Heat crept from my core, seeping down my spine, and into my panties.

His face dipped down to my height, brushing his soft lips against mine; I hadn't expected them to feel so soft. They did not press into me until I nodded.

I was never going to be the same after feeling his lips against me.

My legs buckled the second his lips pressed against mine. He slid his thigh between my legs to prevent me from falling to the ground. I grunted into his mouth, feeling the fabric of his pants unintentionally hit the spot I needed him most.

My head fell back, hitting the wall. He pushed his lips harder into mine, biting, and tugging at me. He was so rough, so aggressive. I was going to crumble in a bathroom stall.

I pushed harder into his mouth, sucking on his lips like they were my lifeline. And, him, the same.

Another first. Bishop was the first boy I've ever kissed. I was horrendous at the motions. It didn't matter, though. Every time he moved his mouth against mine, I mimicked his action, memorizing every movement he made.

When his tongue slid into my mouth, I did the same into his, meeting him in the middle. I trembled at the feeling of his rough tongue rubbing against mine. If it weren't for him pinning me to the wall, I would be a pile of mush at his feet.

I whimpered, though it was muffled by his mouth. The bathroom had turned into a divine chorus; the noise of our lips smacking together, and heavy breathing filled the empty space. I trailed my hands up to his hair, grabbing a fistful of the messy black locks.

His hair was soft.

I didn't think it would be soft. Just as I hadn't expected his lips to be.

"Ethel?" I nearly jumped out of my skin. Grandma's voice pierced through the bathroom, following the heavy door shutting.

My eyes widened. I jerked Bishop's hair to pull him off of me. I physically had to pry him away from my mouth. Why did that feel so good? I didn't recall the girls in books saying how good making out felt.

"Yes, Grandma?" I replied, trying to calm how unstable my voice sounded. I reached over for the stall lock, moving it in place with a click.

I looked down at the gap between the floor and the stall; there was a large trash can blocking her view of two sets of feet.

God truly worked in mysterious ways.

"Are you feeling alright? You've been in here for a while."

Soft lips pulled me away from her question.

My back arched, my stomach hitting his. His lips quietly clamped down on my neck, sucking the skin as hard as I had done his lips. I bit my lip, attempting to mute the noises that were about to slip from my mouth; I could feel his teeth grazing the sensitive skin, biting down every few seconds.

My entire neck was going to be purple.

"Yes, Grandma." My hands went back toward his hair, but I didn't pull him off of me. I pulled him deeper into my neck, silently urging him to keep doing exactly what he was doing. I didn't even think it could feel that good on your neck; it was like he found some special spot or something of the sort.

"Me and Grandpa were talking about going to Harry's for lunch. That seafood place. We don't have a good one back home." I could barely stand, let alone think about lunch right now.

"Sounds good, Grandma."

Bishop's lips moved lower.

And lower.

He planted a trail of open-mouthed kisses down my cleavage. When he reached the end of the neckline, I looked down at the top of his head, afraid he was about to yank my dress down. I wasn't wearing a bra, so if he did, he would have a full view of my breasts.

He took my entire nipple in his mouth, through the dress. Fabric and all.

"Your Grandpa is irritating the Devil out of me right now."

I cupped a hand over my mouth, biting into the skin of my palm. Bishop closed his lips around my nipple, tugging the bud in between his teeth. A flash of pain rolled through me, but he swirled his tongue around the bud to ease it immediately after.

There was going to be a wet stain through the dress if he didn't pull away soon.

"I know Grandma," I replied, holding my gaze with Bishop. The sight of him with my breast in his mouth, looking up at me through his eyelashes, almost made a whimper slip loose. This was torture. Pure, absolute, torture.

"He keeps nagging me about selling his stupid car for some truck."

Bishop's mouth left my nipple.

He kneeled in the stall, planting a kiss on the area above my knee. The dress was covering his head, concealing him beneath it. He reached for the hem of my dress, pulling it up toward my hips. He only made it to my upper thigh before I stopped him.

My eyes widened. Did he think he was going to go down on me as I spoke to my grandma? In church?

I shook my head, tugging at his hair to pull him back up.

He grinned, returning his lip to my neck. It was coated in saliva, and I could feel a dull throb from where the bruises were forming.

"That sucks," I replied. What was I supposed to say? I didn't even remember what we were talking about.

"Yeah. I'm going to meet you in the car. They should be there soon. Alright?"

"Alright," I replied, arching my body harder into his. The moment the bathroom door shut, and I could no longer hear my grandma's footsteps, I pushed Bishop off of me.

His back hit the wall opposite the wall I was currently molded against. His mouth was swollen, and red bruises formed on his upper lip. Did I do that? Holy shit. I gave someone a hickey.

"No," I panted, staring up at him. I pointed my finger in his direction. His hair was a disaster. I could only imagine how terrible I looked right now. My left nipple was tight and wet. The right was erect, but nearly as prominent as the one Bishop had been working with. My legs were still trembling so badly, I wasn't sure I was going to be able to walk out of this stall without falling over.

"No? Am I a dog?" He looked down at my feet, sliding his gaze back up toward my face. I shuddered, afraid he was about to pounce back on top of me. I wouldn't be able to push him off if he did. "I love doggy."

"Yes. In heat." We both were. I scowled, opening the stall to get out of the small space we were confined in.

He followed close behind. He breathed heavier than I was, granted he was doing most of the work. "I'm coming to your house."

I whipped my head around, looking up at him. "No."

"Where?"

I hesitated, turning back around toward the door. I debated whether I should tell him to leave me alone or push him back into that stall and continue our make out session. I've come many times in my life, from myself, but nothing will ever compare to how good that just felt. How good he felt.

"Wednesday."

I didn't need to reiterate what I meant. He knew. "Wednesday," he repeated. I caught a glimpse of him in the mirror, following behind me with a smile painted across his face. We both looked like a panting disaster.

We both left the girl's bathroom, going our separate ways as if nothing had happened. For the rest of that day, I hadn't been able to keep my fingers off my mouth, grinning at the memory of him against me.

VERSE NINE

B ishop.

Bishop. Bishop. Bishop.

His name has been replaying in my head, like a chant. It had been since I left that bathroom stall. During the tense lunch with Dad and my grandparents, Bishop was all I could think about. And, now, a day later, I couldn't get the vulgar boy out of my head.

I looked over at my lamp.

The necklace glared from the dim light, that damned name crossing my mind again. Next to it, a cross necklace dangled down the lamp, coiling with the one he had given me. I'd given up on wearing the crosses outside of the house. He had proven that he could, and would, appear at any moment, and yank it from my neck.

I looked down at my phone and the text conversation already pulled up. Am I making you wet? It was the last message sent, over a day ago.

He hadn't texted me once after the make out session in the bathroom stall.

How did I go from forbidding him to have my number, to wondering why he wasn't texting me?

My thumbs hovered over the keypad. I should be grateful he was letting me breathe, rather than following me around like some dog in heat. He was suffocating. Lord forgive me, I really wanted him to suffocate me right about now. With his hands.

"Screw this," I scoffed, tossing my phone behind me. No message was sent, and none would ever be sent. I didn't want him. But, I did. I think. This was confusing; this was why I never tried with boys.

The door swung open behind me. I gasped, turning around to see who had barged into my bedroom without knocking. Grandma stood in the doorway, letting out a silent laugh. She stumbled into the doorframe, nearly spilling the glass of red wine in her hand.

"Sorry, sweetheart. Family down in Florida doesn't knock much. Bad habit."

I let out an unsteady breath. "It's okay. You scared me."

Grandma gently shut the door this time, taking a seat beside me on the bed. We both stared out at the window; I didn't have that good of a view, just a large tree, and our neighbor's house.

My eyes darted back to the necklace. What would she say if she saw it? I doubt she was that observant; but if she did notice it, I could lie and say it was some childhood friend. She didn't know that much about me. The last time she had seen me was when I was thirteen.

"I'm leaving tomorrow morning." They announced it at lunch yesterday; however, I had been distracted thinking about someone else. Dad had visibly relaxed when Grandpa said they had a flight at seven in the morning.

"I wish we could come visit you more often," I admitted, leaning my cheek on her shoulder.

I felt her tense beneath me after I uttered the words. "If you ever need a place to stay, you are always welcome. I will buy you a flight and everything. Just say the word. Or if you ever need me to come back up here, for anything."

I nodded against her shoulder. She was still staring out the window, but my gaze was locked with the name living in my head. Bishop. "I miss it down there. Maybe during the summer, I can come."

"You would love them. Everyone has gotten so much closer, compared to the last time you saw them. We all live beside each other. We walk into each other's houses like they are our own. We are a family." My stomach sank; she was talking to me about home like I had never been there. It was only a few years since I last saw them, not my entire life.

"If you and Dad ever fight—," Grandma hesitated, her eyes meeting mine from the reflection of the window.

"What happened between you two?" It was out of my mouth before I could stop myself, and before she could finish her sentence. In the eighteen years I've lived, I knew some things were just meant to go unspoken about. Grandma and Dad's relationship was one of those things. But, it was hard to ignore the tension in this house right now.

Her muscles tensed so tightly it felt like I was resting my head on a rock. I pulled my head off of her shoulder, turning to meet her gaze.

She was uncomfortable.

I'd never seen Grandma uncomfortable.

"He just wasn't right growing up." Her words were so clipped, I would have missed them if I wasn't sitting on the edge of my seat, waiting for the answer. "Who was the boy you were with this morning?"

My cheeks have never felt so hot in my life. Guilt, shame, embarrassment, and the memory of his tongue came creeping across my face. I gulped, staring out the window with rounded eyes. The memory of his lips, his hair, his hands.

The flush he caused me concealed the embarrassment I was feeling.

Damn him for having such control over my body, when he wasn't even here.

"What?" I croaked, blinking a few times.

"The boy in the bathroom. The one you were trying to hide."

Everything about him was so asphyxiating. Even the mention of him.

"I don't know what you are—."

"Don't lie to me, Ethel." I looked up at her, knowing the color of my face was giving away all she needed to know about the boy from the bathroom. I wanted to laugh, badly. If Bishop knew I was sitting here, talking to my grandma about him, he would have an absolute field day. Arrogant bastard.

"He's bad," I admitted, letting out the breath I had been holding. "Like, really bad. His friends are terrible, he is terrible to Dad, and this entire town hates him. Besides the women, probably. He's all too good in that department."

I said the last part under my breath. My stomach buzzed with the bad type of heat at the thought of him, and another woman right now. Was that why he wasn't texting? Was he between another woman's legs? Had I not acted quickly enough?

Everything I said was true, to an extent. It was all rumors and whispers among the students at Northside High School.

At Northside, his friend group was nothing but a group of bullies in their teenage years. However, after graduation, it escalated exponentially. It was Cain; everything led back to Cain. The boy who hadn't spoken a word, suddenly blackmailed every powerful figure in this town. Politicians, police, everyone.

They were able to do anything.

According to the whispers, Baylen and Bishop were the ones who took advantage of that. Baylen, specifically; I had seen his snuff videos firsthand. I knew the rumors about him were true. I had unfortunately stumbled across a video of Baylen burning a boy alive.

Even if Cain was gone, and that life was a year behind them, it still tainted Bishop's soul.

"Is he bad to you?" Grandma asked.

I didn't look away from the necklace. "Quite the opposite. We've known each other for what feels like two days, but he is acting like I'm the love of his life." Sure, that was an exaggeration, but it wasn't far. I didn't blame him; it feels like we've known each other for so much longer. Lifetimes.

Was this normal?

"Time is bullshit," Grandma cursed. I flinched, jerking my gaze back toward her. That was the first time I've ever heard her cuss. I needed to see her more; I needed some form of woman to look up to in my life. "I married your Grandpa after a month of knowing him."

My eyes widened. I knew that they had gotten married early on, but not that early. "Really? Did you fall in love with him that fast?"

She shook her head, laughing beneath her breath. "No. I just wanted to fuck him and not go to hell for it. I told him, you want to fuck me, you have to marry me first. Next day he proposed."

My jaw might as well be on the floor.

When I was twelve, the day I started my period, I had been lectured about waiting until marriage. Grandma was one of the people who sat me down, talking to me about it. I never would have imagined her of all people to marry for the sole purpose of sex.

I thought of them when thinking of love. I thought of the way he had carried her over puddles, even at the age of seventy. And, the way he learned to paint nails, and apply makeup, just so when she was sick he was able to make her feel beautiful.

Odd. I never would have imagined them sealing the knot in such a peculiar way.

"I wasn't expecting that," I admitted.

She laughed. I needed to visit her more; I missed my family. I loved Dad, but I wasn't able to see family due to whatever was happening between them. "Me neither."

I sucked in a breath, before continuing. "Did Dad ever tell you about someone terrorizing his church?"

Grandma shook her head.

"He used to do really bad things to the church. He hates Christians, or it's just a way to let out his anger. I don't know. Today was the first time he's been in the church without trying to burn it down." I twiddled my fingers together, holding off on mentioning the actual reason he terrified me. His friends; the power Cain once had over this town.

"Well, maybe you are doing something good for him."

My heart skipped. Was she right? Bishop sat in church yesterday, without releasing snakes or burning a bible. He actually sat in the congregation. He wasn't paying attention, but he was there. There truly was a first for everything. "But Dad would never forgiv-."

The air went cold, and Grandma snapped her head toward me. "Your dad deserves everything that comes to him. As terrible as it is to say. Karma is real, baby girl."

"But, he is your son." As much as I loved Grandma, it was always Dad by my side. I didn't want to jeopardize that. I'd always choose Dad over anyone. No matter how badly we fought.

"Was. Your dad has as much of the Devil in him as he does God."

With that, she stood from the bed, gently patting my cheek. "Have fun with your boy. Life is too short to worry about what others will think. Just be careful. You know what is best for you."

She made her way to the door and left me sitting alone on the bed. My heart was pounding so hard. What did Dad do to upset her so badly? Why wouldn't Bishop just leave my head for five minutes?

I huffed, falling backward onto the bed. They needed to sort out whatever was happening between them. I loved them both to death.

I reached for my phone, quickly sending a message to Bishop before I could talk myself out of it.

ME: wednesday?

He responded immediately.

BITCHOP: obviously.

I rolled my eyes.

ME: my grandma just asked who i was with in the bathroom.

BITCHOP: good.

BITCHOP: tell her to go fuck herself. you would have been dry fucked against that wall if it weren't for her.

BITCHOP: actually, that would be a great sight to walk into.

Following the last message was the moaning emoji, a church, and a rosary.

I gasped, clamping my hand over my mouth. How can someone possibly be so vulgar? Not to mention how disrespectful he was towards my grandma. Tell her to go fuck herself.

I chewed my bottom lip and rolled onto my stomach. I raised my feet into the air, slowly kicking them above me.

ME: you're disrespectful.

BITCHOP: what are you going to do abt it, pretty girl?

ME: good night.

BITCHOP: come over.

I rolled my eyes again, locking the phone. Pretty girl. My cheeks were pure flame at this point.

After a few seconds, another message came through.

BITCHOP: good night, church girl. dream of me.

VERSE TEN

Wednesday came fast.

Too fast.

My stomach was invaded with nerves the moment Dad and I stepped through the church doors. What if he didn't show? What if he was out there right now? God, almighty, why did I agree for him to meet me in the alley? This felt like I was doing a drug deal.

Once I heard Dad's office door shut, I made my way toward the back door. I didn't bother to grab a bag of trash and attempt to be semi-productive. I simply went straight to the door.

I adjusted the skirt I wore, looking down at my outfit in the process. On Wednesdays, I usually wore something simple; a pair of jeans, matched with a loose sweatshirt. But, tonight, I decided on something different.

I wore a tight, white lace-trimmed tank top, with a thin black cardigan to cover my arms. The tank top dipped low enough to show my cleavage.

Cleavage was one of the perks of being plus-sized; I would never need to worry about wearing a pushup bra.

Paired with the tank top was a pleated black skirt; I wore sheer pantyhose beneath the fabric, squeezing my thighs in place. There were rips in some spots due to how aggressively I had been pulling the stockings on. I mentally scolded myself; this was too much effort for a few minutes with a boy who wouldn't even notice.

Was I dressing up for Bishop? Of all people, Bishop?

Before opening the door, I reached for the cross necklace dangling on my neck. I placed it on a nearby pew; he was not going to steal another one from me. It was starting to get expensive.

"He's just a boy," I reminded myself, beneath my breath. I sucked in one last breath of air. His presence was going to take it from me. I reached for the door handle, pulling the back door open.

I didn't walk through the door frame. If I did, I would have my back to the door. As he had gracefully proven so many times, I had a little habit of standing with my back to doors.

Immediately, my eyes locked with his. Shit. I would prefer him standing me up rather than him actually showing up. It was too real now. He was here, and I had no idea what to do next.

Bishop leaned against the wall across from the backdoor, a cigarette dangling between his lips. One of his long legs was propped up on the building wall, supporting him against it. My eyes went to his lips next; only a slap would wipe off the grin he wore.

I moved down his body. He was wearing a tight black shirt that ended just below his belly button and a pair of baggy cargo pants. He had black combat boots on, a satanic pendant hanging from his neck, and various chains dangling from his belt loops.

I gulped, attempting to moisten my mouth. Due to his lengthy legs, the hem of his pants lay low on his hips. I could see the V line of his abdomen before it disappeared into the darkness of his pants.

Bishop wasn't beautiful; he was ethereal.

"You are here," I pointed out, pressing my lips together in a firm line. I forced my eyes back up toward his face. I was staring at the V line of him a little too long; the smirk on his face, and the blaze in his eyes, confirmed that he noticed.

"You don't have trash. So, you came looking." Bishop held his gaze with mine as he snuffed the cigarette out against the church wall. I didn't protest the action; I was too cautious of him walking toward me.

"Did you drive?" I asked, looking down the alley. There was no car in sight.

"No." He kept walking toward me. My attempt at changing the subject was not doing anything. Every step he took toward me, I had to tilt my head further upward to meet his gaze. "I live close."

He was right. All four of them lived in the home a few minutes away. The home that Cain bought and lived in when he was still in town. I'd forgotten just how close the house on top of the hill was; the big one, that only Cain could afford.

"Oh," I replied. I crossed my arms over my stomach. There was a foot of space left between us, and he didn't seem to have any intention of leaving it there.

"Stop changing the subject, Ethel."

"I wasn't," I lied.

"Dinner." He was right in front of me when he said this. So close, if he just leaned down a foot, our lips would be against each other. There was still a faint mark on his lips where I had left a bite, branding him in the same way he had me.

"No," I replied.

He leaned down. I almost shrieked. I pulled away. This was terrifying, why did I think I was going to be able to do this? I wanted to, but I didn't. Shit, why was it so confusing to be a girl?

"Are you a tease?" Bishop asked. His jaw was clenched. The way he looked at me was a mix of two things; he looked down at me like he was ready to rip my head right off of my shoulders and fuck me during the process. His eyes were hooded. We both were here for one reason, and it wasn't to chat.

I shook my head, propping the door open with my foot. The warm air of the church caressed my back, whereas the cold air between Bishop and I caused me to shudder. It felt terribly ironic.

I reached for his hand. The touch caused both of us to flinch, but he intertwined his fingers with mine. My small, warm, baby fat-covered hands fit against his large, thin, cold fingers. His fingers looked like they would be cruel, in the best way possible.

"I'm cold," I admitted, pulling him inside the church with me. We both watched the door shut behind us, trapping us inside. His eyes felt a thousand times heavier when they landed back on me.

We stared at each other, silence passing for a few minutes. He was looking at me, waiting for me to do something. Our hands were still intertwined; his black-painted nails were digging into the top of mine. I felt like he was waiting to see what I did. Like, if I had a conversation, he would have a conversation. If I took off my shirt, he would take off his shirt.

What was I supposed to do now? What would Briar do? She was the most confident girl I knew.

I pulled him toward a pew in the back of the church. It was the furthest one from my dad's office. I let go of his hand once we reached the pew.

I kicked off my shoes, not looking away from him as I did. He stared down at me, his lips parted, as I laid my back down on the pew. It felt as if he were taking the image of me in. I was lying down on the pew, pantyhose ripped, looking up at him through my eyelashes. If he had a spank bank, this was going to last him a year.

"Don't just stand there, Bishop. We only have a few minutes."

He didn't need to be told twice.

VERSE ELEVEN

Bishop's eyes stayed with mine when he pressed his front side down on top of me. My fingers dug into the collar of his shirt, pulling his chest harder against mine. It felt so right, his body against mine. He was heavier than me, but it felt like the perfect amount of weight pinning me to the pew.

We both let out a shuddered breath before he leaned his lips down into mine. His breath lingered against my lips; I propped myself up on my elbows, closing the space between us. He bit my bottom lip so hard I tasted blood in my mouth. "This." Kiss. "Is." Kiss. "A." Kiss. "Bad." Kiss. "Idea."

I was talking to myself. I knew this. To Bishop, this was far from a bad idea; his swelling bulge pressed into my thigh confirmed this.

He responded by sliding his tongue into my mouth. Our tongues slowly rubbed against one another, before he slipped his entirety into my mouth, exploring every last inch. Every tooth. Every taste bud. Every inch. He touched it, claiming it as his own.

His tongue tasted of alcohol and cigarettes.

I dug my fingers deeper into his shirt, arching my back upward to press my stomach into him. My eyebrows knitted together when I felt his cock pressed against my stomach. It was much harder than it had been a few seconds ago.

I gasped into his mouth as he slowly ground it against me.

It felt so good. Even if he had only rubbed against my stomach once, the feeling had gone straight between my legs.

My head fell backward, and my lips parted; his mouth did not stop, even after I pulled away. He moved his lips lower, trailing away from my face, and toward my neck.

"Bishop," I cautioned, wrapping my fingers around his hair. I gently tugged his hair upward, pulling his face back above mine. I narrowed my eyes, looking up at his face hovering above me. Our breaths were coming out as pants, fanning against each other's faces. I licked the excess saliva from my swollen lip.

"Don't do that," I continued. My tongue tasted of blood, from where he had bitten my lip.

"Do what?" he asked, tilting his head. A single dimple revealed itself on the left side of his face. Grind into me. I couldn't force the dirty words to come out of me. From the smirk he wore, I assumed he knew what I meant.

"Why are you being good to me?" I propped myself further up on my elbows, our lips brushing against each other in the process. Heat shot down my spine, causing me to shudder. "I don't mean to be rude, but you tend to be a jackass. But, you aren't to me. Why?"

"I already told you this." Bishop leaned back down, threading his fingers into the hair at the base of my skull. He squeezed the strands, forcing me to tilt my head further upward at him. I recalled the day outside of the church after I had helped him in the alley.

You knew that blood was not mine. You saw blood on a man who had terrorized your father for years. I was drunk and vulnerable, but you still helped me. I'm going to have you for that.

Our lips brushed together when I spoke. "I don't believe that. It can't happen that easily. It's not that simple."

"Do I seem like the type to overcomplicate things?" Yes. Bishop continued, nonetheless. "Despite contrary belief, I could give two fucks about women. Fuck, I could give two fucks about anything. I fixate on things, Ethel. Obsess over things. You just happened to become one of those little fixations when you stepped out into that alley."

He looked down at me like he meant every word. This felt so abnormal, how natural it felt. As if I have known him for so much longer. I've known of him for some time, but this felt like I've known him.

I grabbed the back of his neck, pulling his face back down into me. I was afraid the moment was going to slip away, too fast. Twenty minutes. That's how much time I estimated we had. The church was a mess; I really should have tried to do something more productive than making out with Bishop on a pew.

This felt better, though.

I whimpered as he grabbed a fistful of my hair, tilting my head backward onto the pew. My neck was craned, giving him the access he wanted; his mouth moved from my chin, my neck, and then to the cleavage.

But, not once did he grind into me. As I had asked. I could feel him on my stomach, throbbing, aching, and painfully hard, but he did not cross the boundary I had set.

A male was able to respect a boundary? Truly, there was a first for everything.

His lips left the top of my cleavage, moving lower down my torso. I arched my torso further into his mouth, holding onto his black curls like they were the only thing keeping me from falling off this pew.

When his mouth reached my belly button, above my tank top, he lifted his eyes toward me. He watched every breath I sucked in, and every quiet pant I let out. He lifted the hem of my tank top above my belly button.

His warm lips came down on the sensitive flesh of my stomach, directly beneath my belly button. My back came off of the pew. I was surprised by the feeling of lips in such an intimate area. He sucked, and bit at the inch of the skin, slowly making his way toward the place I needed him most.

I jerked my hand away from his hair, biting into my palm. I needed to stifle the noise I was about to let loose. Why did this feel so good? His mouth alone was turning my body into mush against this pew; my core was releasing more heat than I knew possible. Goosebumps spread across every inch of my body, despite how hot it was getting.

I panted. Again. Why did Bishop keep making me pant? I was the dog in heat, not him.

His lips lingered around the waistband of my skirt, though he didn't dare dip where he didn't belong. I was about five minutes away from begging him to.

"You're a virgin." He smirked against his stomach, tugging more of the skin between his teeth. He looked up at me through his eyelashes; I looked away, embarrassed by how hot my face was getting. Could he tell from how sensitive my body was?

"Shut up," I replied. He did. He shifted his focus back to my stomach, littering every inch of it with kisses. His fingertips gently traced my waist, up to my ribs, and then back to my waist. It was overwhelming how good his touch felt, without any effort at all. I was a trembling mess.

"Say the word and I will make you see your God." The vibrations from his lips went straight through my stomach, zinging my core. A quiet gasp left my lips and I arched my back up further. I tried to focus on suppressing how heavy my breath was coming out.

"Bishop." My voice came out as a mixture of plea, and heavy breath. He pulled my skirt down an inch, to expose my hip; he left a kiss on it. I could feel his smile against me.

"Say my name like that, again." He sucked the skin of my hip between his teeth. He worked with it until it began to throb, then he released it. Over. And over.

My leg slid off of the pew, but Bishop caught it before it was able to hit the ground. His hand wrapped around my ankle, returning my leg beneath me. His fingers lingered on the pantyhose, grinning as if it was the most amusing thing he'd ever seen.

His hand trailed higher; his fingers made their way up my calf, so light my muscles were starting to spasm. My body was begging for him to just clamp down onto me and have his way with me.

He pulled his face away from my hip, returning it above my face. His fingers were at my knee now, tracing light circles around the bone.

Buzz.

My breath was coming out in soft pants. My eyes were locked on his fingers, now trailing up toward my inner thigh. My legs parted, just enough for him to trail his hands between my legs. My thigh was trembling from his touch above the pantyhose.

He would not look away from me. He was watching me attempt to conceal how he was undoing me.

Buzz.

"Someone is calling you," he said, nodding his head in the direction of my phone. I stared at my dad's contact illuminating the phone. I looked back to Bishop, his hands, and then back to the phone.

Buzz.

"Don't talk," I told Bishop. His fingers stopped moving, but they were still clamped down on my thigh. His hands were so cold, despite how close he was to the heat coming out of me.

I cleared my throat before picking up the phone.

"Hi, Dad." My voice was steady, and my eyes were still on Bishop's. This must be divine intervention. First my Grandma, in the church bathroom, and now Dad?

His fingers started to move closer toward my core. It was a frightening sight. Bishop on top of me, his hand between my legs. He had a glare in his eyes. I'm going to break you, was what I read. And, I was ready for it.

"I just wanted to let you know that I'm almost done. I just need to wrap up a few more things. Might be a few minutes late."

"Take your time," I replied. Bishop grinned at this, planting a kiss beside my earlobe. My back curved into him, again, once his fingers reached the apex of my thigh. He was close; painfully close. Just a few more inches, and he would be right there.

He caressed the pressure point of my thigh. It felt like he was already there.

"I can actually get work done. Seeing as your bitch of a grandma isn't nagging me every five seconds." I frowned at Dad's words. They spoke about each other like there was never love between them. There had to have been, once.

His hands continued to rub against the apex of my thigh, but his head moved to rest beside the phone. He was listening to everything my dad was saying. If Bishop speaks, I'm going to kill him.

"Well, I liked Grandma's nagging," I countered. I reached up for Bishop's cheek, trailing the tips of my acrylic nails down his skin. He tensed but let me touch his face. He shuddered once my touch moved down to his neck.

Then his chest.

I wrapped my fingers around the satanic pendant hanging from his neck, jerking it off of him before he could notice what I was doing. He jerked his head up, narrowing his eyes into slits. I grinned, tossing it far into the sea of pews.

"Karma," I mouthed. His hand moved from my thigh, leaving me feeling empty beneath him. Bastard.

"Of course you do. I've got to go now," Dad said, before hanging up the phone. You know, despite Bishop's terrible past with Dad and his church, the two would get along great. They were both assholes when they wanted to be.

I threw my phone down, recalling how much he hated Dad. "Are you doing this to hurt my dad?"

I moved one of my knees upward, resting it beside his hip. He looked down at my legs as I moved; it was placing him directly between my legs, now. "I've known you were his daughter every time I came into this church. If I wanted to get at him, through you, I would have fucked you in front of him."

He leaned down beside my ear, sucking on my earlobe. "I'm not that type of person. Besides, I prefer vandalism. I hate this place more than I hate your father," Bishop continued.

I opened my mouth to ask him what he meant by that, but he rolled us off the pew before I could. He landed beneath me, on his back, whereas I straddled his stomach. I gaped at the new position but leaned down to reconnect our lips.

I liked seeing him under me.

His hands slid up the tops of my thighs, then under my skirt toward my hips, and finally to my ass. He grabbed a rough handful of the meat; his nails dug so hard into the pantyhose, I felt them rip where he touched.

His hand fondled my ass for a second before he brought his palm down on it. Hard. The slap echoed through the quiet church, followed by my gasp.

I braced my hands on either side of his head, looking down at him through narrowed eyes.

"Karma," was all he said.

I leaned back down to his neck, but this time it was me who was leaving marks against pale skin. I bit, sucked, and licked every inch of his neck like he had done moments before. His breathing was getting heavy, and his hands were caressing every inch of my ass.

He grabbed onto my ass, slowly rocking me against his bulge. My mouth was still on his neck. My eyes and stomach fluttered, confused by the new feeling in my belly. This felt so much better than it had when he rubbed against me.

I didn't stop him.

In fact, after three more rocks against him, I started to do it on my own.

I planted my fingers on his abdomen, continuing the slow rocking motion against him. His stomach was as tense as mine had become. I pulled away from his lips, looking down at him as I moved against his erection.

The friction was starting to feel really good. If I didn't stop soon, there was no way I would be able to stop.

Heavy breaths started to come from his mouth, intertwining with my own. I reached for his hand, holding onto it as I continued the motions. His other hand was on my hip, but it was me moving them. "Bishop," I whimpered. "This is wrong. Doing it here."

I didn't stop. And, the friction only intensified.

"But it feels so good, doesn't it pretty girl."

I dug my fingers deep into his hand, moving faster and harder against him. I was close. Shit, he was going to make me come just from sitting there. Was I going to make him? I could feel him throbbing beneath me. Did that mean he was going to come?

I tilted my head backward, staring up at the ceiling.

His hand reached for my throat, grabbing ahold of it. I let out a quiet, choked moan; he was squeezing hard enough to make my head spin. The fear of losing my oxygen made me move faster against him.

"Shit Ethel," he grunted, bucking his hips upward to meet my movements. I felt something wet between his crotch and mine. I couldn't tell if it was from him, or me.

I was definitely about to come. There was no stopping now.

"Pastor Fields wasn't here. I'm just going to call him later." I quietly gasped as a male voice rang through the church. It was coming from where Dad's office was, but it wasn't Dad.

VERSE TWELVE

I clamped my hand over Bishop's mouth. I leaned down toward him, looking up toward the aisle as the voice came closer. Shit. Whoever it was would walk right past us.

I was still straddling his throbbing crotch, but I was no longer grinding into him. My stomach was pulsating. I had been so close to what was about to be the best orgasm of my life.

Bishop tilted his head backward, looking at the aisle.

A man in baggy jeans and a plain white tee shirt walked past. Preacher Jones. I recognized him. He was one of Dad's friends. He worked a few towns over, but I hadn't seen him in ages. Occasionally, the two would meet up for coffee; however, the last time they did was years ago.

Why was he here? Why wasn't Dad in his office?

Mr. Jones was oblivious. He walked past the pew, like he had not interrupted a dry humping session, moments before.

"Yeah, sounds good," Mr. Jones spoke over the phone, disappearing out of the church.

I knitted my eyebrows together, looking back down at Bishop. "He just said my dad isn't in his office. He's supposed to be there right now."

I ran my hands down Bishop's torso before pushing myself off on him. To his horror, I sat on the edge of the pew, slipping on my shoes, and readjusting my clothes. He groaned under his breath, laying his head flat on the ground.

"He's out touching little altar boys." Bishop grinned, propping himself up on his elbows. I kicked his ribcage. Not hard enough to hurt him, but hard enough to prove my point.

"Do not say that," I hissed.

He didn't respond, thus the tense silence returned around us. We were both still breathing heavily; the silence was a reminder of what had been interrupted. I ran a hand through my messy locks, staring down at him on the floor. It took every bit of self-control I had to not look where his pants were currently tented.

"I didn't think you had that in you."

"Me neither," I admitted. I looked over at my phone. Dad should have been here any moment; though it was not his office he would be coming from. Where was he? The church was small, there wasn't anywhere else he could be. "You should go. I'm going to go look for him."

Bishop leaned upward toward my leg, planting a light kiss on my ankle. He stared up at me through those god-forsaken eyelashes. My stomach fluttered. Maybe it wouldn't be such a bad idea to jump back down there and finish what we both wanted.

"Okay," he said, leaving a kiss on my calf. This was going to escalate again if he didn't stop looking at me like that.

"Okay." I gulped, looking down at him as he planted another kiss. Neither of us made any effort to stand up.

"Why won't you let me take you to dinner?" Bishop asked, moving to my other calf. My nails dug into the side of the pew as his lips lingered above my pantyhose.

"Because," I began. "This is abnormal. Unnatural." It was unnatural how well we were fitting together. But, I didn't say that out loud.

"You bend over that pew and I will show you just what unnatural feels like."

I choked, rubbing my hand down my face. "Maybe."

Bishop's eyes widened and he bit into my calf, kissing it after. "Maybe to the anal, or dinner."

"Dinner. Oh, no. Never the first. That shouldn't even be going through your mind." I rested my hand over my face, trying to cover how red I was becoming. The thought of having anal sex felt similar to a very, very bad nightmare. I don't understand how girls would like things up in that area.

Bishop smirked, standing up from the floor. It only took him a few seconds before he found his sigil necklace. I walked behind him, following him toward the backdoor.

My legs were weak. I could still feel the throb between my legs, reminding me of how good he felt between him. And that was with multiple layers of protection between us. I couldn't imagine how he would feel without the clothes separating us.

"There is no way you don't care about being with women," I blurted, once we reached the doorframe. Bishop turned around, leaning against the door, his front to me.

"And why is that?"

I crossed my arms over my chest, looking up at him. How do I say this without complimenting his ego? "Well, you are very proficient with your mouth and hands. That usually indicates that you have had experience. Currently, I am assuming, because you are not rusty."

I didn't care how many people he had slept with. What I did care about was whether he was entertaining both me and other women, simultaneously.

Bishop laughed, propping the door open. "Are you telling me I know how to make you feel good?"

I bit my tongue, looking up at him.

"Coen practically drew a diagram of exactly where to touch a woman when he lost his virginity. He presented it to all of us over dinner, and everything. I mean, the boy would take it personally if one of us left a girl unsatisfied." Coen. The owner of "Crimson." The nymphomaniac himself.

"Oh," I breathed.

Bishop grinned, stepping out the back door. "Let me know if you catch your father touching altar boys."

I reached for a nearby hymn book, throwing it in his direction with a scowl. But, he was already out the door. Jackass.

After I knew Bishop had left, I made my way toward Dad's office. I knocked on the door, but there was no response. "Dad? Father Jones came in looking for you."

I twisted the handle, walking into the office.

Dad was nowhere to be found.

In fact, there was no evident sign that he had even been in his office in weeks. There were no papers on his desk, his chair had collected dust, and the lights were off. The window was propped open. When I looked out the window, his car was no longer in the parking lot.

I always respected his privacy. I wouldn't ask, or pry if it meant digging into something he wanted to keep to himself. But, if he was lying to me? I hoped he had a good reason to. I put all my faith in Dad.

I pulled out my phone and texted him.

ME: are you still here?

DAD: Obviously. In the office. A few more minutes.

VERSE THIRTEEN

I t'd been days, and I could still feel him.

I groaned, rolling onto my side. I grabbed a hold of my stomach and readjusted my head on the pillow. The ache that was left in that church, in that pew, was making me ill. I couldn't sleep after feeling what he felt like. The throb. The bulge.

We'd been texting, but it wasn't the same. I wanted him here. Despite my better judgment, my body was craving him here. Beneath me. On top of me. Whatever, as long as he was here.

I stared out the window. It was around ten at night. This was usually when I would be freshly showered, and ready for bed. I used to go to sleep the second my head hit my pillow. But, for the past few days, I saw my window more than my eyelids.

He lived close. A fifteen-minute walk, at most. That big house, on top of the hill, was right beside the church.

I could walk to his house. If I was desperate.

I ran a hand down my face. I would never, in a million lifetimes, go to his house. The place Cain used to live. The house Baylen, Coen, and Solomon currently lived in. Why did that even cross my mind?

My phone buzzed as if the Devil himself was listening to my thoughts.

BITCHOP: did you ever find your dad that one day? i forgot to ask.

ME: no. he wasn't at the church.

BITCHOP: where was he?

ME: i don't know.

BITCHOP: you didn't ask?

I chewed on the inside of my cheek. No. Whatever he was lying about, he had good reason to. It was the only reason he would lie to me; we told each other everything. Even after our fights, we would always be truthful with each other.

Sure, sometimes we withheld the truth. For example, I was not going to mention the fact that I nearly dry fucked Bishop in the back of his church. It was unnecessary.

BITCHOP: coen is having one of his sex parties tomorrow. you should come.

ME: lol.

BITCHOP: not joking.

ME: no. i would catch a disease just walking into that place.

Crimson was already a sex club, at heart. But, annually, Coen would intensify it by throwing one of his sex parties. It was around the time of his birthday, and half the town would attend. Even people from other towns.

Coen brought Crimson to this town. Crimson was the most exciting thing that ever happened to our town, Death Valley. But, I would never step foot in that place; the thought of someplace dedicated to sex, and just sex, was horrifying.

BITCHOP: i don't have any disease.

ME: bold of you to assume you are coming anywhere near me.

My stomach fluttered as I watched the typing bubble at the bottom of my screen.

BITCHOP: oh, plz. you def wanted to be near me a few days ago.

BITCHOP: i have seen rabbits hump slower than that.

I gasped, clamping my hand over my mouth. I rolled onto my back, cursing under my breath. "Little shit!"

ME: i can't believe you just said that.

BITCHOP: am i wrong? never.

ME: no to crimson. never to be precise.

ME: good night.

BITCHOP: dream of me.

I rolled my eyes, locking my phone. My face was still heated from the rabbit comment. Vulgar bastard.

∞

At three in the morning, I decided I was not going to sleep. Whenever I dozed off, a certain gothic-looking boy came into my thoughts. I felt like I needed to scrub my brain to get him out of it; he wouldn't get out of my head.

I sat up in my bed, pulling my knees to my chest. I reached for my phone, pulling up the text thread with him.

I hovered my fingers over the keypad. He had to be asleep by now. It was three in the morning.

ME: are you awake?

I locked my phone, throwing it onto my bed. It felt like every message I sent made butterflies set loose in my belly. Every message I sent to him, and every message I received, felt like I was reliving the day in the pew. I had the urge to squeal, and pace around my room in anticipation; though, I remained seated on my bed.

Buzz.

I flinched, pulling my lip between my teeth. I felt like a giddy little school girl, in high school, waiting for their crush to text them; I never had crushes like that in high school. I could imagine this was what it felt like.

BITCHOP: alwayds.

BITCHOP: always.

I chewed hard at my cheek. Why was I even texting him? Was I supposed to respond with what was currently going through my head? Dang. I literally can't sleep thinking about you. Screw you. Lol!

ME: i can't sleep.

BITCHOP: thinkinn of me?

BITCHOP: thinsing

BITCHOP: tHinki

BITCHOP: you know what I'm trying to say.

If only he knew just how true that was.

I frowned, watching the next message come in from him.

BITCHOP: let me come over and pwut you to sleepp.

ME: no.

BITCHOP: i mean that's thwe oneely reason you're texting me thiss late.

A ping of emotion jolted through my stomach. I blinked, staring down at the words. Not only did he sound like an absolute dick, but he also sounded inebriated. Even through texts.

It was a Saturday night, maybe he was partying. But, it didn't explain every other time I had seen him. The lingering taste of booze on his lips every time I tasted him. My heart sank to my stomach. Why did he drink so much?

Do not pry, Ethel, I told myself. I was just going to be annoying; it would push him away. When did that become a bad thing?

ME: you're drunk.

I loathed being that person. The person you could never take to parties, because they were too worried about everyone's safety. Too anxious. But, he was self-destructing. When people spiraled, like Bishop appeared to be doing, they never noticed until they hit the ground. I wanted to at least make sure he was prepared for impact. If I didn't, I would never forgive myself if he did something to himself, because no one was there with him.

I hated that I was making him my responsibility. But, I needed to.

Maybe this was the reason God put Bishop on my path.

BITCHOP: yuh. come over and get this sloppy dick, bitch.

I scrunched my nose at the word. Bitch. I bet this was how he texted all of the girls on his phone; the ones he claimed he had no interest in. For a split second, he had made me feel different. Like, I wasn't like a notch on his bedpost.

I guess alcohol brings all of him to life. Even the worst parts.

ME: don't talk to me like that, bishop. i don't like it.

BITCHOP: whatever, bitch.

He followed the messages with two emojis. A church, and the fire emoji.

ME: are you somewhere safe?

He didn't respond to me anymore. I pulled my knees tighter into my chest, staring down at my phone.

Bishop was a different person when drunk. He was the person that made me shriek the first time I saw him. In high school, there was a boy a grade above me. He had told me how when he was a freshman, Bishop and Baylen had both attempted to drown him in the toilet. All because he told a teacher that Solomon was giving out answers for the finals.

That was the person Bishop became when drunk; the boy I had heard stories about. The person following loosely in the footsteps of Baylen.

Was that why he drank so much? To become that person?

He had been such a terrible person in high school. Was a terrible person? I didn't know. I didn't want to care about him. But, I wouldn't be able to sleep knowing what could be happening right now. He could be drinking alone, until the ache dissipated, as he had been doing that day in the bar.

I should at least be with him. To keep him company as he numbed the ache.

VERSE FOURTEEN

I had fallen asleep at some point.

I only knew this, because I was abruptly woken up by the sound of a loud creak, followed by a thud.

I jumped up in my bed, pulling the covers to my chest. My eyes widened seeing someone climbing through my window, rolling off the edge and onto the floor with a thud. The silhouette was tall, and lanky; I only knew one person with a body type as such.

I reached for the string of my lamp, pulling it so my room was illuminated by a soft light. But, by the time the light came on, Bishop was already climbing into the bed. His hood was pulled up, so I could not see his face. And, when he collapsed into the bed, he had his back toward me.

My mouth was ajar as I looked down at him. My fingers were still tightly fisted in the comforter.

I listened to his breathing. His breath grew steady the second his head hit the pillow. His body was trembling, but his tremors calmed once he slid into unconsciousness.

He smelled of his spirit; weed, alcohol, and cigarettes. It contrasted with the vanilla-scented candle on the nightstand beside my head.

Bishop just broke into my room— holy shit. He was lucky he guessed which room was mine; I assumed the lace white curtains gave it away.

My gaze was locked on the back of his head, where his hoodie concealed him. I looked down at my cotton tee shirt dress next. I looked like a grandma; I would have worn something a little more attractive if I knew there was a chance Bishop was going to break into my bedroom.

I reached for the lamp, turning it back off. I pushed myself from the bed, rounding the mattress. I reached where his feet dangled from the bed. He was tall enough that his long body wouldn't even fit the length of my queen-sized mattress. The bed swallowed me whole every night.

I wrapped my fingers around the bottom of his black combat boots, gently pulling them from his feet. I kept my eyes locked on his sleeping face to make sure he did not wake up.

Even in the dark, and beneath the shadow of his hood, I could still see his pale face. He looked at peace when he slept, much like he had in the alleyway that first night. I could see his parted lips, his cheeks flushed, and his messy curls under the hood.

He was wearing a black hoodie and a pair of black skinny jeans. The jeans had to be uncomfortable, but I refused to remove them. He could deal with it, especially after referring to me as a bitch.

I dropped both of the combat boots to the floor. I returned to my side of the bed, quietly slipping back over the covers. My bedroom was growing hotter, and hotter by the second; his aura and body heat was slowly taking over every inch of this room.

I didn't lay beneath the covers; it was getting too hot, just from his mere presence.

I laid on my side and faced his back. The first boy to ever be in my room. The first to ever lay beside me. The first to ever crawl up that old, dainty tree, and roll through my window.

The thought of Bishop, drunk, attempting to climb the tree outside of my window made me wince.

Bishop shifted in the bed, rolling to face me. He wasn't awake; his breathing was steady, and quiet snores were coming from his mouth. My breath became unsteady in my throat. He was as intimidating unconscious as he was conscious; I swore he was staring holes into me, in his sleep.

He shifted again, burying his face into the crook of my neck. We both went still against each other; I listened for his snores, making sure he was still asleep. His hot breath was seeping into the sensitive part of my neck, causing me to tremble against him.

He still had his hold on me, even when completely out cold. He was intoxicating, even when intoxicated.

I tensed further. He shifted his face deeper into the area where my shoulder met my neck. The area was now slick; my skin had become wet, and slightly sticky. His cheeks and eyelashes were wet, rubbing his dried tears against me as he slept.

I moved my hand to his back, pulling him closer to me. He was trembling.

My other hand reached for his hair. I gently traced the tips of my acrylic against his scalp; he shuddered against me, and his breath grew heavier. I would believe he was awake if I couldn't feel his silent snore against me.

He was upset about something. Was he coming to me for comfort? Was he even aware he climbed up my tree, and into my bed? Or, had the alcohol already taken over his consciousness, and taken control of his memory?

I didn't move for the few hours left in the early morning. Neither did he. I woke up occasionally, and we were still in the same position as we had been since he slipped into my room.

But, when the sun rose, Bishop was gone. The only memory of him was the crease in my bed, and the tear stains on the crook of my neck.

VERSE FIFTEEN

Dad paced the stage, preaching something regarding Cain and Abel. I zoned in for a second, and the topic was regarding envy and our feelings toward people close to us in life.

I couldn't even pretend to concentrate. I felt the presence in the back pew, burning his into the back of my head. I hadn't turned, yet, but I knew if I did, Bishop would be staring.

It was unsettling how quietly he had been able to leave this morning. I was a light sleeper, yet he hadn't woken me when he departed. Plus, it was disturbing thinking of him and my dad under the same roof; Bishop was only a few feet away from him last night.

When I woke up this morning, I first texted Bishop to ask if he was alright. But, he never responded. Secondly, I had to check to make sure Dad hadn't been murdered while I was sleeping.

Buzz.

ME: are you okay?

read 7:34 am

BITCHOP: i like your hair like that.

ME: you already said that.

BITCHOP: so, you wore it like that on purpose?

I gnawed at the inside of my cheek, pushing up my glasses. I stared at the phone in my lap; I hoped my hair was hiding how red my face was getting. I had thought of him when putting my hair up this morning, knowing he might just find himself in the back of the church again. But, he didn't need to know that.

I looked back to the previous message I had sent; the one he completely ignored.

ME: no.

ME: you ignored my question.

I did not want to nag. Genuinely. I winced, knowing I was just some annoying girl, trying to get under his skin. But, he came to me, vulnerable this morning. Some part of him wanted me to latch onto him, otherwise, he would have stayed with his friends.

Did he remember?

BITCHOP: peachy.

All morning, while waiting for his response, I had imagined him drunk in some alley. All I got was "peachy"?

BITCHOP: sry for calling you a bitch.

He replied to the message from the previous night. I wondered if he was rereading the messages.

BITCHOP: now come to the bathroom and i will show you how good i am feeling.

It was very tempting to play along and pretend as if nothing had happened; to go into that bathroom and touch him until he made me forget every minute from this morning. He was either an absolute master at avoiding how he felt, or he truly had blacked out last night.

ME: no.

ME: did you blackout?

The second I watched the message send. I gulped and locked my phone. Guilt crept up my throat; I should not have asked that. I didn't know how to even begin to approach a topic as sensitive as this; however, I knew that was not the way to do it.

Or was it? I've never had an alcoholic in the family. Gwen drank the most out of everyone I knew, and she barely drank.

Buzz.

I couldn't look at my phone. I stared at my dad, imagining the worst message possible waiting on my phone. I should have at least eased into it. I mean, I might as well have said "Oh, by the way, you climbed into my bedroom last night. Drunk off your ass. Post cry. Remember?"

I unlocked my phone and checked the message.

BITCHOP: i didn't blackout.

BITCHOP: drop it, ethel.

Drop it.

I jerked my head around, narrowing my gaze in his direction. His jaw was clenched, eyes already set on mine. I could give two shits if someone noticed I was looking at him.

Drop it. I looked back to my phone, turning my back to him. He was defensive over last night, even though nothing happened; that he was awake for, at least. Did he not like how vulnerable he was?

I debated what to reply, but I decided on nothing. Instead, I stood up and walked toward the bathroom.

I chose the aisle that would walk directly beside Bishop. We did not break our intense stare as I walked past him, toward the bathroom. My heart was pounding in my chest, but I kept my chin high; I couldn't breathe under his stare.

Once I made it inside the bathroom, I ducked down to make sure no one was in any of the stalls. Mid bending over, the door swung open, and combat boots slapped against the floor. My breath hitched. I twisted my head up to face him.

I knew he was going to follow, but not that fast. If Dad hadn't noticed Bishop in his congregation before, he had now.

"That was qui—," I began, my voice shaking. All confidence was lost; Bishop took up the entire space. There was no room for confidence when someone like him was in the same vicinity.

His fingers wrapped around the back of my neck, and in one quick breath, his lips came down on me. I gasped, digging my nails into his wrists. I backed up against the tiled wall, his body pressing me flush against it.

This was not what I was planning on doing here. I had been planning on slapping him across the face for calling me a bitch last night, as well as telling me to drop something as serious as that.

But, now that his lips were on mine, they were all I could think of. I slid my lip against his, tugging at him. I opened my mouth for him to deepen the kiss and slip his tongue inside. His other hand landed on my thigh, pulling it over his hip.

We weren't in the confinement of a stall anymore. If someone were to walk in, they would see everything. And, there was no doubt in my mind they would recognize Bishop.

Shit, we should stop.

I grazed my hand up his cheek, recalling how the skin felt hours ago. I moved to his hair, resting my fingers in the thick curls. I was slowly slipping down the wall, but his tight grasp on my neck held me in place.

He felt so good. His lips almost felt as good as his bulge, when I grinded against it a few days ago.

I moved my thumb back to his cheek, cupping the skin. My thumb gently traced the pores of his soft skin. The same skin that was slick, only a few hours ago; the skin that was tainted with tear stains.

It took every cell in my body to pull myself away from him. Our foreheads rested against each other. Our heavy breaths intertwined together; his hot breath fanned up and down my face.

"Bishop," I began, looking up at him. "I don't want to pry—."

"Then don't." He pushed himself off of me; he acted like my body had just burned him. He put at least a foot between us.

Bishop stared at the floor by my feet with a tight jaw.

If something happened to you, and I didn't do anything, I wouldn't be able to forgive myself. I said nothing. I stared up at him, waiting for him to speak first. He stared at my feet, unable to meet my eyes.

He looked up at me for a second, but he instantly looked away. "Jesus Christ, stop looking at me like that."

"Like what?" I asked, tilting my head. Like I was worried for him?

He looked back up at me. This time, he was able to hold my gaze. But, he looked as if he was ready to sprint out of this bathroom. I didn't want to make him uncomfortable, I wasn't trying to.

I looked down at his collar. Again, he had taken off all his religious sigils, respecting the House of God. I reached up for him, but he slapped my hand away.

"Bishop, are you okay?" He clenched his jaw so tight that his teeth had to be on the verge of breaking. He looked down at me in a way no one ever had; he looked down at me like I was the bane of his existence. As if, I was taking everything he loved from him, just for asking if he was okay.

My stomach twisted.

"Stop. Fucking stop. Everything is fine. You don't want to pry, then don't fucking pry," he hissed, pushing past me. I stared up at him, letting him get the harsh words off his chest.

He bumped into my shoulder as he walked toward the door. His steps were stumbled and he was unable to walk straight. "I just wanted to get between your legs. Not all this. I will just fuck someone else tonight, and boom! You're out of my system. Have a good life, Ethel."

I stared up at the back of him; he opened the door and walked out of the bathroom. "Predictable prude," was the last thing I heard him say before he left me in the bathroom.

My eyes started to sting, and my throat tightened. No, Ethel. You will never cry over a boy like that.

I crossed my arms over my stomach, leaning against the tiled wall. It wasn't him speaking. He may have worn his skin and walked his steps, but Bishop was more than that. Bishop was the boy who crawled into my bed, quiet, seeking comfort over whatever was happening behind his eyes.

If he truly wanted to "get in between my legs", he would have tried last night. He wanted comfort. Yet, when I tried to give him a sliver of it, it was as if the world was going to end for him.

I swallowed the bundle of needles coming up my throat. Grandma wouldn't cry over a boy. I walked in front of the mirror, adjusting my outfit.

SACRED TIES

The "predictable prude" was going to Coen's party tonight, without Bishop.

VERSE SIXTEEN

I stared at my reflection. My chest was heaving from how frustrated I had become.

I narrowed my gaze at the pile of dresses behind me, and the loose-fitting one I currently wore. What was I even supposed to wear to a club? In movies, it was always tight little dresses. Was that what I was expected to wear? I've never owned a dress even close to that.

My stomach turned. I was actually going to go to a sex club. All for a boy. I had half my closet on the floor, all because of said boy.

I shouldn't be changing myself for him. He did not deserve my energy or time.

I was about to rip out my hair. Nothing fit the way it did other girls.

With a groan, I collapsed onto the bed. I debated calling Gwen and asking for her help in the matter. She would look at me sideways for wanting to go to Coen's party. It was not our type of crowd. Plus, she knew as much as I did about the matter.

Why was I even doing this?

I should just let it go. Have a good life, as he had so politely put it.

My phone illuminated my last Google search. When looking up clubbing outfit ideas, it was the same as the movies. Tight little black dresses, with women's pussies one moment from slipping out from the dress. I didn't care if it was Timothee Chalamet himself, I would never put a dress like that on. I wouldn't be able to pull it off; I would be too self-conscious of every movement.

I scrolled through my small selection of contacts. Most were from church, and others were classmates from high school. None of which would be remotely helpful in my current dilemma.

There was Janyce, a widowed elder who brought my dad cookies every Sunday. She would scream if she knew what I was planning on doing right now. Gilly, our mail delivery driver. And, of course, Gladis; she picked up the trash from church.

Am I boring?

Why do I know no one my age?

Maybe Gwen could help. No. I could see her now if I asked her for one of her dresses. She would look at me as if I had taken hard drugs and killed her entire family.

I loved her. Even if she never talked when we were together.

My finger landed on another contact; a name I hadn't spoken to in over three months.

Briar.

The last time we spoke, we were catching up about how we were doing after high school. I used to help her with homework, and essays; in exchange, she would pay me beneath the table.

She was also incredibly hot.

She never left the house without the best outfit on her body, her hair fully done, and lip gloss painted on her lips. She had been the cheer coach in high school. The stereotypical "queen bee." Though, despite contrary belief, she was one of the nicest people I've ever met.

When she wanted to be.

With who she wanted to be.

She could be a bitch, but she never had been to me. It may have been because I was the reason she passed her senior year; I had been very talented with essay writing, back in the day.

Most importantly, the boys loved her.

My cheeks heated as I clicked on her icon. Could she make me hot for the night? Just for the night, to spite him; to show him that his words didn't affect me, as he wished. After, Briar and I could go our separate ways again.

ME: can you help me with something?

——

An hour later, I no longer recognized myself.

Briar had come to my house, with a large bag of clothes, and at least a thousand dollars' worth of cosmetics. She had scowled at the large pile of clothes in my room, before throwing some of her choices onto the bed.

I was wearing the most conservative of them. And, even then, the black skirt was barely reaching my thighs. Paired with it, I put on one of her mother's black lace-up corsets; my breasts were to my neck.

"So, who are we making jealous?" Briar asked, tilting her head to the side. She continued to straighten my hair, staring at me through the mirror.

She was wearing a tight, black dress. It was similar to the dresses I saw in my Google search earlier. It matched her voluminous, black curls.

Briar was beautiful; bombshell beautiful.

"It's stupid. He's stupid." I ground my teeth together. He was stupid. She smirked, slowly running the straightener through my natural waves; I preferred my natural hair, but this was way too much effort.

"You know, this might be a sign from the universe." She blew her bubble out of her mouth, popping it, before continuing. She was just like how she was in high school. "I wanted to go to this, but all of my girlfriends are out of town. And my stupid stepbrother was saying he would lock me in my room if I tried going alone."

Briar huffed, looking to the ceiling. She rolled her eyes and continued. "Then I was like, well why don't you go? You know, get out of the house some. You know what the jerk said?"

"What?" I replied. I felt like I was just in the room. Briar could make conversation with a wall.

"He said bite me!" Briar exclaimed, jerking the straighter away from my hair. I winced, afraid she was going to burn me. "What a fucking ass."

Briar was an only child. She always had been. Politely putting it, she was a spoiled brat in high school. People often associated that with her lack of siblings. She didn't have a dad, but her mother was incredibly rich, despite that.

"I didn't know you had a stepbrother," I said.

"Unfortunately, Mom got married over the summer. Now, up!" Briar exclaimed.

I didn't question it any further.

I stood up, checking my figure out in the mirror. The black, lacey, corset was flattering; it squeezed me together and pressed my breasts far up. The skirt reached a few inches below my hips. It was long enough to bend over... once. If I bent over twice, though, everything would be out for show.

I traced my fingers on the fishnets.

"This is a lot," I sighed. My eyes widened as I turned around, looking at the outfit from the back. She threw a lacey cardigan in my direction; when she originally arrived, I told her the only way I would wear a corset, was if I had something to cover myself up. In case I got cold.

"I'm a lot. That's why you texted, is it not? So, who is it? Do I know him?" She bit her lip, leaning over the vanity to reapply her clear lip gloss.

I looked at my makeup. My eyelids were painted with a subtle shimmer, eyeliner paired with it. She had curled my eyelashes, and applied so much mascara I could barely blink without them sticking together.

But, it worked.

I looked hot.

"Probably," I started. "He graduated just before we went to high school. I don't know how I feel about him. He is very rude."

It felt good to be able to talk about it. I needed to hang out with Gwen more often. She was the best listener. But, ever since her brother died, she barely left her house anymore.

"Well, you clearly like him. I mean, look at you. You're stiff as a board. Only a boy makes you do things you don't want to do."

I laughed, sitting on the edge of my bed. She was right; I would have never done this if it weren't for the jackass himself. I shouldn't be doing this, but there was no going back now.

"Beautiful," she squealed, looking at herself in the mirror.

Briar turned around, facing me. I let out a gasp as she reached for my breasts. She slid her hands beneath the corset, grabbing a handful, and pulling them upward. "You have nice tits," she started, moving to the other breast. "Show them."

Whatever she had done worked. The tight corset was pushing my breasts further up my chest. It looked like I had a boob job.

"Are you sure this isn't too much?" I asked.

She shook her head, perking her breasts up. "No. Have you ever been to Coen's club? Half of them are naked most of the time. Plus, it's dark. No one cares what anyone is doing."

I take it back. This is not a bad idea. This is a terrible idea. This might actually be the worst thing I've ever done in my life. It wasn't just any night, it was Coen's birthday night; sex party night.

"You're nervous. We are taking a shot." Briar pulled a bottle of Fireball from the front of her dress. She filled her mouth full of the amber liquid, swallowing it in one hefty gulp. She didn't wince once.

I was going to spit that out. I could smell it from here.

It smelled of Bishop.

To that thought, I filled my mouth full of the liquid. Just for tonight.

VERSE
SEVENTEEN

"Crimson" was as intense as I expected it to be.

It may have been a little more traumatizing if I was being honest.

Once I stepped through the doors, it was clear there were no rules. I couldn't see much due to the dim, red, lighting; however, I was able to make out multiple figures from my peripheral.

Specifically, their skin sliding together; there were multiple couples, having sex wherever they wished.

If you wanted to have sex at the bar, you could have sex at the bar. If you wanted to have sex on the dancefloor, you could have sex on the dancefloor.

I kept my gaze upward, ignoring some of the activities we walked past. There was no way to recognize anyone in this club; the red hue was barely illuminating the large club. I was grateful for this, it made it easier to ignore the sex happening, every so often.

There were two rules in the club. It was plastered on a large board, beside the entrance. Non-consensual activities and date drugs were prohibited from the space. All goers that broke this, would be dealt with by the owner.

I shuddered, imagining Coen summoning Baylen to deal with rapists. My mind conjured a horrific, well-deserved, image.

"Holy shit," Briar cursed. Her short, French acrylics, dug into my skin as she held tightly onto my arm. I was grateful she was clinging to me; I would get lost within a minute. Crimson did not look this large from the outside. It was two stories, at least.

She pulled me toward the mass of dancing people. The bass thumping through the speakers was so loud my head began to rattle. "I wasn't expecting this many people," she admitted.

The low lighting did not bring justice to how many people were currently in this club. Our town did not even have this many people.

Briar reached for her flask, downing another shot of fireball. She passed it to me; this time, I gladly flung the liquid into my mouth.

The shots were becoming easier against my gag reflex. My head was spinning, and a gentle buzz was spreading across my skin. Was this why he drank so much? It felt so numbing; I felt like I could do anything right now, without getting hurt.

"This is insane," I gawked.

This had to be the biggest building we had in Death Valley.

Briar pulled me closer to the music. She and the chaos were star-crossed lovers; wherever loud music, dancing people, and parties were involved, she would follow. It was where she belonged. A place like this.

I squinted up toward the second floor. There were balconies overlooking everything. A few men dressed in suits sat on the balconies, with a whiskey glass in their hands. Coen was someone I had never seen before in my life; however, I imagined him to look like one of those men.

I've seen the rest of them, though. Unfortunately.

There was a bar, twice the size of my bedroom. Beside the bar was a staircase; it was blocked off, leading to an entirely different area of the club. This place was like a maze. How did people not get lost here?

Tucked in the corner were large, circular booths, for clubbers to eat, or chat. A few couples were sitting there, eating over a dinner, as they talked over the music. Other couples rolled around, atop the tables, fucking each other into oblivion.

In the very back of the club, there were multiple rooms blocked off by a red rope. They were shielded by crystal clear curtains. There were at least seven individuals in one room; the curtain allowed anyone who wanted to watch, to watch.

"Have you been here before?" I asked, yelling over the music. She nodded; her eyes lit up as she scanned the crowd of moving bodies. It was overwhelming, but the buzz from this space was absolutely electric. That was the only way I could explain it.

What would have happened if I went here clinging to Bishop, instead of Briar?

"Yeah," Briar continued. She looked like she was in a trance. "Just not to one of these events. God, I don't think I've ever seen so many people in one place. This is breathtaking."

Breathtaking. That was not how I would describe it; I would say shocking. Pulsating. Electric.

This had to be twice our town's population. I wondered, if beneath the lighting, there were people here that no one would expect. I mean, I was here, there had to be others like me. Outcasts, hiding in the shadows and dim lighting of Crimson. Letting go for the night.

Just for tonight, I reminded myself.

Briar squealed, before jerking me into the crowd with her. My eyes rounded, watching her pull us deep between the bodies. She smiled, looking back at me. She bit her lip and said something beneath her breath, but I couldn't make out what she was saying.

From the way her lips moved, it looked like she said "This is my wet dream."

Briar settled us in a spot, in the center of the crowd. She started to dance, showing me how to move like her. At first, I had no idea what I was doing, but she moved her body against mine, showing me how she moved.

It didn't feel erotic in any way; however, people gazed down at us like it was arousing.

We didn't stop.

VERSE EIGHTEEN

B riar and I both giggled. The back of her head rested against my shoulder as she threw another shot of fireball back into her mouth.

I wondered what it would be like to be Briar; to live this wildly, boldly, every day. To never feel stiff in a crowd. She could have anyone. Since we made our way into the crowd, people had been staring at us through the lighting.

It was Briar they stared at.

She did not give anyone a second glance.

Whoever was going to have her heart was going to be lucky. She was fun.

"Do you see your boy thing yet?" Briar asked, yelling over the music. Even then, I couldn't hear half of what she was saying. I only understood her because of her lips, and the way they moved.

I shook my head.

I'd forgotten about Bishop.

I was having more fun in this crowd, with Briar, these sweaty bodies, this short skirt. Stepping on his toes was not nearly as exciting as I currently felt.

Then again, I did want to make sure he saw the "predictable prude" before we left.

"Help me look," I yelled, wrapping my fingers around her bicep. "It's Bishop."

The name was out of my mouth before I could bite my tongue. I felt myself get hotter, though it wasn't the fireball, nor the mass of people. Bishop. He was the reason I was here; the jackass was the reason I was stepping out of my comfort zone, dressed in this tight little outfit, and dancing in a sex club.

Shit, maybe he had more control over me than I wished to admit.

Her jaw dropped to her chest. She smiled hard, her eyes lighting up when she realized what name I had spilled. "Bishop!"

I pushed my lips into a thin line. I shook my head, trying to hide the smirk creeping up my face. God, help me. Briar was never going to let this go. Even if we only spoke once every three months, she was going to remind me of this every time.

Bishop. Bishop. Bishop. Bishop. My chant, repeating in my head like a mantra. My stomach fluttered, but sunk, all at once. Bishop, the dick that had spoken to me in the bathroom this morning. Bishop, the boy who climbed into my bed last night, upset.

Briar grinned. She wrapped her fingers around my hand; she pulled us out of the crowd, and toward the outer ring of people. I felt disappointment wave over me as we left the liveliest area of the club.

It was still loud where we currently stood, but I was able to hear my heartbeat now.

"Bishop?" Briar exclaimed, again. She clasped her hands together, jumping from one foot to the other. Suddenly, she frowned, as if realizing something. "Oh, fuck, Ethel. He will rip you apart. I'm surprised he hasn't already."

"Yeah," was all I could say. I once believed the same. I believed it this morning when he left me in the church stall.

She smiled, sucking in her bottom lip. Her gaze moved behind my head, toward the bar.

My breath hitched. Her eyes lit up, and her smile deepened so far into her face, that dimples came to light. What was behind me that was making her smile so hard? I was scared to turn around and see.

"He's there. With my stepbrother."

I twisted my head around, fixing my eyes toward the bar. Small lights were hanging above the bar top, making it easier for the bartenders to see. Sure enough, Bishop sat on the corner of the bar. Two of his best friends sat on either side of him.

To his left, Solomon sat with his fingers tapping against the edge of his glass of water. His natural curls were cut close to his head, but long enough to cover the light blue of his eyes. His skin was a light shade of brown, contrasting with the dark shade of his hair.

Solomon was gorgeous; being out of high school gave him a new glow. I hadn't gotten a good glimpse of him in the alleyway, I was too distracted by hauling Bishop into the car.

He looked as stiff as I had on the dance floor. He was close beside Bishop; Solomon fearfully eyed every woman that passed as if they were trying to kill him.

I moved to Bishop next. The back of his head was a mess; it was his constant hairstyle, apparently. He reached over the counter, jerking a bottle from the bar. The bartender narrowed her eyes at him but allowed him to refill his glass.

Lastly, to his right, Baylen sat. I felt the fireball rise up my throat.

He had his face tilted to whisper something into Bishop's ear. I was able to see half of his face; he was the youngest of all of them. He was still in high school, at seventeen years old. Well, he would be if he hadn't gotten arrested a year ago; he was a dropout now.

Thankfully, the years he did attend were at Southside. Otherwise, we would have been in school together.

He wasn't fat, nor was he thin. He had some baby fat on his cheeks, and hands still, but the rest of his body was relatively lean.

Baylen smiled at whatever he was whispering into Bishop's ear. I watched a dimple sink into his cheek, and his plump lips brush against Bishop's ear.

I frowned, zoning out on Baylen's image. This was the first time I've seen him since he got released from juvie.

He looked up at me like he knew I was staring at him. His eyes looked as if they had died, a long time ago. They were black; not a glint of light rested behind them. His hair was thicker than Bishop's and much messier. Streaks of red were scattered throughout his mop of black hair.

Baylen wasn't beautiful. He was rotten. He may wear the face of a charming boy, but something was wrong with him. Deep inside of him.

I shuddered, looking away. "Which one is your stepbrother?" She had to be talking about someone else at the bar. If it were Baylen, she would have already been murdered, or committed suicide. If it were Solomon…

"Solomon."

My jaw hung low as I looked up at her. "You did not mention this."

"You didn't ask," she began. "Say something to Bishop, then we leave. After that, you never speak to him again. That's how you play with boys, Ethel. Now let's go."

She slapped my ass, pushing me forward.

"Say something good," she added, trailing behind me.

What was I going to say? Hi. No. As Briar kept mentioning, I was someone else tonight. What would Briar say in this situation? She would not even be in this situation if it were Briar; half the men in this club were staring at her like they wanted to eat her.

"I'm nervous," I admitted, turning toward her. I stopped walking. I couldn't do it; I couldn't approach him after he practically told me to "go fuck myself" in the church bathroom.

She grabbed her flask, pushing it toward my chest. "Fireball solves everything."

It doesn't, it was only making me nauseous. But, I took the shot anyway.

"I'm more scared of Baylen. Why does he look like that?" I asked. The kick of the shot helped me move my legs closer to the bar.

"Yeah, I can't help you there. Not stop fucking stalling." She slapped my ass again.

We were at the bar before I could back out.

She slid beside Solomon, snaking her hand around his bicep. She reached for his drink, downing the water in two gulps. "Hey, step bro," she purred. She pulled her lip between her teeth, returning the empty glass to the table.

Solomon looked like he was going to strangle her.

"What the fuck are you doing here?" Solomon hissed.

I looked away from them as they began to argue. I positioned myself between her and Bishop; my eyes didn't leave the side of his head. He was completely uninterested in the warm body that was pressed against him.

At least I didn't need to worry about him being with a girl. He didn't give a fuck about two girls sliding beside him on the bar.

"You're devious, big man," Bishop said to Baylen, continuing their conversation. Big man. He was the smallest, and the youngest of their group.

I tensed as Baylen's eyes moved down to meet mine.

When he was looking at me, it felt like it was just us in the room. But, not in the way Bishop made me feel. It was a terrible, indescribable feeling.

Baylen was every Devil in existence. Every religion's sin, hell, and Devil, combined into one flesh. His stare was so dark that I almost whimpered under it. Anytime Bishop looked at me, it was a mixture of pain and pleasure.

Baylen looked like he wanted everyone to suffer.

I gulped, looking back up to Bishop. Briar and Solomon were still arguing behind me. And, the bastard was still not looking at me. He had to have noticed his friend's gaze on me. Did he just not care about the two females beside him?

Just for the night, I reminded myself.

I stood on my tiptoes. Even with him sitting down, and Briar's heels on my feet, I could not reach his ear.

I placed my fingers on his forearm, steadying myself as I whispered into his ear. "I may be a predictable prude, but at least I am not a douchebag desperate to get his dick wet."

His head jerked in my direction. His eyes lit up, surprise filling the green hues.

His mouth parted. His eyes were only on my face for a second; he spent the rest of his time raking over every inch of my body. He looked at my chest, then my ankles, and then back to my chest. Every inch of exposed skin was touched by his eyes.

Bishop's eyes darkened. He met my gaze, again.

He looked like he was one second away from jumping me.

I grabbed ahold of Briar's arm. "Oh shit!" She cackled, pulling us away from the bar. I grabbed ahold of Bishop's drink in the process, taking it with me wherever we were going.

"Where are we going?" I asked once we were a few feet away from the bar. My heart was beating hard in my chest; Bishop had never looked at me like that. My legs were getting weak with every step.

I downed the whiskey. My face contorted at the taste. How do people enjoy drinking that?

Briar muttered something, but I could not hear her. I turned back around, looking in Bishop's direction as she pulled us through a crowd of people.

His eyes were already pinned on mine.

I flashed him a smile, before looking over to the other boys beside him. Baylen was staring at the bottles, zoning out the mass of people behind him. He didn't even look present; he looked like he was breathing. Existing.

Solomon was as tense as he had been before. He was looking in our direction, but it wasn't me he was looking at.

Once Bishop was out of sight, I turned back toward Briar. Our fingers were intertwined together. My body was trembling, pure adrenaline pumping through my veins. Even though half the people in this place were currently having sex, openly, this was the most fun I've had in a while.

Just for the night.

We didn't leave the actual club, as I was expecting.

Instead, she pulled me into a private room. There was a black lace curtain concealing the room, and a black rope blocking off the area. A woman covered in tattoos stood in front of the room, her arms crossed over her chest.

She narrowed her eyes on us, before moving the rope aside.

VERSE NINETEEN

Every step I took deeper into this club, the more intense it became. I noted to be prepared the next time I walked into a private room. This once was dimly lit, like the outside, though it was more of a purple hue in this room.

And it was just women.

There was not a single man in sight.

The room was small. There was a tiny bar in the corner of the room; a woman with pink hair was currently constructing a margarita. She placed it on a tray, before walking out of the room.

Scattered through the room were multiple seating options. There were love seats, beanbags, a strangely constructed swing, and plush chairs. There was even a stripper pole in the center of the room.

Briar moved us to the pool table. She turned around, looking at me with wide eyes and a cheeky smile. "You should have seen his face. Oh, fuck. I was scared for you."

I was out of breath. Twenty more shots of the fireball would not erase the sight of Bishop when he realized who I was. His face was priceless; I bit my lip, laughing. "Do you think he is still irritated with me?"

I was still irritated with him; he had been such a dick, but he had a reason. I shouldn't have pried. If he didn't want to get better, I couldn't force him to; it would only push him away. He would retreat, into the confinements that made him happy. Alcohol.

She shook her head. We both scanned the room, watching the various girls making out with each other. There were two people in the corner, rubbing themselves against each other, letting out soft pants. I tried to look away, but the sight was mesmerizing.

"No," Briar continued, looking back at me. "He looked like he wanted to fuck you."

I pushed myself up so that I was sitting on the edge of the pool table. I was still out of breath. I didn't ever want to leave this room; he hadn't seen where I went, but the thought of seeing him after that made my stomach flip.

No one has ever looked at me like that.

"What did you even say to him?" She asked.

I grabbed the bridge of my nose, recalling what I uttered. God, forgive me after the night I've had tonight. "I said, 'I may be a predictable prude, but at least I am not a douchebag desperate to get his dick wet'"

Was I being immature?

She clamped her hand over her mouth, stumbling into the pool table. She nearly fell over. Briar was beyond inebriated; she thought this was the funniest thing anyone had ever said to her. "That is so funny."

My phone buzzed.

We both looked down at the phone with wide eyes. I didn't open it; I looked up at her. My face was pale as a ghost. Maybe I should have never spoken to him again like he wanted; it would avoid having to face him after this club.

"Open it!" Briar exclaimed. She tried to reach for my phone and do it herself, but I beat her to it.

BITCHOP: come here.

I showed her the text, biting hard into my lip. It was bleeding; it had been bleeding since I entered this stupid club.

She held up a finger, telling me to wait where I was. She disappeared to the bar. I didn't respond to Bishop; I impatiently kicked my feet in the air under the pool table. My fingers were digging into the side, watching all of the couples around the room.

It was loud, still. I could barely hear the noises coming from the two girls scissoring a few feet away. Occasionally, the bottom would cry out, and buck her hips up.

It felt peaceful here. Safe.

Briar returned with a shot glass full of some dark substance. "Lay down," she instructed. "And give me your phone."

I shook my head. "Why?"

She smiled, a devious light glinting behind her eyes. "To step on his toes a little more. It's my expertise, of course."

Briar was the perfect level of brat, and bold. It was exactly what I needed. Without her "expertise", I would have been curled up in bed with a book; sulking over what could have been.

Hesitantly, I unlocked my phone and laid it on the pool table. The other girls in the room were too distracted with each other to even look in our direction. It was just Briar and me on this pool table; the camera of my phone was our only witness.

She wedged the cold shot glass between my thighs. Half of the glass disappeared beneath my skirt. My chest was moving fast, heaving, as I looked down at what she was doing. She smiled up at me and pressed the record button; she captured everything that was about to occur.

Briar planted a kiss on my inner thigh. After, she wrapped her lips around the shot glass. Her face disappeared beneath the hem of my skirt. She locked her gaze with mine, not breaking the stare once as she threw her head back.

She licked her lips and turned off the recording.

"This is going to be so hot," she said, collapsing onto the pool table beside me. We lay beside each other, taking up the entire table. It wasn't like the people in here were going to play, anyway; they were only interested in each other's pussies.

We watched the video over. Again, I've never watched porn, but this looked like how I imagined a lesbian film to begin. She was staring up at me, eyes laced with sex, and I was looking down at her; I was trembling, with my eyebrows tight together.

I didn't even want Bishop to have a video like that. What if he sent it to someone? Would he?

She sent the video. I did not feel regretful. I felt ecstatic seeing the message sent to him.

He viewed the second it went through.

"Now we wait," she instructed, locking my phone.

We both stared up at the purple lights. Everything in my vision was starting to sway. I might have been tipsy. Maybe drunk. My toes were starting to tingle; I was indeed tipsy.

"He can't come in here. Right?" I asked.

She shook her head. "It's the ladies section."

Briar's intense voice softened, and she crossed her arms over her stomach. She let out a huff before spewing. "You know, Solomon doesn't even live with us, but he is still so protective over me. It's like borderline possessiveness. I never would have thought he'd be like that. You know, the guy we went to school with."

Solomon was a sophomore when we entered high school. Bishop, Cain, and Coen were graduated by the time we started freshman year. Thankfully, we had missed them by a year. Baylen was a year beneath our grade; he didn't attend Northside, though.

I couldn't imagine Solomon like that; he never acted like that in high school.

I was quiet, but she kept going. "It's annoying. Oh, Briar, your skirt is too short. Oh, Briar, you can't go to that party. Like, he only comes to the house once a month. If he needs to concentrate on whatever he does with those computers. He's probably watching porn or something. Gross."

She continued to ramble about her stepbrother, even after another long stretch of silence passed.

"Like, three months our parents have been married, and now he thinks it is like his duty to watch everything I do. You know, one time he hacked into my phone, and threatened to send my nudes to Mom if I went to a party?"

"Solomon?" I asked. I looked over at her. Maybe he was different with her, that was not how he acted in high school. Solomon was the boy who was too good at math for his own good; the boy all the teachers liked.

"Exactly! I mean, he was a fucking nerd in high school. I never would have expected it if I wasn't living with him." A groan came from her throat; I watched her eyes flutter. "God, I hope he doesn't sleep at our house tonight. He does it just to spite me, I swear."

"Strange," I said, looking back to the ceiling. The alcohol was beginning to wear off. I was slowly becoming more and more aware of where I was right now. What was I doing?

My mouth dried as guilt took over my thoughts. Dad must not be home, otherwise, he would have called asking where I was. If he saw the pile of clothes on my floor, he would think I'd run away.

"You know what is strange." Briar rolled onto her stomach, looking down at me. "You and Bishop. I mean, opposites really must attract if that is happening. Didn't he like graffiti on your dad's church? And, release snakes in it? A bible on fire, too, if I recall."

Shit. No need to remind me.

I nodded, rubbing my eyes beneath my glasses. Briar rarely went to church, but she had been present for those horrifying days.

"Damn. I mean, you go gir—."

"Your brother is looking for you."

Briar and I both shot up from the table, gaping. On the edge of the table, Bishop stood. He was talking to Briar, but his eyes were on me. He snaked his arm around my waist, hauling me from the table, and onto my feet. "Something about calling your boyfriend," Bishop continued.

Briar was off the table in a second. "The little shit," she hissed, running out of the room.

She left me alone with the thick tension circulating between Bishop and me.

VERSE TWENTY

I stood in front of the pool table. My back was pinned against it, and Bishop's hands fell on either side of my hips, keeping me in place.

He didn't speak. Nor did I. I let out a shuddered breath, staring up at him through my heavy eyelashes. What was I supposed to say? 'Sorry for pushing such a sensitive topic, but also fuck you for being so rude in that bathroom.'

I cleared my throat. "You can't be in here. It's only for girls."

As if that had stopped him in the girl's bathroom. Many times.

Bishop laughed, tipping his head down lower. It felt like he was currently looking inside of me; if that were even possible. "My best friend owns this club. I can be anywhere I want."

His hand landed between my thighs, without a single warning. Two fingers had landed over my clit with such precision it felt unnatural. I let out a choked gasp; my body folded over, stunned by the sudden feeling.

My stomach became hot. Arousal pooled in my panties. It was like he activated my core from a single touch.

I slid my hand between my legs, grabbing tightly ahold of his wrist. I jerked his hand away, narrowing my eyes up at him. "No," I snapped. I squeezed my fingers tighter around his wrist.

"Just testing the waters," he replied. His lips perked up. He opened his mouth to continue, but I pulled him forward, stifling whatever remark he was about to make.

I pulled us out of the room, leaving the scissoring women to their privacy. I looked back to see if Bishop was watching them. To my surprise, he hadn't looked at the woman once. I thought this was every boy's wet dream.

He only looked at me.

We made it a few feet away from the private room before I was pushed against a nearby wall. This time, it was me that pulled him down onto me. I grabbed the collar of his shirt, pulling his mouth onto mine.

I kissed him once. But, once he tried to slip his tongue inside my mouth, I pulled away. I wouldn't be able to stop if he started with his tongue; it felt too good.

"You were rude today." My lips brushed against his as I spoke. It still felt like we were kissing, even after I pulled away.

"I'm sorry," Bishop began. His body tensed against mine. But, despite the discomfort, he continued. "There are things I really, really do not want to talk about. Not yet. So, if that's going to be an issue—."

I shook my head. "It won't. I won't pry. I'm sorry for being pushy about it." I hesitated, thinning my eyes into slits. "Just don't be a dick about it."

"I'm sorry, Ethel. Truly. There's just too much going on in my head. I don't want to think about that."

Bishop's lips were back against mine. His hips pressed hard against mine, rolling slowly against me. A moan slid out my throat, but his mouth stifled the noise. My head fell backward, hitting the wall.

His lips moved down my neck. He moved his hips, groaning against my neck. The vibrations against my skin made me shudder.

I grabbed ahold of his hair, pulling his face deeper into my neck. His teeth bit down harder against the flesh, responding to my action. Our bodies were so responsive to each other; it felt like we were made for each other, physically.

"You look different," he said, against my throat.

His lips brushed against the crook of my neck. The same area he had burrowed into when he crawled into my room, covered in sorrow.

"I don't like it," I admitted. It looked better on Briar; I didn't look like me.

"Me neither." His fingertips landed at my knee, slowly trailing up my inner thigh. His touch was gentle; however, the second he reached the apex of my thigh, he grabbed a harsh hold of my flesh.

A soft moan came from me. I leaned forward, sucking on his neck to silence any other noises that he brought from me. He lifted my leg to rest against his hip, giving him easy access to my soaked panties.

From over Bishop's shoulder, I caught a glimpse of the bouncer still guarding the private room. She didn't look over at us once. She had likely seen everything there was to see. Twice.

His hand moved from my thigh. He didn't stop at the apex of my thigh, like he had before. The tip of his thumb landed directly above my clit, sliding it down my slit, and then back to my clit.

My fingers latched onto his back, holding onto him as he worked me through my panties.

I was trembling, and he had only stroked the length of my slit once. If he ever was to make it inside of me, I would combust. I doubted we would make it that far, though.

Bishop kissed my ear. His lips brushed against my earlobe as he spoke. "I like your little church girl skirts." He slipped his thumb up, and down my folds again. I let out another muffled moan. His smirk intensified after the noise.

I was wearing cotton bikini panties; they were molding tighter against my pussy, the more his thumb moved. I hadn't expected anything to happen tonight. Briar offered to bring me some sexy, new underwear; however, I promised her he wouldn't be going anywhere near my panties.

He pulled his thumb between us. It was glistening. Even if he had only touched me through my panties, my wetness was dripping from his finger.

He took it between his lips, licking every drop off of him. His eyes never left me.

"Do you want to go to dinner?" I asked. My voice resembled a pant. His chest was pressed hard against mine; he had to feel how fast my heart was pumping.

I slid my hands up his chest. Every muscle tensed under my fingertips; I reached his neck, brushing the tips of my nails across his pulse. It was moving as fast as mine was.

"Now?" Bishop asked.

I nodded, sliding my leg away from his hip. He nodded, intertwining his fingers with mine.

He abandoned his best friend's party, taking us away from the god-forsaken club, the second I asked. He never pleaded to stay a few more minutes or say goodbye to his friends. He was acting like I was his priority. Not his friends. Not his endless supply of alcohol.

For that, I was going to have Bishop.

VERSE TWENTY-ONE

Thirty minutes later, Bishop was across from me, two plates of food settled between us. Gianno's was the only restaurant open at this time of night. I felt guilty, imagining Dad and I sitting at this exact table.

"Stop looking at me like that," I huffed, stabbing my Caesar salad with my fork. We had been here for a total of twenty minutes, at max, and all 1200 seconds, Bishop spent his time staring at me. He stared at me like I was more appetizing than the food in front of him.

I had to look like a disaster. Why was he staring at me? My hair was a frizzy mess, I was sweaty, and the entire club smelled of cigarettes. Crimson smelled of Bishop, minus the smell of sex. The corset was digging into my sides when I sat; it was leaving red marks under the straps, and around my rib cage. Not to mention the makeup. I've smeared it everywhere by now.

Bishop looked at me like none of it existed.

"How am I looking at you, Ethel?" I gulped, looking up at him for a split second. The way he said my name made me tremble. He could make anything sound like it was related to sex, even if it was as simple as my name.

"Like that," I replied. I stared down at my salad, unable to even look at him right now.

Everything was hot. I had to take off my cardigan the second I sat in front of him; I was barely wearing any clothing in the cold restaurant, but I was still sweating. It was the Bishop effect.

He picked at his pasta before biting into it. Even when eating, his eyes were on me. I've never been so nervous to eat; he was watching my every move.

"I did not like that place," I admitted. My ears were ringing from how loud the music was. I could still feel the thump of the bass in my heart, even though we were far from Crimson.

"Careful," Bishop began. "Coen put his heart and soul into that place."

He grinned, biting the pasta with his white teeth. I was grateful for the tablecloth covering my thighs right now. He couldn't see me clenching my legs together. God, how did he make every possible movement so seductive?

My gaze slid down to the lower half of his face. I watched his jaw, clenching as he chewed. Then, at his lips. His tongue slipped out of his mouth, collecting a stray drop of marinara; the movement of his tongue running across his lips was so slow, and subtle. It was painful to watch.

I looked back down at my food, forgetting that I was mid-bite.

Bishop was going to make me explode.

"You're beautiful," Bishop started. I moved my eyes back to him. Was Bishop calling me beautiful? There had to be a but... "But, you look better when you are not trying to dress like a slu—."

I scoffed, cutting him off. "I am not. I just wanted to wear something different. Thank you for your input, though." I rolled my eyes, jabbing my fork hard into my salad. I reached for my water, attempting to quench how Bishop was making me feel; my insides felt like they were melting.

"Can I take it off of you?"

I choked on my water.

Bishop let out a silent laugh, looking up toward the waiter standing beside our table. I was too flustered to even realize the bill had come, and Bishop had paid. Tonight, I made myself one with the salad in front of me.

Once the waiter left, I responded to him. "Bishop, we are in a restaurant."

Bishop turned around, looking toward the bathroom behind him. He looked back at me and dipped his head down. He looked through his thick eyelashes, flames flashing behind his sage-colored eyes.

I couldn't breathe.

His eyes told me exactly what he was thinking; that fire behind them was showing me what he wanted to do. To me.

The waiter returned, giving Bishop a copy of the receipt. I cleared my throat, pulling my eyes upward. I wasn't going to be able to sit in this restaurant again, without thinking of the look Bishop just gave me. The sin and lust, possessing a green hue.

Shit, I wasn't going to be able to sleep without thinking of him.

I did not ask Bishop to walk me home. He followed me out of the restaurant, walking beside me. Silence and tension lingered between us, intensifying with every step toward my house.

Occasionally, a few people walked past, glancing at Bishop. There weren't many people out this late; those that were out, and about, were partiers returning from Crimson.

Dad's car was not in the driveway when we arrived. Where in the world was he this late at night?

I spoke once we walked up the steps, toward my front door. "I have a question."

I pulled my cardigan tight around me, preparing for the conversation I was about to invoke. I turned to face him, leaning my back against the door.

He tilted his head, looking down at me. "I most likely don't have an answer."

I wrapped my arms right around my stomach. His stare was making me more, and more, conscious of what I wore. I had texted Briar that I was leaving early; she said she would come over another day to pick up the small pieces of fabric.

I cleared my throat; this was something I'd been afraid to ask. I didn't want to know the answer. It would ruin this image I had of him if he confirmed it to be true.

"When Cain was still in town—." I hesitated. It felt wrong to speak of Cain. He was a ghost now. Nothing but a memory, from the darkest days our town had ever seen. "There were a lot of rumors about you and Baylen taking advantage of the situation."

Murdering for fun was what the people said. It was completely true for Baylen; he'd posted the videos online, sharing them as if it were a funny clip he'd seen. Some people on the streets even muttered the horrifying word "rape" beneath their breaths.

I leaned my head against the door, staring up at him. His fingers reached up for my jawline, lingering on the bone. His jaw was flexed, given the topic I'd just brought up. Don't pry, I reminded myself. But, if it were true, this was the last time I would allow myself to look at him.

The time Cain was in this town was a dark dark time. For every person in this town. He, and his friends, were able to do anything. Cain had the law wrapped around his finger. They could do whatever they wished, without the fear of arrest.

Cain was a false god.

Bishop shook his head. "Baylen," he muttered beneath his breath. He wasn't lying. He didn't look away from me. He lied to me in the church bathroom a few days ago; he couldn't look me in the eyes when he did. Now, though, he was staring into the deepest parts of my soul.

"I've hurt people, but never for fun. I never wanted to. That's all Baylen."

I've hurt people. That alone should have made me open the door and disappear into the safety of my home. I knew he had hurt people. He had blood on his hands the first time I spoke to him, directly. But, I always believed what the people said; that it was for fun. By choice.

Baylen and Bishop were often mistaken for each other. It made sense why they associated one's actions with the others. They both looked like they belonged in a Metallica concert. Plus, for a few years, the two were attached at the hip.

I should go inside.

An image kept popping into my head. Bishop, drunk against a dumpster, with someone's blood on his hands. He had hurt people.

I tilted my head to the side, urging his fingers to slide lower. My eyes fluttered, along with my stomach; he traced the pulse of my jugular. "Thank you for being honest," I whispered. If I spoke any louder, I'd be a nervous wreck.

His fingers wrapped around my throat. The grasp was not tight enough to hurt, but firm enough to pull my face to him. He covered my mouth with soft lips, swallowing the noise I made upon impact. I slid my tongue against his. He didn't taste of alcohol, as I expected; mine still tasted of fireball.

He pressed his hand against my stomach, pushing me harder into the door. I held onto his hair to steady myself. My legs were already becoming wobbly.

"Again," Bishop started, moving his lips to my jawline. "I am not good with opening up. Is that going to be an issue?"

I shook my head. "You will. When you are ready."

He returned his mouth to me. His hand tightened around my throat. "Just like you were going to wear my hands around your throat?"

Fire.

Pure fucking fire boiled at his words.

I wanted him. Needed him. Right now. I pulled him into me, sliding my tongue into his mouth. I kept him planted against me, biting rough and fast at his lips. He slid his thigh between my legs, rubbing it against my panties.

I groaned at the friction he made.

Whenever he touched me, without cloth between us, it was going to be loud; he was able to find a voice deep inside of me. He effortlessly pried it out of me, and he hadn't even been beneath my panties yet.

"I want to wait until marriage, for full-on sex." Kiss. I tugged at his shirt, slowly rolling cunt down his thigh. "Is that going to be an issue?"

"I will wait," he promised, kissing me harder. I expected him to leave or say that being inside of me was the only reason he was interested in me. His words sunk deep into my soul. Even if we never spoke to each other again, I would never forget what he just said. I will wait. Not, 'oh I will convince you otherwise, you prude.' I will wait.

His fingers reached for the back of my corset, frantically unbuttoning it. My head hit the back of the door, arching myself forward to help his fingers. We were still outside; completely open to the public.

"Other." Kiss. "Things." Kiss. I said it while opening the door to my house, pulling him inside with me.

VERSE TWENTY-TWO

I walked backward toward the stairs that led to my bedroom. I jerked at his shirt, pulling it over his head; I tossed it somewhere near the front door. He was somehow able to completely unlatch my corset, and throw it beside his shirt, without breaking the kiss once.

His cold fingers reached for my breasts, grabbing two full handfuls of the fat.

He grinned against my mouth, deepening the kiss further. My lips were throbbing, but I didn't pull away. If one of us pulled away, our oxygen would cease to exist. It was like we needed each other's mouths to survive.

The back of my Achilles hit the stairs. I fell on top of the first four steps. I still did not dare pull my lips away. We both grunted when he fell against my front. The position pinned me to the uncomfortable edge of the stairs.

I guess this was where this was happening.

He pulled away first and moved his mouth to my breasts. The stairs were jabbing into my back, but the more his tongue worked against my nipples, the less I noticed. I arched myself toward him and reached my shaky fingers toward his hair.

"Jesus fucking Christ, Ethel," he cursed, looking down at my breasts. I wanted to cover myself up; he was staring down at my chest, his swollen lip tugged between his teeth.

He leaned down, sucking my entire nipple into his mouth.

"Don't say that," I gasped. My stomach bucked up into his as he worked at my sensitive, tight nipples. He licked, bit, and sucked the flesh. His other hand moved toward my left breast, kneading it with his hand.

My head fell backward against the stairs; I panted, trying to catch my breath.

Bishop was made for me.

I looked down toward him. It was the most glorious sight I've ever seen in my life. His lips were wrapped around my breasts, tongue circling the bud.

What Bishop did to my father was a memory. My salvation was no longer the priority for my soul; it was Bishop.

"What can I do?" Bishop asked. He moved his mouth to my other breast, giving it as much attention as the other. My nipples were throbbing. A gentle breeze would make the sensitive peaks ache. Only his mouth, and hands, were soothing what he had caused.

"Nothing inside," I panted. My head fell to the side. My cheek rested against the flat of a stair. Soft, breathy moans were slipping from my lips.

At some point, his hand had slipped between my thighs, stroking my clit with his thumb.

I was drenched. I could feel it collecting on the apex of my thighs.

"Nothing inside," he echoed, biting at my nipple. He stared at me through his eyelashes, similar to how he had at the restaurant.

I never wanted to look away from him, especially when he was looking at me like that. But, I couldn't keep my eyes open. I clamped them shut, arching my hips into his hand. His fingers slid beneath my panties.

He applied two fingers to my clit, rubbing slow, hard circles against the swollen nerves. I moaned, reaching for his back; I dug my nails into his bare back, holding onto him.

"I can work with that," he continued. My lips wrapped around his neck, muffling the moans and cries slipping out of me. I was going to come. So fast. He used his index finger, and thumb, to gently pinch my clit. Whenever it started to hurt, he pulled away, massaging me back into bliss.

"Bishop," I groaned. I opened my eyes to meet him, but they rolled backward in my head. My teeth dug into his skin, fingers still holding onto his back for dear life. I was shaking, trembling. I'd never felt so good in my life.

I was embarrassed by how fast he was going to push me over the edge. My stomach was coiling, and releasing, in fast spasms. Everything was throbbing, and the blink of pleasure was building in my core. I was so wet; arousal was dripping out of me, trailing toward my ass.

"Look at me, Ethel," Bishop instructed. My stomach coiled tighter. I almost came after hearing him say my name like that. He was fulfilling the promise he made every time he said my name so erotically.

I did. I pulled my face from his shoulder, staring up at him. My mouth was rounded; pants and moans were coming out of me like a song. Despite how far my neck and back were beginning to arch, I kept my gaze on him.

He pressed harder against my clit and added a third finger.

I tried to clamp my thighs shut and ease the buildup happening between them, but his hips prevented me from doing so. His other hand made its way to my face, gently caressing my bottom lip with his thumb.

A car door shut, and keys jingled outside. You have to be fucking kidding me. I moved my head in the direction of the front door. Luckily, I had locked it behind me, but Dad had a key to get inside.

Bishop didn't stop rubbing me, nor did he look away. If I hadn't pushed him off of me, he would have kept going. He would have taken me right in front of my dad. Did I really have to debate stopping him? I almost let him.

"Upstairs," I panted, pushing him off of me.

I couldn't move for a second. My legs trembled, even though he hadn't made me come yet. Once I gained my balance, I grabbed a hold of the corset and his shirt. I chased Bishop up the stairs, leading him toward my bedroom.

I barely had time to lock my bedroom door behind me before Bishop grabbed hold of my hips, throwing me down onto the bed. I squealed at the sudden action, landing on the back of my elbows. He smiled, climbing back over me.

He pressed his lips back against mine.

His fingers dipped under the waistband of my panties, and skirt. He yanked all layers of clothing downward. I lifted my hips, helping him discard the rest of my clothing; first boy to ever see me fully naked.

He looked down at me, to my breasts, and then to my splayed pussy a few inches from his crotch. He ran a hand through his hair, looking back up to me. "You're beautiful, Ethel." There was no 'but' this time.

Three fingers returned to my clit, continuing the pace he had been at before.

I looked down at his tight jeans. The denim was tented, a large bulge visible beneath the dark cloth. I licked my lips and reached for his belt.

"Nothing inside," I reminded, reaching for his belt. My fingers were shaking as I fiddled with the leather. First time I'd ever taken off a boy's belt.

"Nothing inside," he repeated, helping me remove his belt and pants. We threw it somewhere in the room, reconnecting our lips.

Bare.

We were both completely bare and vulnerable against each other. From his neck, his sigil hung. My cross dangled from mine. Other than that, we were nothing but skin and sweat.

I pulled my lips away, looking down between my legs. He rubbed slowly at my clit; it felt better when he went slow, and hard. I whimpered, moving my gaze between his legs.

His cock was huge. I don't understand how in God's name that could possibly fit into someone without it hurting. The heavy sex was poking into the apex of my thigh; he was so close to being inside of me.

The tip of his cock was glistening, precum already leaking out of him.

I don't know how to do this. But, all the books I read helped prepare me for a moment like this. Gwen's books specifically; she always read the most erotic books she could find.

I collected the precum with my fingers, stroking the lubricant toward his balls, and back up toward the tip. More precum beaded out of him; I continued to repeat the motion, readying him for me to jack off his cock.

I looked up at him; he sucked in a breath, bracing his free hand beside my head.

I was doing something right.

My fingers grasped tighter around his shaft, stroking him in hard movements. He stopped working on my clit, focusing on what I was doing to him. But, once he adjusted to the feeling of my hands around him, he returned his fingers to my clit.

He matched the speed of his fingers to my hand.

My stomach started to convulse. The thought of him, feeling as good as I was, nearly sent me over the edge. I pumped my fist harder, and harder. I gritted my teeth, panting; he was going to make me come.

A few drops of precum slid off of his tip, landing on his working fingers. He collected it, using it as lube against my clit. My back arched up on the bed, and a silent cry left my lips. No book would ever do justice to how good Bishop felt.

"Fuck, Ethel," he groaned. He looked between my cunt and his cock, watching his fingers play with my clit, and my fist pumped him. I wanted to come with him. At this rate, I was going to; he was leaking drops, and drops of precum.

My back came off the bed, and then back down. Over, and over. But, not once did I look away from him. And, neither did his leave mine. My mouth was ajar, but nothing but gasps were coming out now.

"Bishop," I cried. The pleasure was becoming too much; my thighs were shaking around his hips, and his cock was throbbing in my hand.

Even the weight of him felt perfect in my hand. The pressure of his body against mine felt even more divine. "I'm going to—."

He nodded, letting out a groan. It took us both five more strokes before we came undone, together. He leaned now, resting his head on my neck as he came, groaning into my neck. I bit into my pillow, muffling the cry that came out as I shattered. Hot cum dripped out of him, every drop falling onto my throbbing pussy.

He collapsed beside me after he rubbed me through the aftershocks and helped me clean myself off.

"Shit," I cursed. Bishop panted beside me, almost as hard as I was.

Bishop turned his head to face me. "You were good at that. Have you done that before?"

I shook my head, pulling my comforter over my body. Gwen's little books did come in handy. She told me a story of how she'd been eaten out as a freshman, but it was so boring and unpleasurable she started reading one of her books during it.

Should I tell her about this?

Bishop's finger landed on my nipple, tracing gentle circles around it. Vulnerability scared me, terribly. And, Bishop hadn't just seen me naked, he'd seen me vulnerable. The thought of having sex scared me because of how vulnerable I would become during it. With Bishop, he somehow made vulnerability feel good. Comforting.

He could make anything feel good.

I looked over to him. He tensed, looking away from me. Something shifted in his eyes; the light, and desire fading. He looked away from me and pressed his lips into a firm line. He was slipping away, again. Going somewhere in the depths of his mind. Somewhere he only wished to numb, rather than cope with.

He pushed himself off of the bed, reaching for his clothes.

Once he slipped on his boxers, I grabbed a hold of his wrist. "Will you stay?"

Something was upsetting him. I wouldn't pry about what exactly it was, but maybe if he was with me, it would offer some form of distraction. The same distraction alcohol was giving him.

He nodded, joining back on top of the bed. I adjusted myself and laid my head against his stomach. I could hear his heartbeat; it was beating fast. I listened to it, memorizing it; I tried to match it with my own.

"Why does it feel like that with you?" I asked, staring at the foot of my bed.

"Like what?"

I hesitated. Vulnerable. He made me feel so vulnerable; I hated it. I didn't feel like I could speak, without my soul feeling as though it was opening up for him to crawl into. "Like I've known you longer than this."

He didn't respond. He threaded his fingers through my hair, caressing my scalp through the night. I fell asleep memorizing his heartbeat.

He didn't leave through the night, again. He slept beneath me through the full eight hours I slept. I would check when I woke up, to ensure he was still with me, entangled in my limps. He had even showered at some point and returned to the bed beside me.

In the morning, he was gone.

VERSE TWENTY-THREE

"I'm not going to be home till late. I have to go out of town after church," Dad informed, packing a sandwich and water bottle in his backpack.

I stood beside the sink, pulling large bowls from the cabinets. "Out of town?" I asked. "You've been out late a lot recently. What is out of town?"

Dad snapped his gaze in my direction. He narrowed his eyes, before shoving a few more items into his bag. He was leaving to prepare for the sermon this morning; the sermon he was "supposedly" preparing for last Wednesday, when he was nowhere to be found.

"What happened to respecting each other's privacy? If I have something to tell you, I will tell you." I frowned, watching my phone buzz on silent beside the sink. I ignored it, looking back up toward him.

"I'm sorry, you're right. I trust you," I replied. I bent over, pulling a stack of pans from the cupboard. "But, you can talk to me. If you are seeing another woman."

It made the most sense. But, it also made no sense at all. He'd told me of the women he dated after Mom; why would he keep this one from me? If there even was a woman. It didn't make any sense.

"Ethel," Dad warned, zipping up his bag. "Mind your own business. No one likes a woman who can't mind her business. Wouldn't it upset you if I asked who kept calling you?"

I looked over at my phone. Five times my phone rang, going unanswered. Bishop arrived back in town last night, after a week away from me; he'd been calling all morning, desperate to come over.

"It's Gwen," I lied. "She's coming over for the bake sale. I'm sorry. You're right. I trust you. If it is important, you will tell me." We always respected each other's privacy. If I ever questioned him, that was how he responded. If it is important, I will tell you.

Dad stepped forward, planting a kiss on my forehead. I tensed, looking over at my phone again. "I love you. You're such a good girl. Have fun at the bake sale after church."

He wasn't even going to be there; the entire reason we were doing it was to raise funds for the church. And, the preacher of the church, was going to disappear after. Where was he going? Shit, Ethel, mind your business. If it is important he will tell you.

Dad left, going to church to finish his sermon. Was he lying about that too?

I looked down at my phone; it buzzed for the sixth time in the past fifteen minutes. I reached for it, answering it. "Good grief, Bishop. I was talking to my dad." I smiled, leaning down to collect more pans and trays.

"Is he home?" Bishop asked.

The night after our interaction, he had texted, saying he was going out of town with Baylen. I refrained from asking about it, knowing it couldn't be good, but Bishop reassured me that he wasn't murdering anyone. Cain and Baylen needed to talk about something, but Cain refused to speak to him without someone else there.

A witness.

To make sure Baylen didn't rip his head off.

Cain disappeared from the face of this earth, but apparently, they knew where he was. I didn't ask any questions about it; I wanted no involvement in anything to do with Cain and Baylen.

"No, he isn't home. He just left. But—."

"Wonderful," Bishop interrupted. "I'm coming over."

I bit the inside of my cheek. For the past few days, we had been sexting. Every night, and occasionally in the mornings as well, Bishop and I would call each other; he would whisper dirty things through the phone as I touched myself.

We were both very eager for him to arrive back in town.

"No. Not today. Someone is coming over." I propped my phone between my shoulder and my ear; I wiped down the counter with a rag of soap and water.

"Is it a boy?" Bishop asked. I scoffed and rolled my eyes.

"Yes, Bishop. I have a boy coming over. I think we are going to have sex on the stairs! Such an arousing spot, is it not?" My voice was thick with sarcasm.

"Ethel," he warned. "Joke about that again and I will make you squirt on those stairs. Then you will never be able to fuck another boy without thinking of me."

I dropped the rag I was holding. I was already one step ahead of him; I couldn't look at those stairs again, even without the "squirting" part. "It's Gwen. We are having a bake sale after church."

Was the Bishop jealous? I smiled, leaning over the counter. My stomach flipped. Would it be bad if I canceled on Gwen, and asked Bishop to come over? Half the time we hung out, she slept through it.

"Ah yes. Because poorly made cookies are exactly what will bring you people closer to your God." This time, Bishop's voice was laced with sarcasm.

"Oh, shut up. It's for the finances."

"So, money isn't the root of all evil? Does it bring you closer to your God? That is fascinating, church girl." I could hear his grin, even through the phone.

"No," I snapped. "I'm going to hang up."

"Let me come over. I can add my sticky special ingredient to whatever you are giving out," Bishop began. Vile. He was so vile.

"That is not funny," I groaned. I wouldn't be able to look at the batter Gwen and I made this morning; all I would imagine was him, adding his 'special ingredient'.

"It is. I'm feeling like a douchebag desperate to get his dick wet."

I grinned, pursing my lips to repress it.

The doorbell rang. I pushed myself from the counter, making my way to the door. Gwen was an hour late; however, it was impressive she was able to wake up this early. She usually slept through the entire day.

"Shame. I'm feeling like a predictable prude on this fine morning."

With that, I hung up the phone and made my way to Gwen.

156

VERSE
TWENTY-FOUR

After the church service and hours of attempting to bake, Gwen and I sat at a table outside the church. We accepted money for the goods we baked, organizing them in a metal container. Half of the goods we baked; however, the other half we bought from the grocery store. We both agreed we didn't know how to bake, and it was too much work.

Gwen sat beside me, her arms over her stomach. She had a pair of sunglasses over her head, and a hood pulled to shield her face from the sun. She tried her hardest to stay awake, but every time I looked over at her, she was falling asleep.

Gwen didn't speak much. She rarely did. But, today, she was extra quiet.

"Are you okay?" I asked, looking over in her direction. Her hair was in two messy braids, falling down her back. She had two loose strands of hair framing either side of her face. When she arrived at my house this morning, her eyes were bloodshot, and her shirt was on backward.

"Tired," she yawned. She slumped the side of her head on my shoulder. I mean, at least she was here, for moral support. She planned the whole thing while I was distracted, similar to her own.

My phone buzzed.

DAD: leaving now. good luck with the bake sale.

Jackass. He couldn't even say goodbye in person?

I scowled, locking my phone and placing it flat on the table. He would tell me if it was important, I reminded myself. He never lied without reason. I imagined him driving off to see some secret lover that he didn't wish to tell me about. Maybe it was getting serious; was he ashamed to tell me?

Something was off. Shit Ethel, stop doubting him.

"Are you alright?" Gwen asked, still trying to stay awake against my shoulder. She must have felt how tense my arm became.

"Fine," I bit out.

Gwen shifted, hugging her stomach. She'd lost weight in the past few months. A lot. I tried to talk to her, so many times, but she always changed the subject. She shut down. Whatever was going on, she didn't want help.

She was a lot like Bishop, in that way; she was trying to deal with whatever was happening in her head, alone.

"How is school going?" I asked. She graduated a year early and was already in college. We didn't go to the same high school, but she was top of the class from what she told me. Academically, Solomon led Northside, while Gwen led Southside.

When Gwen first started college, she complained about how Solomon and she were fighting for teachers' attention. They were both top of the class for math. She would tell me every Sunday of how annoying he was, and how much better she was at the class.

Then, she stopped talking about it.

She stopped talking about everything.

"Stupid," she replied. She shrugged, huffing a breath out of her. Don't ask Gwen about college. Noted.

A finger swiped a cupcake directly in front of me, removing a wad of icing. I jerked my head up toward Bishop; he was towering above us. He stuck the finger covered in icing into his mouth, licking it clean.

"Sweet," he said, biting his lip as he looked down at me.

Gwen muttered something under her breath about being immature. She was still against my shoulder, unfazed by Bishop standing in front of us.

"Bishop," I hissed, slapping his hand away. He was reaching for another cupcake, to collect more icing.

"Church girl," he replied, pulling his hand away. I stared up at him, narrowing my eyes. Gwen still hadn't said anything; maybe I could have come to her about Bishop. I thought she would have judged me over it.

Bishop reached for a cookie. He bit into the sugar cookie; it was one of the ones Gwen and I attempted to cook. I tried to reach for it, but he yanked his hand away. "This tastes like shit," Bishop spat, returning the destroyed cookie to the platter.

"Don't curse here," I replied.

Gwen shifted, her breathing growing steady. Did she fall asleep?

"Shit. Fuck. Bitch. Cunt." I interrupted Bishop by grabbing the cookie he bit into. I threw it hard at him, watching the flour stain his black shirt. "Oh, that wasn't nice Ethel. I think I need to bend you over my lap now."

My eyes widened. He had zero filter. How did he not get slapped daily?

Gwen jerked her head upward, a soft gasp coming out of her. She wasn't asleep. She was wide awake now.

I followed her gaze, searching for whatever had startled her.

A man stepped beside Bishop, but his eyes were on Gwen. She shifted in her seat, clearing her throat.

Bishop spoke, introducing the man. "Church girl, this is Coen. I don't think you've met him yet."

VERSE TWENTY-FIVE

I'd never seen Coen once, despite living in this town for so long. He never left his club. Bishop, I'd seen from church; unfortunately. Baylen, I'd seen from the violent videos he posted on social media. I had seen Solomon in high school. But, Coen?

This was not what I was expecting him to look like.

He looked so casual.

He was fit, but not bulky; his black shirt clung to his torso, outlining his light abs hidden beneath. He wore a pair of ripped blue jeans, with a pair of tennis shoes to match. His dark, toffee-colored hair was lazily parted in the middle; the straight, soft locks fell on either side of his head.

At first glance, this did not look like the man who owned one of the most intense clubs in the state; he looked so laid back.

He wore a pair of sunglasses, but his head was directed right at Gwen.

She shifted in her seat, dusting nothing from her shirt. "Hi," she squeaked, jerking her sunglasses above her head. Now that was fascinating; Gwen rarely spoke of boys, let alone became flushed over one.

Coen said something in response, but Bishop spoke to me before I could hear what he said. "I think it would have tasted better with my special ingredient—."

"That is disgusting," I hissed. "And perverted."

"You give me five minutes and I will show you perverted, church girl."

Coen looked at Bishop sideways, the corners of his lips twitching. He returned his gaze to Gwen within a second.

I scoffed, looking back over to Gwen. She was laughing nervously, slowly sinking into her chair. I tried to listen to what they were saying, but every time I heard a few words, Bishop started talking again.

"I like filled cupcakes," Bishop began, shoving his finger into the bottom of a store-bought cupcake. I narrowed my eyes, slapping his hand again. He dodged the palm of my hand, shoving his coated finger into my mouth. "Mouths, if that is okay with your little book."

I bit his finger and stood from my seat. I looked down at Gwen, but she was too entranced with Coen to even notice I'd stood from my seat. Coen's gaze flickered to mine for a second, but he returned it to Gwen.

I grabbed Bishop's hand, pulling him into the alley a few feet away. Once we were out of sight, I turned to face him, dropping his hand. I pressed my back against the wall and stared up at him.

Shit, he was gorgeous; even when he was grinning like an absolute maniac.

"You didn't answer my question," he stated. He tilted his head and leaned down into my face; I stood on my tiptoes, meeting his lips halfway.

No amount of dirty talk over the phone would compare to this. To his warmth; to how full he made me feel.

When did he even ask a question?

"Hmm?" I hummed.

His lips moved to my cheeks, planting a hard, slow kiss against the skin. "Is the mouth okay, according to your "nothing inside"?"

Oral. He was talking about oral. Outside of my dad's church. Forgive me.

"Maybe." His mouth moved down to my neck; the bruises were starting to fade, given I had a few days free from him.

"Can I come over tonight?" He pushed himself off of me, bracing a hand on the wall beside my face. He tilted his head down to meet my eyes.

"I don't know. I have a boy coming over tonight," I teased, tipping my chin upward. I smiled and his jaw flexed. He leaned down, biting my bottom lip.

"Hm," he hummed, against my lip. "Three's a party, isn't it?"

I shook my head, pushing him off of me. "I'm going to make sure your friend didn't kill my friend."

Bishop laughed at this. "Coen? He is harmless. He's fisted more people than he has punched." He slapped my ass after he finished speaking.

I twisted my head around, looking up at him. "Fisted? As in like—."

Bishop's fingers wrapped around my waist, leading me out of the alleyway. "Would you like me to do it to you?"

I shook my head, frantically. "Absolutely. Not."

Once we came into view of the table, Gwen's terrified eyes met mine. Her eyes were rounded, her lips pressed into a firm line, and her foot tapped anxiously against the cobblestone ground.

"Go," I told Bishop before we were within earshot of Coen and Gwen. "She's nervous."

"Because they had a little moment at his party."

"Really?" I asked, my eyes widening. She was there? Coen? I had a thousand questions, and then some more.

Bishop leaned down, kissing the back of my neck. "I will tell you all about it tonight." Even if he was a foot taller than me, he always seemed like he was looking up at me. I wondered if he knew how weak it made me.

I shook my head, sitting down beside Gwen. Bishop did as I asked, taking both Coen and himself away from the table. The two lingered on a rock, many feet away, bickering about something. Coen had a slice of cherry pie in his hand; once Bishop noticed, he took it from him, eating it in two bites.

"Are you okay?" I asked, looking over to Gwen. She was wide awake, now. I'd never seen her so alert in my life.

"Yep," she croaked. She crossed her arms over her stomach, sinking further into her chair. She pulled her hood up over her head, trying to block her face from Coen, a few feet away.

Once her breathing steadied, I spoke. "You know Coen?"

"Never." Her voice was clipped. She ran a hand down her face, breathing heavily against her palm. There was not a single woman in this town who had a bad thing to say about Coen (when it came to the bedroom). They said it was life-changing.

"Bishop and you?" Gwen asked.

I looked up toward Bishop. He was already looking at me. Coen was close beside him, scrolling through his phone. "Never," I lied.

Bishop grabbed his phone, looking away for a second to type something. My phone buzzed once his eyes met mine again.

Gwen was zoning out, staring at a piece of cake on the table. Her cheeks were flushed, and her breathing had grown heavy. I looked over to Coen; he was staring at her. He looked at her the way Bishop looked at me.

"He's looking at yo—," I started.

"Do not remind me. I do not want to think about it," Gwen snapped. It was incredibly odd for Gwen to be going out to a party if what Bishop had said was true. The church was her only form of social interaction; I got out of the house more than Gwen did.

She deserved something exciting, like Coen.

BITCHOP: when you say nothing inside, does that include my tongue?

Virginity was interpreted in many different ways. Some believed even sticking a tampon inside of you would count as losing your virginity. I interpreted it as any bodily part inside of me.

I pushed my lips into a thin line, concealing the smile that was spreading across my face. I slowly looked up at Bishop; he was looking at me, two fingers in the form of a 'V'. His tongue flicked between the digits.

Coen only looked away from Gwen to see what he was doing. He looked at Bishop, and then me. He smirked, looking down at his phone.

ME: nothing inside.

ME: you can put it somewhere else though.

I looked up at Bishop. He looked as if he'd seen a ghost when he read the message. His lips parted, and I swore a little blush crept up his neck. I gnawed at my lip, texting him something else.

ME: and anything in my mouth.

Bishop looked like he read the text three times. His eyes were dark when they met mine; I could see the desire, even from this far away. He grinned, before typing something on his phone.

Gwen was still staring ahead. She was oblivious to Coen's gaze; she had to be ignoring it. Her knee was bouncing up and down. She looked like she was about to make a run for it inside of the church.

BITCHOP: come to coen's car.

ME: no.

BITCHOP: let me come over.

ME: maybe.

Coen whispered something in his ear and the two left. Before they disappeared into the parking lot, Bishop looked over his shoulder, narrowing his gaze at me, and shooting me his middle finger. Ass.

Gwen and I both let out a breath we had been holding.

VERSE
TWENTY-SIX

M E: when will you be home?

Delivered 3 hours ago.

I frowned, staring down at my phone. It was almost midnight, and Dad still hadn't responded. He was gone early before church and had disappeared the rest of the evening. He was only present to preach. What could he be doing?

I needed to respect his privacy. I knew I should be; if it was something worth telling me, he would tell me. He wouldn't lie to me. Dad never lied.

I placed my phone face down on the floor. The TV was playing "A Christmas Story", though I hadn't watched any of it. I was too distracted, worrying about my dad.

The only theory I had was him meeting with a woman. It made sense; he told me he was going out of town. She could live out of town. Was he too ashamed to tell me? I wouldn't judge him; he had a right to move on from Mom. It had been years.

I rested my chin on the pillow, zoning out to the movie. My stomach was flat against the living room floor, a bowl of popcorn in front of me. I wore an oversized shirt, with a pair of cheeky black lace trim panties beneath. My hair was still damp from the shower, and my skin had a few remaining droplets of water on it.

Today was a long day. After the bake sale, Gwen insisted that we go shopping. Something about wanting to "spice" up her wardrobe. She only wore baggy sweatpants and ripped T-shirts. The entire time, her face was pink; I wondered if she was thinking about a certain toffee-haired boy.

A heavy weight came down onto my back. I shrieked, but a hand clamped over my mouth, muffling the noise. Panic rose up my throat and tightened the air in my lungs; however, I looked down at the fingers around my mouth and recognized the rings my appendage wore.

Soft lips brushed against my ear. I shuddered under Bishop.

"Hello, church girl." His lips sucked on my earlobe, tugging at it.

I moved my head to the side, forcing his hand to slip from my mouth. "If you are going to break in, at least go through the front door." The front door was a few feet behind me; I would have heard him if he had come in.

"I don't know. I like climbing that little tree and sneaking into your room." I grinned, imagining him and his long limbs climbing the frail tree outside my window. I still couldn't fathom that he was able to do it while drunk.

His lips moved to my neck, sucking on the sensitive areas. My mouth parted and I sucked in a sharp breath. My forehead fell to the floor, allowing him more access to the area where he worked. "What are you watching?"

I dug my fingers into the carpet below us. Besides my head, his entire body pinned me to the floor. His lips were keeping my forehead in place, against the floor.

"Nothing important," I said, tilting my head to the side. His lips moved to the area I opened for him.

"I don't know. Looks kind of important to me." His fingers slid down my spine, and then to my ass. He gave it a firm squeeze, before continuing his path. The tips of his digits traced a slow circle around the back of my thigh.

"How was your stupid little bake sale?" Bishop asked, tracing the tips of his nails along my thigh. I smiled against the carpet, digging my fingers deeper into it.

"I think my friend likes Coen."

"Fascinating. I think my friend likes your friend."

"Her name is Gwen."

Bishop's hand grabbed a hold of my waist. He flipped me over, onto my back. I sucked in a breath, looking up at him above me. His sigil dangled above my face; I was tempted to rip it off of his neck like he did mine. "I don't give a fuck what her name is."

One of his hands landed beside my head, helping him hover above me. The other hand was on my stomach, fingers digging into the t-shirt I wore.

Bishop dipped his head to my chest, kissing my nipples through the cloth. He spoke into the breasts. "Coen came home asking about the girl that was always with you." Did Bishop talk about me to him? How did Coen know to ask Bishop about me?

My cheeks were sore from how hard I smiled. He pulled his face back above mine. "What is so funny?"

"You are gossiping with me," I stated, reaching for his shirt. I fiddled with the buttons, slowly undoing them.

"No," he bit out. He narrowed his eyes into slits.

I continued down the line of buttons. We should have gone into my room. Dad wasn't responding, the front door was unlocked, and he could arrive at any second. And, we had terrible luck with family members interrupting "Bishop time."

I pulled his shirt over his head.

"How did things go with Baylen and—?" I didn't say Cain's name. It shouldn't be on my tongue. He was a ghost now; just a memory. He should be. Cain shouldn't even be in the equation anymore.

I trailed my fingertips down his chest.

"Terrible," Bishop admitted. He reached for the hem of my shirt, fiddling with it. His knuckles brushed against my thighs; I bucked my hips upward, reaching for more of him. "Baylen couldn't keep his fucking mouth shut. As soon as he saw him, he started running his fucking mouth."

I looked up at him, my stomach sinking. "Did anything happen?" Did you hurt anyone?

What did Baylen even want with Cain?

Bishop shook his head. "No. Cain doesn't put up with Baylen. He left as soon as he was interrupted."

I never met Cain. But, I lived in this town when he ruled beneath the city. It was terrifying how fast his name became known. One day, he was a quiet high school kid. Then, the next day, you couldn't walk outside without the fear of your life being taken from you.

I didn't want to know the involvement Bishop had in it, during that dark time. It was in the past.

My phone buzzed. I reached for it, fast. It was a text from Gwen; I didn't read it.

"Expecting someone?" Bishop asked, removing his hands from the hem of my shirt. He looked at my phone, and then my face.

"My dad is being weird."

"Touching little altar boys."

I slapped Bishop's bare chest. "Stop saying that. It's not funny."

Bishop rolled his eyes, threading his fingers through my hair. He squeezed at the strands and pulled my face closer to him. "I can give a picture to Solomon. He can have every camera that picked up his face in town."

"No," I snapped. "That's an invasion. I wouldn't do that to him."

Bishop lowered his lips to my cheek. He placed an open mouth kiss on the skin. "Promise me you won't do that," I said, arching into him. That was a complete invasion; I'd never be able to forgive myself if I knew I did that to him.

"Promise," he mumbled, his words muffled against my face. My stomach started to heave, the lower his lips moved down my body. He pulled the shirt around my waist, leaving kisses on the bare skin above my belly button. "Stop talking about your dad now, Ethel."

I nodded, grabbing ahold of his hair.

His mouth reached the waistband of my panties. The cheeky black cotton was trimmed with lace; he kissed the lace, looking up at me. I propped myself on my elbows, looking down at him.

"Nothing inside," he stated. His mouth moved to my inner thigh, biting hard enough to make me gasp.

"Nothing inside," I repeated.

VERSE TWENTY-SEVEN

Bishop grabbed hold of the top of my thighs. He yanked me toward him, his head now residing between my legs. I shuddered, feeling his breath fan over the sensitive area, covered by black cloth.

His eyes fluttered shut. He lowered his lips to my pussy, leaving an open-mouthed kiss over the throbbing area. He sucked it inside of his mouth. Panties, and clit. I squeezed his hair hard, letting out a strangled moan.

That felt good. That felt really good.

"Ah," I moaned, throwing my head backward. My mouth hung open, vocalizing to him just how good he felt. He ran his tongue up, and down, my clothed folds. My thighs shook around his face. He dug his nails into my thighs, steadying them.

"Does that feel good, pretty girl?" Bishop hummed, against my clit. I bucked my hips upward, trying to get his mouth back on me.

"Mhm," I whimpered. I looked down at him, watching his eyes as he slid my panties to the side. I was panting, loudly; it felt like I was gasping for air, so desperate to feel him trail his tongue against my slit, without panties separating us.

"If you look away from me, I am going to stop. Okay?" His lips grazed against the ones between my legs. I rolled and bucked my pussy toward his mouth, nodding my head.

"Okay," I croaked. One of my hands was holding onto his hair, while the other caressed my breasts. I kneaded my breasts, trying to ease how hard and sensitive my nipples were. He grinned, dipping his tongue back between my legs.

His rough tongue slid down my slit. I bucked my hips upward, but his hand kept me steady against the ground. Curses, cries, and moans were coming out of my mouth in a jumbled mess. He was so good at this; not a single movement he made strayed from pure euphoria.

"Shit, Bishop," I cried out. I threw my head backward, clenching my eyes shut. The second I looked away, his mouth left my cunt, and bit my inner thigh.

"Ethel," he cautioned.

I returned my gaze to him, nodding. This time, he clamped his lips over my clit. He sucked the nerves between his teeth. It was unlike anything I had ever felt before. I'd heard of girls squirting before when it was too good. Overwhelming. If I ever squirted, it would be because of his teeth, and tongue, massaging my clit.

"Can I—." He sucked my clit harder, letting it go with a pop. "Do something." Pop. I started to shake. "To you?"

I nodded, frantic for the coiling in my stomach to burst. I was already so close. Again, Bishop found a way to push me over the edge in record time.

I whimpered when he pulled his mouth away from me. His face left my heat entirely, and he returned above me. I was about to yell at him for stopping when I was that close to coming. Hard.

My panties were back over my pussy, covering my throbbing and soaked clit.

He pulled his pants and boxers down. My legs were still spread, even after he removed himself from me. He kneeled between my legs, slowly stroking himself. I watched the head of his cock slide between his fingers, collecting the cum; he fisted it, pumping it three times.

I was throbbing. Desperate for something. Anything. Watching him jack off was only making the ache worse.

I reached down to rub my clit, but he grabbed my hand, stopping me.

"Nothing inside," he promised. He lowered his cock between my legs. I watched him, fascinated by how he stroked himself. It looked so fluid compared to how rigid I had fisted him. "I promise."

I nodded, trusting him. He could do it. If he really wanted to. It'd be so easy to slip in; the tip of his cock was a few inches away from my entrance. Nothing but thin panties were separating him from it.

He lifted my panties, just enough to slip his cock inside. He let the panties go, trapping his cock inside, with my throbbing pussy. The heaviness and heat of him rested against my slit. The ridges of his cock lined perfectly in between my folds. His length was parallel to my own; not once did he try and push himself inside of my entrance.

Nothing inside.

His palm pressed against his cock, pushing his length harder against the middle of my folds. He locked his eyes with mine and started to roll his hips.

I groaned. His cock was slowly rubbing up and down my length, with enough pressure to make me see stars.

The tip of his cock landed around my clit; the glistening head nudged against my clit with every movement. Around half of his length was pressed against the remainder of my slit, slowly grinding against it.

I took it back. This felt so much better than his mouth. His heat, his slick head rubbing against my throbbing bundle of nerves, and his heavy length rubbing against the remainder of me.

My folds even felt good, feeling him grind in between them.

"Fuck," I cursed. I reached a trembling hand behind me, bracing myself as his thrusts became harder. Fuck. Fuck. Fuck. I couldn't remember the last time I said fuck; but, it was coming out of my mouth like a chant now, the harder he grinded against my folds.

He did not stop his thrusts as he adjusted me on his thighs. My ass was now resting on his thighs, giving him easier access to hump me beneath my panties. His breathing was coming out heavy, deep groans rumbling through his chest.

"Shit, Ethel. You feel good." His voice was raspy, coming out as a heavy breath. He leaned over me, continuing to rub himself against my pussy. I could feel my panties sticking to me, from the precum leaking out of him, mixing with my wetness. Squelches were echoing through the room. It was so fucking sticky.

"Fuck. Fuck." I cursed and cried, squeezing the carpet hard. His face hovered above mine, watching every contortion my expression made. Half of his length wasn't even inside of my panties; he was so big.

He pressed his palm harder against his length. The pressure intensified in my belly. I wanted to clamp my eyes shut and take in the pleasure that was tightening in my core. I couldn't. I couldn't look away from him; he was so ethereal.

His lips parted, groans coming out of him. He looked down at me like I was the only person in this world. Fuck, that was enough to send me over.

"Bishop!" I cried out. I forgot how to breathe. Moans, groans, and pants were taking up my airways; I could barely get a second to breathe with him rubbing against me. My hips lifted further up his thighs. The angle strained my lower back, but I did not care; it was aiding in the bliss.

"Fuck, Ethel. I'm going to come."

I nodded, groaning loudly. His cock was twitching, and throbbing against me. His precum was seeping down my clit and dripping in between the folds of my cunt.

I pulled his face down to me, trying to kiss him through the orgasm. Both of us kept our mouths ajar, groans and moans slipping into each other's lips. His warm cum filled my panties, slipping down my folds, seeping inside of me.

I cried out when I came, my legs and cunt tightening hard. I saw black and stars for a split second. There was so much cum. Not just from him, but also from me. I could feel his hot seed spreading across every inch of my slit, seeping inside of me.

But, not once, did his cock slip inside of me.

"Stay with me tonight," I panted, into his mouth. His cock was still throbbing against me, twitching through the aftershocks. He nodded, pulling himself from my panties.

After we both showered and changed, we lay beside each other in my bed. My head was on his bare, wet chest, listening to the sound of his heartbeat. My fingers traced a few scars on his chest, outlining them with my fingertips.

"Do you know the story of Adam and Eve?" I asked. I reached for the sigil around his neck. I fiddled with it, examining the markings. I wondered what it meant. Was it for a Daemon? Or was it something else?

"I think even an infant knows that story. You Christians sure do love to shove that one down people's throats, specifically." I gently slapped his stomach. I readjusted myself on top of him. My leg was between his; it was hard to ignore the feeling of his soft cock pressing against my hip.

"I feel like I've known you for so long. I think I know why." I traced along the ridges of his ribs; they bulged out from his skin. "When God made Eve, she came from Adam's rib. A lot of times, people think that's how everyone after was made as well. In soul I suppose. I think I came from your rib."

Bishop was quiet, tracing my spine with his fingers. I looked up at him, afraid this was where he was going to reject me. But, he didn't. He was grinning. Ear to fucking ear. "Are you saying we are soulmates, church girl?"

"It's not funny," I scoffed, looking down at him. His lip was between his teeth; I was about to lean down and bite it for myself.

We stared at each other. Too long. The grin faded, and something flashed in his eyes. He frowned, looking up at the ceiling.

"Are you okay?" I asked. It was the same darkness that flashed after the club when he tried to leave me.

"I haven't drank since the night of the club."

That was a week. He had been sober for a week. Holy shit. What changed? Was it something I did? Him?

I opened my mouth, but he stopped me.

"Don't," he bit, pulling me by my hair to his lips. He kissed me, slowly, before putting my head onto his chest to rest. I didn't say anything; he didn't want me to.

We both fell asleep soon after that. Unlike last time, he was there when I woke.

VERSE TWENTY-EIGHT

"Did you have a good night?" I asked. I reached for a mug in the cabinet. Dad was at my back, sitting at the counter. I heard him sip his coffee and flip the newspaper. I looked back at the living room a few feet away; my cheeks heated remembering what had happened last night.

"Yeah," Dad replied. I reached for the coffee, filling my cup to the brim. "Father Rowans was in town. We were catching up."

I froze. I looked at him through the reflection of the window, checking to see if he was joking. He stared at his paper, sipping away at his cup like he hadn't just lied to me so effortlessly.

My hands shook as I placed the coffee down.

Lying was one thing, but using Father Rowan as an excuse? Dad couldn't be that desperate to cover up whatever he was doing.

Father Rowans was dead.

He had been dead for over a year. I saw it on Facebook a few months ago; I never mentioned it to Dad. I didn't want to open up a wound he was mourning over. He never brought it up, so neither did I.

Dad continued the lie. "We went to Gianno's, just like you and I do. Was great. We split a pizza too."

His lie was covered in the tone of truth in his voice. When did Dad become such a good liar? If I hadn't seen that Facebook post, I would believe every word he was saying.

"Sounds nice." I sucked in a breath, turning to face the liar sitting a few feet away. I sipped my coffee and watched him. Father Rowans and Dad had been close. He was a good man. What was worth using a good man's name to lie?

I looked over to the steaming cup of coffee in his hand. If I pushed any further about his business, he would throw the liquid in my face; Dad hated it when I asked questions. He always had.

Trust and privacy were what our family had been built on. If I walked past a suspicious figure, Dad would teach me to trust in God. That if something were meant to happen, it would happen. Mom didn't raise me like that before she died.

"Speaking of, I'm not going to be here tonight, or tomorrow. Father Rowans and I are going out of town. We've been talking about maybe building a prayer garden by his church. I told him maybe we could help with the money we raised. What do you think of that, sweetheart?"

He spoke as if he were talking about the weather. Something factual. His eyes didn't leave mine once, as one did when lying. He hadn't even hesitated or debated how to continue the lie. It was like he believed what he said.

Father Rowans, dead at the age of thirty. Suicide. I reminded myself of the article when listening to Dad speak. He spoke of him as if he were still alive.

"That would be great," I replied, continuing with his lie. I looked at the rug behind him. My stomach clenched; Bishop and I had rolled around the rug a few hours ago.

Last night was the best sleep I've ever had.

Dad smiled, looking back down at his newspaper. He looked happy. Genuinely happy. Did it not eat at him? That he was lying to me? I wouldn't be able to forgive myself if I used someone like Mom to lie.

I should have told Bishop to stay. He wanted to stay, desperately, but I practically forced him out of my window. I expected a morning of talking with Dad. Maybe he would tell me of the woman he was seeing if it were the case. Not this.

I cleared my throat and walked past Dad. Lying was far from talking. I wasn't going to waste my breath in this kitchen.

Dad caught my bicep before I could pass him. I looked down at him, holding tight onto the hot coffee in my hands. His fingers were tight around my bicep, so tight I winced.

He reached up for my neck, brushing the sore area from last night. Shit. I forgot how bruised Bishop had left me.

"I hope it's Simon," Dad began. Simon was a boy from our church. I'd never spoken to him, but he was my age. I tried to pull my arm away from his grasp, but his fingers tightened. "You're maturing in all areas. He would know how to appreciate that."

His eyes slipped away from my face.

"Yeah. I've got a book to get to." I laughed. It was a nervous habit. And, right now, Dad was making me very nervous.

Dad smiled, letting go of my arm. I practically ran up the stairs. Why was that so weird? Speaking a dead man, alive, was one thing. The conversation after was beyond strange. That was not normal.

Trust, I reminded myself.

Grandma's face came to mind. Specifically, the day of my mother's funeral. Dad and her had been arguing, when neither knew I could see them. I thought he was going to hit her. It was the worst argument I'd ever seen.

I never asked him about it. He would just yell at me when I did. "If you are meant to know, you will know," was what he would have told me.

My fingers grazed my bicep. There was a light pink mark forming from where he held me in place. Was he angry I asked him about his night?

My phone lit up. I looked down, seeing Bishop's name illuminating the screen.

BITCHOP: can i come over?

He only left a few hours ago. Did he already want between my legs?

ME: my dad is here. no.

BITCHOP: okay. can you come over?

My blood ran cold. To his house? Where Baylen lived? The house that Cain bought them, before disappearing from existence? Solomon could get information within a second. That was terrifying. Coen, well I didn't know much about him. But, Baylen? That house? I couldn't step foot into that place; I would have a heart attack.

ME: baylen scares me.

BITCHOP: please, ethel.

This had to be God's way of telling me to stop trying to think about Dad's life. If he wanted to tell me, he would; I needed to mind my business.

ME: okay.

VERSE TWENTY-NINE

I stared at the large house, unmoving.

It didn't look like it belonged in our town. It was three times the size of any house in this town. Cain made sure everyone knew he was no longer from the trailer park; he was the biggest force this town had ever seen.

There were various sports and luxury cars lined up on the circular, bricked driveway. A motorcycle sat in the very back, a black helmet hanging from the handle.

I wondered which one was Bishop's. I never saw him driving. Anytime we saw each other, we walked.

I walked up to the front door. I debated whether to knock or call Bishop.

This was terrifying. My stomach was flipping, afraid to even move. This was more frightening than being splayed, and vulnerable, to Bishop.

This was the house. This was where Cain and his "associates" would meet, discussing what would be done beneath the city. Mafia. The word that made every person in this town shudder, remembering what we never thought would come to this town.

I frowned as I zoned out on the door. This was where Baylen filmed some of his videos. The law was a fucking joke in this town. He documented himself torturing, and killing, with a smile on his face. Nothing. The system did nothing.

There weren't any gates guarding the house. No one would dare try and break in. People in this town were not suicidal.

I hit my knuckles against the door. My heart rattled against my ribcage, pounding in my ears.

I should have just let Bishop risk stumbling across my father.

The door swung open a few minutes later. It wasn't Bishop who opened the door, though. It was Baylen.

My face went pale as a ghost. Even the red cheeks I had from the cold, paled. My breath was lost in my throat.

I wasn't afraid of Bishop anymore. Cain was gone. Solomon never spoke or showed his face. And, Coen didn't even glance over at me. They weren't nearly as bad as I had expected them to be.

But, him?

I trembled. "I'm here for Bishop," I bit out. I could barely force the words out.

He didn't move.

There was something wrong with Baylen. You could see it. There was something distorted, shifted, in his eyes. No light existed. No joy. No love. Baylen couldn't love. It would be like asking a rock to love someone. If Baylen felt anything besides hate, I'd consider it an anomaly. The stories Gwen had told me about Baylen when he was in high school were demonic.

Baylen was unlovable.

His soul, if it existed, was pure black. Darkness.

I stared up at him, still unable to breathe. His eyes were black, matching the strands of his hair. The dark, crimson-colored streaks in his hair matched the blood he had seeped into his soul. His fingers wrapped around the door, tightening against the wood.

His hands.

He was so young. He still had baby fat on them. Those were the hands that had committed so many atrocities.

Gwen had an experience with Baylen in high school.

At the time, Gwen was a sophomore, and Baylen had just entered his freshman year. He tried to touch Gwen, but she shoved him away and gave him the dirtiest look she could muster. As a result, Baylen forced her to watch a video, warning her of the last time someone looked at him that way.

According to her story, Baylen had broken into a single mother's home. At the time, her eighteen-year-old daughter, and her son-in-law, were in the house. They were comfortable on the couch, watching a movie with their mother.

Gwen had explained exactly what the low-quality video showed. Baylen tied the daughter to a living room chair. He held a gun to the fiancé's head, forcing him to take his soon-to-be mother-in-law.

All were stabbed fifty-seven times. Their bodies were dismembered to the point that police couldn't recognize them. But, due to Cain's power at the time, Baylen walked out of that house a free man.

Gwen said it was because the mother looked at Baylen "funny".

Baylen was thirteen at the time.

Age didn't matter, though. If you had a gun, and something wired wrong in the head, you could play God. No matter what the age.

Baylen looked to my feet, and then to my face. His nose scrunched up; he looked at me the way I looked at a piece of gum I stepped on. He didn't have hate in his eyes, nor desire. His eyes were just dead. Like he wasn't even here.

"No, kid." Bishop pushed past Baylen and slipped through the doorway. I let out the breath I was holding. He grabbed ahold of my hand, pulling me inside of the warm home. My shoulder hit Baylen's in the process; he gritted his teeth and twisted his head in my direction.

Bishop spoke before he was able to pounce. "Off limits."

"I really don't like him," I whispered to Bishop, once we were moving up the stairs. He felt so safe, even in this house.

"You aren't the only one."

VERSE THIRTY

B ishop's bedroom was exactly as I expected. It smelled of cigarettes, with a hint of his cologne beneath the toxic scent. There were multiple metal band posters covering his walls. The sunlight was the only light in the room; a few red lava lamps provided some glow to the room. He even had a few guitars hanging from his black-painted walls.

A TV was mounted on the wall across from his bed, but it was unplugged, with a black screen. There was a pile of clothes near the foot of his closet, and a dresser with clothes spilling out of it.

I liked it. It was Bishop, in the materialistic form of a bedroom.

I traced my nail along the dresser. There was a picture of him, with his family. I sucked in my lip. Even as a child, he stood out amongst his family. He wore all black, despite their church attire. In every photo, he pouted with his arms crossed over his chest.

"Were you busy?" Bishop asked.

I turned around to look at him. He was sitting on the edge of his bed. His elbows were propped on his knees, and his fingers intertwined in front of him. He was watching me. I liked the feeling of him watching me.

"No." I turned away, trying to conceal the frown deepening. Dad. His cruel touch still stung against my bicep. If someone were to hurt me, I would go to Dad. He was my safety. My home. I never would have imagined that foundation crumbling; where was I to go now?

I turned back toward Bishop, walking toward him. I stood between his legs, looking down at him as he sat on the bed. Even sitting, he was almost my height. His face landed in the area between my chest and stomach.

On the dresser beside his bed, I noticed a silver glint. There was a collection of cross necklaces. They weren't the ones he had stolen from girls in high school. They were all silver, with a dainty chain holding onto the charm; they were my cross necklaces.

Bishop dug his fingers into my waist, squeezing a fistful of the sweater I wore. I looked back down at him, surprised by the sudden feeling.

He wasn't smiling. Nor was he trying to slide his hand down my pants.

"Did Bael say anything to you?" Bishop asked. Bael. Baylen.

I shook my head, still staring down at him. He wasn't looking at me; his eyes were trained on where my jeans squeezed my thighs in. I wrapped my fingers into his locks, and gently massaged the strands.

This felt intimate. This felt vulnerable. Why did it feel like this?

"No. He just stared. I think that's worse," I admitted.

Bishop let out a soft, breathy laugh. They were once so close; it was strange seeing him push past Baylen as if he were an appendage.

He leaned his head down, resting his forehead against my abdomen. He planted a slow kiss against my stomach. I was wearing a sweater, so I couldn't feel his lips, but he planted another kiss, nonetheless.

I wrapped my other hand around the back of his neck. I dragged my nails gently across his neck. Goosebumps spread beneath my nails; at least he knew how I felt in his presence.

"I'm sorry for asking you to come over. I know you don't like it here. I just didn't want to be alone. Not today."

Vulnerable.

There was that silly word again. It echoed in my head when I looked at him. When I was with him. I straightened my spine, continuing to stare down at the top of his head. He planted kisses along my stomach. There was no sex, or lust behind his mouth; it was touch. Comfort.

He was being so gentle.

"Are you okay?" I regretted the words the second they slipped from my tongue. The last time I uttered those prohibited words, it triggered him into something. He had retracted from me, last time; over three words.

I knitted my eyebrows together, slowing my movements against his neck. His breathing was growing heavy; I could hear him shudder with every breath.

He shook his head.

I noticed something move in the corner of his room. There were brown shards of glass, shattered, in a pile beside a puddle. The amber liquid continued to move, bringing some of the glass with it. The wall had a slight dent in it, likely from where the beer bottle had collided with it.

It had to have just happened. The liquid hadn't soaked into the clothes a few feet away.

Was this why he called me? I should have let him stay with me; something had triggered him into another spiral.

"Bishop," I started. I didn't know what I was planning on saying. His body started to tremble beneath my fingers. It was so faint, I would not have noticed if my fingers weren't sunk into the back of his neck.

He left another kiss on my stomach; he looked up at me through his eyelashes. "Do you want to know why I drink so much?"

I didn't answer. I was afraid to say yes, but too worried to say no. I waited for him to speak; if he wanted to speak about it, he would. I wasn't going to push him past a boundary he had set between us.

Kiss.

"A year ago, I killed my mother and brother. That's why I drink so much."

VERSE
THIRTY-ONE

"**A** year ago, I killed my mother and brother. That's why I drink so much."

My fingers went still.

I felt his body tense. He planted another kiss on my stomach, before burying himself in the heat of my aura. My blood was cold, and my body had gone as tight as his.

No matter what caused the deaths, I understood why he drank so much. That had to be so grueling to forget. It was his own mother and his other half. The two that stood beside him in all the photos on the dresser and hugged him despite the frown on his face.

He dug his fingers deeper into the wrinkles of my sweatshirt.

"Bishop," I repeated. Again, it was just his name; I had no words to offer him after the sound. I needed to say something, but I couldn't find what to say. The room was thick. The air was thicker than the sexual tension that usually lingered around us. I never thought something could be more suffocating than that. But, his grievance was.

"Don't," he snapped. His fingers flexed against my rolls. "I'm not going to be able to get it out if you start talking."

His face pulled away from my stomach, but he didn't look up at me. I nodded, though he couldn't see me. He didn't look at me.

Shame.

"I was back home for the holidays last year. I drank too much. I got into the car, and I started driving—." The fingers holding onto my waist dug so tight, it started to hurt. I didn't wince or try to push him away. It felt like he was holding onto me, for dear life. Like one of us was going to disappear if he let go.

"And, I hit them. Killed them. I feel like if I don't drink, then it was for nothing. If that makes sense. It probably doesn't. It definitely doesn't make sense. I'm just fucking talking out of my ass right now."

I intertwined my fingers beneath the hands holding onto me. I sat down beside him on the bed, holding his cold, trembling hands in my lap. He still wasn't looking at me. The floor was the most fascinating thing he'd ever seen.

It had been over five years since my mother died. And, I still struggled over her passing. A mother's death, or lack of a mother, was a different kind of hell entirely. The first year was the worst.

Bishop had been in the worst part of the grieving process. Alone.

Fuck, I felt like an insensitive idiot. I offered him no emotional support through it; I should have recognized that glint of loss. It was the same one I wore.

He looked up at me. His eyes locked with mine. His eyes were as intense and electric as before. However, spots of red were starting to form around the green. He was looking at me like I was offering support to him. I hadn't spoken a word, but based on his gaze, that was all he needed.

"It was an accident," I affirmed. I knew he didn't want me to speak, but I had to say it.

His face twitched. He looked down to his feet, grinding his jaw, and then back up to me. "I got behind the wheel, didn't I? I don't consider that an accident. I knew what could have happened." His voice dripped with guilt, matching the look hidden behind his eyes.

I flexed my fingers around his hand.

"I can't even get into a fucking car now. I mean, legally I can. But, I just can't stop thinking—." Bishop sucked in a breath, looking down at our intertwined hands. He opened his mouth to finish speaking, but nothing came out.

"It's okay. I know what you are trying to say." He nodded, tracing the pad of his thumb around my knuckles. He traced gentle, small circles around the bones of my hand.

He pressed a hand to my cheek. His thumb brushed the area of skin right where my glasses ended, beneath my eyes. My head tilted a little, falling into the support of his cupped hand. His hands were cold. So fucking cold. But, it felt comforting knowing it was his cold.

"You're so fucking good, Ethel." He looked at me as if I were the one grieving. Like, he wanted to comfort me even in his time of ache. My stomach sank at the look. I didn't need help. I wanted to help him.

I parted my lips to speak, but the pad of his thumb slid between my lips before I could. He trailed his thumb from one corner of my lower lip to the other, memorizing every crack, and soft spot. They were still swollen from last night, thanks to him.

"Cain and Baylen are the only people who know. Cain was the person I called first. He could get someone on death row out of jail." Bishop muttered the last part beneath his breath, but I heard it.

Cain. I couldn't even remember what he looked like. I'd only seen his videos on social media.

"Do you remember the night outside the church? When I had blood on my hands?" Bishop asked. His hand slid away from my face, and back to my lap. I quietly whimpered, missing the feeling of his touch against my skin.

I nodded. We had never talked about that. I didn't want to know whose blood it was. At the time, I had such a muddy and tainted image of him in my mind; I didn't want to distort Bishop, back to the person I believed him to be. He wasn't Baylen.

"It was Baylen's blood," Bishop admitted. I rounded my eyes, looking up to see if he was lying.

"Really?" I gasped. Whatever happened to Baylen was deserved. Even if it involved that much blood. Baylen deserved to be broken and re-assembled as a doormat.

He nodded, sliding his fingers up my neck. His digits curled around the chain that kept my cross in place, against my chest. It was going to end up amongst the others, beside his bed.

"He said that he wished he was in the car with me that night. He wanted to see the look on my face when I realized what I had done. He wanted to see what made me soft, after all the years we had together." Bishop stopped, flexing his jaw.

"He started talking about my mother, too. Of what he would do to her if I hadn't killed her. But, I was hitting him by then. I've never hit Baylen."

I've never heard of someone hitting Baylen.

"Did he retaliate?" I asked. Bishop wasn't as tense as he had been before, but I was stiff as a board.

"No. He wasn't angry, even after I broke his nose. He smiled through the entire thing. Fucking begged me to hit him harder."

The amount of blood on Bishop's hand that night was abnormal. It was nothing Baylen should have been smiling about. He had to have hurt him, badly. The blood had been all over him, even after the rain washed him clean.

I winced, imagining the picture Bishop had just painted; Baylen, on the ground, muttering cruel things about his mother while Bishop beat him until he matched the red in his hair. I shuddered, thinking of the smile he wore through it all.

"I don't want to speak about this after today. Okay?"

I nodded. "Okay."

"Will you stay?" Bishop asked, pulling his hands away from mine.

"My dad is going to be gone until Wednesday night." Bishop's eyes lit up, and any sorrow was replaced with desire. "Can I stay here until then?"

Bishop nodded. He leaned in for my lips, planting a soft kiss on them. "Thank you, Ethel," Bishop muttered, against my lips. I didn't know what I did for him to thank me. He made me feel like just sitting here, in silence, was enough. Maybe just listening would help him.

I leaned into him, leaving a kiss on his swollen eyelid.

With Bishop, it felt like nothing outside this room existed. Dad wasn't in this world. Mom's death wasn't. Grandma and Dad's feud didn't exist. I didn't need to worry about anything; it was just Bishop and me.

VERSE THIRTY-TWO

I refused to leave Bishop's bed.

The only time I left the comfort of his body was to shower and use the restroom. Luckily, he had a bathroom in his bedroom. So, I didn't need to leave his room through the night, or the morning; Bishop brought food to the room, knowing I wasn't going to go downstairs when Baylen was here.

The side of my face rested on his stomach, rising and falling to the pace of his breath. I kept my eyes on his face, watching him as he scrolled through his phone.

I had spent the night with Bishop. In this house. Holy shit.

For years, Dad had warned me about the people living in it; he told me of the horrors that were happening on the street. This house was where Devils resided, according to him. I wondered what he would say if he knew I was currently sleeping against one of his supposed "Devils."; one that had confided in me, about something so painful.

Compared to him sneaking into my bedroom, this felt different. It was more intimate here; there was no climbing trees or breaking through windows. It was his bedroom. His messy sanctuary with pictures of his family, cigarette ashes on the walls, and various posters.

I was in a large T-shirt; I swam in the warmth of it. The hem ended just below my ass, and it squeezed in at the shape of my breasts.

I shifted on top of his stomach, moving my gaze to a spot on the wall. I wondered where my dad was right now.

He wasn't with Rowans. That was for sure. But, he was somewhere, lying about his whereabouts.

He preached that I respect his privacy, throughout my entire childhood; he told me he would always be truthful. He would treat me the same if I treated him as such. I wasn't given curfews growing up, but I stayed inside, nonetheless.

Dad was a hypocrite sometimes. He insisted that we get a tracking app on each other, once. But, I denied it, saying privacy was what we had. It was as he had taught me; I honored it.

I regretted it.

I wanted to know what he was doing. What was so important that he lied? And, when did he get so good at lying?

"What are you thinking so hard about?"

I looked back to Bishop. His phone was face down on his chest.

"My dad. He had been out late recently. Like, really late. And, he's been lying about where he is going. I don't want to invade his privacy and follow him, but I don't know. He is definitely lying to me about it."

Bishop listened to every word I said, soaking it in with as much attention as Gwen did. "How do you know he is lying?"

He propped himself onto his elbows. His fingers reached for my hair; I bit back a moan when they started to work light circles around my scalp.

"Well, he said he was with a priest today. But, that priest has been dead. For a while. We just never brought it up, I thought he was grieving." My eyes grew heavy from his fingers working in my hair. I couldn't concentrate on what I was saying with his fingers acting like this. "But, he was so good at lying. Like, I never would have suspected it to be a lie if I didn't know."

"I don't know. And yesterday morning, he was being so weird. He said I was maturing in all aspects and that Simon would know how to appreciate that." I left out the part about Dad's grasp around my arm.

Bishop's stomach went hard as a rock beneath me. "Ethel—."

"I don't think he meant to be weird about it. I'm just overthinking it. He doesn't have a filter sometimes. It's fine." I sat up, hoping he would drop it. I sent him a glare, pleading with him to do exactly that.

"Ethel, that sounds pretty fucking weird." My throat burned, recalling the way he grabbed my arm. He wasn't like that. He was just having a bad day. He couldn't be like that. I had to be overthinking it.

I shook my head. "He's like that. Drop it. Please." Drop it. Oh, how fast the roles have reversed now.

Bishop was still tense, but he started to move his fingers against my scalp again. "Okay," Bishop hesitated.

"I never asked you why you hated Christians so much. You went to Northside. A religious school. Why didn't you just leave?" I asked.

"My parents wanted me to go there. So, I did. Plus, Coen and Cain were there, I wasn't going to leave them. But, I was treated differently.

The school treated me differently. They thought I worshiped the Devil, because of the music I listened to, and the way I dressed."

I watched his lips as he spoke. "The school had me go to a mandatory prayer. Whatever the fuck you Christians call it. It was daily, during lunchtime. Your father just so happened to be the preacher they sent me to."

Shit. Was that why he hated Dad so much? "That is corruption if I've ever seen it. Isn't it, Ethel?"

I didn't even know the school was able to force someone into doing that. And, Dad? He never mentioned how he knew Bishop. He had just said the boy hated our God and wanted trouble. "I didn't know that," I admitted. "Dad never told me."

"Your dad is a lying hypocrite. Isn't he?"

The words sunk into my stomach. He was. "I'm sorry," I said. I meant it. If my dad had forced something onto the Bishop that he didn't believe in, I would forever feel guilty. Dad would never apologize to him. But, I could, for him.

Bishop grunted, sitting up in the bed. He leaned against the bed frame, resting his intertwined fingers behind his head.

I pushed myself upward and adjusted my position until I sat on his thighs. I straddled either side of his outer thigh, planting my palms on his chest. His crotch was a few inches in front of mine, but I didn't move toward it.

I leaned down and placed a slow kiss on his lips. In response, his hands slid beneath the shirt I wore. I shuddered at the feeling of his cold fingertips running down my spine.

"You know how to change the subject," Bishop said, in between the kisses he was leaving on my upper lip. I smiled against his mouth, shaking my head.

"I'm not changing the subject," I started. I slid my hands under his shirt, dragging my hands down his stomach. "I'm just taking an intermission."

Bishop grabbed hold of my hips, pulling me upward. I looked down at where I now sat, directly on his crotch. I could feel him growing and swelling beneath me, with each passing second. I applied more of my weight to his crotch; I wanted to feel every inch of him.

"You are very good at taking intermissions," he added, biting my upper lip. I winced at the feeling, but he ran his tongue across my lip, soothing the pain.

Bishop used his hands to roll my hips against him. I wasn't wearing anything beneath my shirt. My folds were bare and wet; my stomach tightened when I felt his clothed length rub against them. I wanted to burn the sweatpants he wore right now.

"Bishop?" I panted. The coil in my stomach tightened as he slowly rocked me against him.

"Yes, Ethel?" His eyes were on our crotches. His fingers were still on my hips, guiding me, but it was me grinding against him now. I was chasing the high building inside of me; the tightness.

"I changed my mind." I dug my fingers into his stomach, continuing to rock against him. Vulnerable. The word repeated in my head. God looking down upon me was no longer my worry, being vulnerable was.

If God can forgive a murderer on his deathbed, then God can forgive bliss.

"I want you to fuck me."

VERSE THIRTY-THREE

Bishop's lips went still against me. I tugged at him, nonetheless. I ran my fingers up his stiffening torso. Once I reached his throat, I wrapped my fingers around him, lingering my touch on his sensitive skin.

I pulled away from him, staring down at him.

"Ethel," he cautioned, sucking in a breath.

I leaned back down, attempting to kiss him again. His fingers grasped my hair, preventing me from disappearing into the warmth of him. I narrowed my eyes, responding to him. "Bishop," I echoed.

Did he not want to have sex with me?

My throat tensed. Was he going to reject me?

"That sure is different from nothing inside," Bishop teased. I watched his gaze drop as my fingers moved from his neck, down his chest, and to his stomach. His breathing was growing heavier with my touch, and his muscles were tensing.

"Yes, it is. Isn't it?" I tilted my head, still looking down at him. My pussy was bare on top of his bulge; there was a throb between my legs, from the mix of ache in my core, and his cock. We were both craving this. I could feel it.

Despite him holding me in place by my throat, I was still able to move my hips. I slowly rolled my hips against him, choking on the gasp that slid up my throat. It felt like an electric current had activated inside of me. Like something was in there, curling and coiling my insides.

Just from a single roll.

It was going to feel good when he got inside of me.

Bishop's mouth hung open, and his hands slid to my hips. His brows knitted together, staring down at where my shirt had risen. My bare pussy was in view, as well as his hard, clothed length. He was tucked between my folds, hitting my clit with every movement I made against him.

This was the hottest thing I'd ever seen.

"Fuck, Ethel," Bishop groaned. He tilted his head backward, against the pillow. His lips parted and a soft growl slid from his mouth. I continued to move against him, watching him unraveling beneath me.

I wanted him inside me.

I needed him inside of me.

My body shuddered the harder I rolled my cunt against him.

"Ethel, if you don't stop doing that, I'm actually going to fuck you," Bishop warned.

I rolled myself against him again, reaching for my breasts. I stared up at the ceiling, trying to steady my heavy breathing.

"That's the point," I said. I moved my hands away from my sore breasts, and toward his stomach again. I braced myself, grinding harder against him.

Roll.

Did he think I was joking?

The green of Bishop's eyes was replaced with a dark shade of dilated black. Desire and arousal were all that was left behind the green.

He tightened his hold on my hips. He didn't stop my motions. Instead, he pulled me harder onto his crotch.

I could feel every inch of his length. He was aligned perfectly against my clit. I whimpered, rolling harder into the length. This may just feel better than his fingers against my clit.

His cock pulsated inside of my folds, even with his sweatpants separating us. It was growing hot between us; the heat between my legs was mixing with his hot cock. He was so close to my entrance. Just one movement, the throw of his pants, and he would be inside of me.

"Don't joke around about that."

"I'm not," I replied.

I pressed harder into him. His tongue against my clit would never fill me the way I wanted him to. I wanted to be stretched, to a girth and length only Bishop could offer. I wanted to be stuffed.

Bishop blinked, staring up at me. I mimicked him, staring down at him with a gaze as intense as his own. We stayed silent, nothing but our heavy breaths echoing through the room.

I shifted my fingers behind my neck. I didn't look away from him once as I undid the clasp of my cross necklace. I let the cold metal pool in the palm of my hands. I placed the necklace on the nightstand a few inches beside his head. "God will forgive," I stated.

Bishop watched me as I pulled the purity ring from my finger. After all the times he had touched, kissed, and ground against me, this was what made him breathe the heaviest. I placed this ring beside my necklace, knowing it would never leave this room.

My innocence was never going to leave him.

The second I saw him in the alley, he already had it.

"Please, Bishop. Fuck me."

In this age, virginity was no longer viewed as sacred. Not in the way I viewed it; I supposed it was the way I was raised that made me see it as something so important. Bishop looked at me as if he knew how important this was; I wanted to have him even harder for that.

"Are you sure?" Bishop asked. His voice was deep and raspy. My legs trembled around his hips, hearing his voice so sex laced.

"Yes," I replied. I reached for the waistband of his sweatpants. I was frantically trying to pull it down his hips. He lifted his hips, helping me spring his cock free.

Whatever he wanted, I was going to give it to him. On my back, hands, and knees, as he had so gracefully stated before; I would give it to him. It didn't matter how. I just wanted him.

VERSE THIRTY-FOUR

I let out a soft squeal when Bishop grabbed hold of my hips, flipping me over. I landed on my back beside him; the second I hit the bed, Bishop crawled above me. I was breathing heavily, staring up at him with rounded eyes.

Holy shit.

I was about to have sex with Bishop.

In his bed.

In this house.

I shuddered, reaching for his neck. He was about to be inside of me.

Bishop let out a heavy breath on my lips, before disappearing down my body. I watched his eyes meet mine for a moment before I lost sight of him between my thighs. He pushed my knees into the mattress, splaying me for him.

He pressed the tips of his fingers against my clit, rubbing slow circles against the nerves. I buried my mouth into his pillow, letting out a soft cry. My back came from the bed, and I arched my pussy further into his hand. I tried to chase the high he was causing me to currently feel, but he slowed, pulling away.

"Shit, Bishop," I gasped, bucking my hips toward him. He wasn't inside of me. Nor anywhere close. But, my entrance was throbbing and contracting like he had been fucking me all day.

Slowly, he started to rub me again. He looked up at me, watching me watch him. He tugged his lip in, suppressing the grin creeping up his face. He sucked in a breath before spitting a wad of saliva onto my pussy.

That feeling alone made me release another soft moan.

"Don't come yet," Bishop instructed. The way he moved his fingers against my clit told a different story. His breath fanned down my clit, continuing to rub me hard. I was going to burst on his fingers if he didn't pull away soon. "I want you to come on me."

"I'm about to come on you," I said. My eyes fluttered shut.

Bishop smirked, pulling his fingers away from me. I was going to hit him if he didn't replace the void he'd caused to lurk between my legs. I needed something. Anything. Fuck, I would settle for a pillow between my legs right now.

"I like how fast you come for me." Bishop planted a kiss on my thigh, inches from where I wanted him most. Needed him. The intensity was starting to fade between my legs. He'd pushed me right to the edge, and pulled away when I was most desperate for him.

Bishop was a dick.

"Mhm," I whimpered.

Kiss.

I tried to clench my thighs together, but his hands kept my knees pinned to the mattress. He bit my thighs, tracing his tongue along the bruises he left. I had them from how hard his fingers were digging into me.

Kiss.

"I don't want you to look away. If you do, I will stop. Okay?"

I nodded, looking down between his legs. He fisted his cock in his hand, stroking it to the pace he currently kissed my thighs. Shit. I was about to have sex. My stomach fluttered. I wasn't just nervous about having sex for the first time; it was Bishop I was about to be fucked by.

God never existed within this home, anyway.

He let out a shaky breath as he fisted his cock. I stared down at the length of him. There was no way he was going to fit inside of me. No fucking way. He was too big.

He continued to stare at me as he pumped himself, frantically. He was so fast. Hard. Rough.

This was going to hurt.

"I'm going to put my tongue inside of you now," he warned. He slid the tip of his hot tongue down my slit, hovering by my entrance. He stared up at me through his lashes, awaiting my consent. I nodded, watching him sink the length of his tongue inside of me.

A strange noise came out of me once he sunk inside my entrance, flicking his tongue around the ring of muscle. I understood what he meant so many weeks ago. When he said, "Say the word and I will make you see your God." I couldn't even moan. Only primal, strangled noises were coming out of me.

He moved his tongue in slow circles, pushing at the tightness milking his tongue. He thrust his tongue in and out of me, all while his thumb continued to work at my clit. My knees were still pinned hard to the bed, allowing him easy access to my cunt.

I arched into him, pushing my pussy harder into his face.

"Now my fingers." Again, he waited. His tongue stilled inside of me, waiting for my consent. I nodded.

He wrapped his lips around my clit, pushing a finger slowly inside of me. It hurt, for just a moment. But, once his knuckle made it past the resistance, he started to work with my pussy. His finger curled up against a spot inside of me, slowly caressing it with the tip of his finger.

I saw stars.

I dug my fingers into his hair, holding him right where he was. This felt too good.

Bishop added a second finger, slowly pumping in and out of me. He curled inside of me once his knuckles made it to my pussy lips. Every movement he made caused me to see black. He was caressing a spot so deep inside of me; a spot I did not realize needed to be touched.

I trembled. I was a complete mess beneath his touch.

"Shit that feels good," I moaned. I had to force my heavy eyelids open. The only reason I had the strength to keep them open was the fear of him stopping the complete, and utter bliss I was currently undergoing.

He spread his two fingers apart, stretching me further.

He was preparing me for his cock. Every inch.

"Bishop," I cried. My stomach rolled and jerked with every thrust of his fingers. It felt like he was already fucking me. Pounding into me. My breasts came toward my throat with every movement of his finger. "I'm gonna—."

He pulled his fingers out of me. "Ah, ah," he warned. He positioned himself between my legs. The tip of his cock collected any wetness that had slipped from my folds. I looked down at his head, seeing how slick it had become. From me, alone.

He reached into the drawer beside the bed. He slid the condom on, drawing out every second of this. I ground my teeth together, impatiently waiting for him to return inside of me. Any part of him could be in me; I would take his fist at this point.

"Ready?"

I nodded.

He braced a hand beside my head, using his body weight to keep my legs splayed. I felt him slap the tip of his cock against my clit, running it up and down my wet stripe. Again.

"It won't hurt as bad if you relax. And breathe," he instructed.

I laughed, looking up at him. "Do you take people's virginities a lot?"

He shook his head. "You would be surprised by what Coen brings up at dinner."

The top of his cock lined my entrance. He pushed the tip inside of me, crowning me. His cock pushed past my folds and he tore through the ring that was causing so much resistance. He held his eyes with mine, sucking in a breath with me. I focused on my breathing as he pushed through the resistance, breaking it.

I gasped, reaching for his back. I dug my nails into his skin, hurting him in the way he currently was me. He continued to slowly seat himself inside of me; it felt like he was reaching my chest. He was so big.

"Fuck, Ethel," Bishop groaned, once his hilt reached my folds.

My eyes rolled backward, taking in the feeling I was experiencing. He was throbbing and twitching inside of me. I was pulsating, tightening, and releasing around his hot length. This was unlike anything I had ever felt before; this was pure fucking nirvana.

My pussy slowly adjusted to him, accommodating his girth. I wasn't squeezing as tight around him, but I still was against his length like a glove. He must have felt me adjust; he slid out of me, to my folds, before hitting his balls against me again.

I groaned this time, my mouth stuck ajar. "Shit, you are big." I moaned into the crook of his neck, brushing my teeth against the soft skin.

Thrust.

His thrusts started slow, letting me get used to the feeling of his cock. Every movement inside of me made my stomach tighten. My core dripped around the condom, soaking both of us. The pain had only lasted for a second. Once it disappeared, moans started to slip out of me; begs even found their way inside of his ear.

His speed picked up. At some point, something had snapped inside of Bishop. He started to pound hard into me. So hard, I couldn't tell when he was inside of me, and when he wasn't. Everything was getting tight, so tight I was on the verge of bursting. My core was tight, and my pussy continued to hold selfishly onto him.

Thrust.

"Ah!" I moaned, looking up at him through teary eyes. Noises were coming out of me; noises only he seemed to be able to bring from my throat. I didn't want my pussy to ever feel empty again. I wanted him to forever be seated, between my legs.

"God, you're so fucking good," Bishop praised, fucking me harder.

My head fell backward, but my eyes stayed on him. The room was growing hotter, and thicker by the second. Our noises were echoing from the walls; a mixture of wetness, moans, and groans. I didn't care if Baylen, Coen, or Solomon could hear us. Bishop could fuck me in front of them for all I cared. As long as he stayed inside of me, hitting the spot that made me see stars.

"I'm gonna—" I croaked, unable to finish my groan.

He pressed more of his weight against me, unable to hold himself up. His thrusts were becoming sloppier, and harder. The condom was growing hotter by the second as he filled it with precum. He was about to come. As was I.

"There!" I cried, feeling his cock hit the spot, yet again. He was so good at this; I hoped it was Coen who had taught him of this spot, not experience.

Bishop slammed into me three more times before we both came. I trembled, holding onto him as he came into the condom with a groan. I was quiet when I came. I couldn't moan anymore, and my voice was taken by the pure pleasure rocking through my body.

I pulsed around him, milking him so tightly. The aftershocks made me feel as though my body had become pure electricity. I was buzzing, from the drug who called himself Bishop.

His thumb ran across my slick cheek. He had fucked me so hard I had literal tears streaming down my face. I didn't even notice, until now. "Are you okay?" Bishop asked, pulling himself out of me.

I nodded, whimpering once he was fully out of my cunt. "That was the best thing I've ever done," I croaked. He collapsed in the bed beside me, disposing of the condom in the trashcan next to his bed. I debated leaning over and cleaning the remaining cum from him, with my tongue.

A shower, with him inside of me, would be better.

"Welcome to the sex world, church girl," Bishop teased, pulling me into his chest.

I no longer understand why sex before marriage was frowned upon. That was the closest I've ever come to heaven.

215

VERSE THIRTY-FIVE

I didn't even attempt to figure out what Dad preached about today.

I watched him, thinking of the previous days between us. He was never home anymore; he was with "Father Rowans" doing something only God knew of. When he returned home a few days ago, he wouldn't look at me. He simply walked upstairs as I ate alone.

The man who preached in front of me was a liar. There had been a point when he was not, but that was far from the case now. He was too good at it; the lies were seamless. What else had he been lying to me about?

My phone buzzed beneath my thigh. The hairs on the back of my neck stood erect; I was pulled from my intense stare up at my dad. I slowly turned around toward the back pew, seeing Bishop sprawled out in the shadows of his pew. He watched me; he had been watching me all service.

I looked back forward, slowly blinking. His face was a reminder of what had occurred nights before. I could still feel him; I could feel the emptiness I did not know existed. He made me feel full; however, I was back to feeling empty.

Because of Bishop. The lack of him.

I rubbed my knees together, brushing off my dress. I reached for my phone, reading the message he had sent.

BITCHOP: did your father ever say what he was doing?

I frowned, looking back to Dad.

ME: no.

ME: no vile texts anymore? am i out of your system?

I quickly sent him a grin, letting him know I was not being serious. Even with an entire congregation between us, I could still feel the intensity and desire behind his green eyes. The heat of it was a different beast entirely.

BITCHOP: you'd still be in my system even if i fucked you every day of your life.

My cheeks heated upon reading the message. I clamped my thighs together seeing the next message, and image roll in.

BITCHOP: as for the vile messages.

One image attachment.

I choked on my breath as a picture of Bishop's thick cock illuminated my screen. His fingers were wrapped around the base of his shaft; from the background, it appeared to be in his bedroom. His painted black nails were chipped, and his knuckles were white from how tightly he was grasping it.

Shit.

I locked my phone, throwing it face down beside me. Another message had come through, but I did not look at it. I kept my palm on my forehead, leaning against the pew; the back of my neck was hot, and my ears were an unnatural shade of red. He had to see how that affected me.

I licked my lips, zoning out on the crucifix that hung behind Dad. Why would he send that right now? My throat and mouth had gone dry, remembering how tight he held himself.

I scratched the side of my head, running my fingers down my face.

Gwen had told me of how horrifying dick pictures were. She was the only one who received them during high school. Briar definitely did, but she never spoke of that to me; Gwen had no filter.

She had told me of a boy who sent her one after he made out with her thigh in an attempt to "eat her out." She had told the boy his cock was ugly, and to leave her alone. When he responded with another picture, she sent it to his mother.

Gwen was wrong. That was arousing, even if it were just a picture.

I crossed my arms over my stomach, sinking lower into the pew. If I could disappear into the hardwood of these pews, I would. His gaze; I was all too aware of his gaze currently.

My phone buzzed, a second unread message floating through the air. I couldn't bring myself to look at the messages. He could see how flustered I was; if I had to bet, he had sent two more just to see how much blood he could send to my head.

I was going to be damned.

I stood from the pew, walking toward the aisle. I made my way toward the bathroom, making sure that I would walk directly beside Bishop.

My eyes only slid down to meet him when I was about to pass him. His knees were spread far and his arms were stretched out on the pew. He looked so casual. As if he were lounging in the back row of a movie.

The sight of him made my stomach liquefy. I tightened my thighs together, walking out of the congregation hall.

Whenever I reached the mirror, I slipped inside, adjusting my appearance. I tugged at the half-up hairstyle I wore, making sure there were no loose strands. I brushed off the front of my loose sun dress, staring at the door from the mirror.

The door swung open within seconds, and a black mass seeped into the bathroom. His shadow took up most of his body; it trailed behind him, making me lose my breath for a moment. His aura was so forceful. Prominent.

I was fully expecting him to follow behind me in the bathroom. But, now that he was here, I froze up.

I continued to adjust my hair. "That was inappropriate," I stated, watching every step he took toward my back. I looked up at him through my mascara-coated lashes, hiding the smirk that was coming up.

This felt so wrong. But, so good.

I recalled a time after Bishop had fingered me. When I had told him it felt wrong. His response echoed through my head daily after that; even today. But, it felt so good, didn't it pretty girl?

Bishop took a step into my ass, his hands landing on my hips. "Did you lure me in here to scold me? Over a little dick picture?" Not little. I looked down at his hand, rubbing wide circles along my hip. The dress was loose; every movement he made hiked it up more.

"I did not lure you," I bit back. "You followed."

Okay, maybe the look I gave him was a come here, type of look. My lips parted as he pressed his cock into my lower back, pinning me to the edge of the sink counter. The door was unlocked. Shit. Before, we had a stall concealing us. But, now?

My fingers dug into the porcelain. I dipped my head down toward the sink as his lips bit into the skin beneath my ear. I think he liked my neck more than the heat between my legs. I had to pound makeup over my neck daily now; it looked like someone had been trying to attack me from all the bruises his lips gave me.

Bishop rolled his hips into the back of me. His entire length rubbed against the soft fabric of my dress. I gasped, watching my face contort in the mirror. My lips rounded, and my brows scrunched together. I didn't recognize the light that flashed behind my eyes; was that desire?

He watched me, biting harder into my neck. My eyelids were growing heavy. I slumped my head backward, hitting the part of his shoulder that met his neck. His mouth nor eyes left me once, even when I was moving.

It took every bit of strength to push him off of me. I wanted to melt into him, mold our bodies together. Even if some parts of us didn't fit. We could force them to.

"Ethel," Bishop growled. I twisted around to face him. My gaze slid down to where his length was prodding out, begging for something to stuff. Anything. I looked back to his face, walking past him toward the door.

I locked it.

"We are not having sex in a church bathroom," I informed. I dropped to my knees as I spoke, sliding my hands up and down his bony thighs. The tiles were cold on my knees; my nipples were already tight, but now they were throbbing from the feeling.

"Nothing inside," Bishop teased, tilting his head. He certainly had been inside.

I reached for his belt. "Nothing inside."

VERSE
THIRTY-SIX

This may have been the most glorious sight I'd ever seen.

Bishop, looking down at me through heavy breaths. His erection swelled in front of my face, inches away from brushing across my skin. I dug my nails into his belt, fiddling with the leather until it came undone.

I threw it somewhere across the bathroom. I tugged down his pants, awaiting his cock to fall out.

I lied. This was the most glorious thing I'd ever seen. His erection sprang out of his pants, slapping across my cheek in the process. He was so big; the sight of him made my mouth dry. He was not going to fit inside my throat. I didn't know how he fit inside of my pussy a few nights ago.

I trailed my acrylic tips along the ridge of his cock. I examined the veins running beneath his shaft, aiding in his twitch. I wrapped my hand around it, groaning at how he felt in my hand. He was so heavy and hot; his cock twitched in my hand.

Bishop bucked his hips forward, forcing his cock inside of my fist.

"Shit, Ethel," Bishop hissed. He looked down at me, out of breath; I hadn't even stroked him yet.

His breathing was heavy and his nostrils flared. He looked down at me in the way I had been looking at him, a few moments ago. It was the most glorious sight he had ever seen.

I kept my eyes on him as my tongue connected above his balls. I slowly slid my tongue along the ridge of his cock. He tensed and twitched beneath my tongue. Once I reached the head of him, I swirled my tongue around it, collecting all of the precum.

I had no idea how to suck a cock. But, the steamy romances Gwen had lent me, went into great detail about how they worked their lovers' cocks.

That's what I planned to do to Bishop. How the people in books did it.

I grazed my teeth over his shaft, watching him continue to unravel above me. Fuck. Bishop was completely, and utterly, perfect.

I made my way back to his tip and rolled my lips over my teeth. I sunk my hot mouth as far as I could, swallowing him whole with a gag.

Bishop let out a growl, grabbing ahold of my hair. He didn't force me further down onto his cock; he simply held onto my strands as if it were the only thing keeping him on the ground right now. I suctioned my cheeks, pulling him out of my throat, before taking him deeper.

Over, and over.

I sucked his cock hard. Like it was the greatest thing I'd ever put in my mouth. If I were being honest, it might have been.

"Fucking hell," he cursed, throwing his head backward. The bathroom had come alive. His pants and groans were intertwingled with the wet noises coming from my mouth. I was sucking, slurping at him, drowning out the noises coming from him. I clenched my thighs together, a moan slipping out of me.

I pulled my mouth away, looking up at him with a narrowed gaze. His cock dripped spit and precum, down my face. I stared up at him, nonetheless, awaiting his eyes.

He looked down at me like he was ready to kill me. My stomach fluttered, a mix of fear and excitement bursting through me. I tilted my head, reciting his own words back to him. "What do you always say?" I asked. It was on the tip of my tongue, mixed with his precum. "Look away and you will stop?"

He ground his molars together, but a grin crept up his face. He squeezed my strands tight as I placed my lips back over his cock. I didn't hesitate, nor gag this time; I swallowed him again, bobbing my head with such force that he stumbled backward into the sink.

He didn't look away from me this time.

And, I didn't stop bobbing my head. Sucking him. Swallowing every drop of him.

Occasionally, he hit my gag reflex; a few tears slid down my face, streaking my mascara. I dreaded seeing how disastrous I looked. The sight only seemed to make him swell more in my mouth. I could feel his throb in my throat, matching the beat of me.

More precum leaked inside of my throat, coating it. It tasted salty, with a hint of lemons. I savored the taste.

He groaned when he burst in the back of my throat. He grabbed the back of my head, pushing me to the hilt when he came. His cum filled my throat; I gagged, but surprisingly, I was able to fit every inch of him. My mouth was wide, sucking every drop clean from him.

I pulled away when his groans became heavy breaths.

"Jesus fucking Christ," Bishop gaped. He tucked himself back into his pants. I shot him a glance for the blasphemy.

Bishop crouched down to meet my height. The pad of his thumb moved across my lip, collecting a single drop of cum that I missed. I wrapped my lips around his finger, sucking the final drop clean. I swiped my tongue across the tip of his finger, similar to how I had done to his cock.

We both shuddered.

I looked up at him through my smeared lashes, still attempting to catch my breath. Even with him crouched down to meet my height, he was still a foot taller than me.

He wrapped his arm around my waist, pulling me from the ground. "What are you—?"

I was cut off by him dropping my ass to the edge of the sink. He positioned himself between my legs.

"Nothing inside," he reassured, with a smirk on his face.

"Nothing inside," I repeated.

Arousal rolled down the length of my spine, causing me to sit upright.

Bishop grabbed hold of my panties, pulling them down my legs. I lifted my hips, helping him remove my cheeky lace panties; he tucked them into the back pocket of his pants.

"Shit, Bishop," I cursed, throwing my head backward against the mirror. He wasn't between my legs, yet his gaze did enough to my cunt.

I could feel my wetness leaking out of me, preparing me for whatever he planned to do to me.

Bishop grabbed hold of my ankles, positioning them on the countertop. The position strained my hips, but it aided with the coiling in my stomach. I was sitting on the edge of the counter, my feet on either side of me, with my pussy splayed for Bishop.

He kissed my lips once before disappearing beneath my dress.

My hands flew out to grab onto something, anything. His tongue dipped inside of my pussy, curling around my heat. I bit into my palm, muffling the groans that came out of me the harder his mouth and fingers worked inside of me.

Bishop held my hips down as he ate me out. His tongue played with my clit occasionally, before it dived back into my pussy. He hadn't used his fingers once; he didn't need to. His tongue was enough to make me come.

Three times.

Bishop made me cream three times. The first was from his tongue flicking against my clit. The second was from his tongue spearing my entrance as if it were his cock. The third was a blur of stars and white light.

He would have kept going, too. I had to force him to stop when the music started playing inside the church, signaling the service was about to end.

I left that bathroom happier than I had ever been in my life. There was no stress from Dad. No stress of anything.

Bishop was my undoing.

VERSE THIRTY-SEVEN

I watched the knife slowly carve into the meat, blood oozing onto the plate in the process. Dad always liked his steak rare; it made my stomach turn seeing the blood.

I stabbed my fork into the salad in front of me.

I wanted to go home, and shower. My thighs were still slick, and I did not have any underwear on to catch the aftermath of my arousal leaking out of me. Bishop had taken my fucking panties.

I protested about going out, but Dad insisted on us going to Gianno's after the service.

"Great service," I admitted, biting into a crouton. I was there for some of it. He had preached for over thirty minutes today; I'd say I spent seven minutes listening to it. The remaining time was spent with Bishop between my legs.

My stomach flipped, and a blush spread across my face.

I looked down at my salad. I hoped my hair shielded the blush that was creeping up. An image of the previous hour came into my mind. I had been sprawled out on the counter, holding onto Bishop's hair for dear life as he brought me to three orgasms. Not to mention the aftermath; I had to clean my mascara completely off my face.

"Yeah." Dad's voice was drawn out. I looked up at him; he was staring at me already. He smiled, tilting his head once we locked eyes.

"What?" I asked. His face went blank. Even if he wore his emotions like a mask, could I even trust him? He was lying about something. God, this was the most frustrating I'd ever been; I knew something was off, but I couldn't ask him. That wasn't how we functioned.

"Nothing." He shook his head, looking down at his bloody steak. He hadn't stopped smiling.

My gut twisted.

Fuck this. Dad had no right to be lying to me. But, where would I begin? I knew I needed to start with the lie and pry at it some; it was my specialty, after all. Prying. "How was Father Rowans? I haven't seen him in so long."

I watched him, waiting to see if his eyes flickered away from me. I waited for any sign of deceit, but none appeared. "He is doing well. He just got back from Italy for a vacation. He showed me pictures of everything. Beautiful city. We could go some summer. If you wanted."

Dad smiled, but it didn't reach his eyes.

Father Rowans hadn't been to Italy; his flesh was rotting six feet beneath the dirt.

"That would be great," I replied, hesitantly. I noticed how white his knuckles had become around the knife that sawed through his steak.

A long pass of silence passed between us.

I listened to my heartbeat, and the crunch of salad with every chew. I zoned in on the buzz of the restaurant, occupying my mind with any thoughts besides the one across from me. How was he this good at lying? Did he know I knew he was lying?

I opened my mouth to speak; however, Dad did as well.

"Are you seeing someone?"

"How long have you been with that boy?"

I think I stopped breathing.

We stared blankly at each other, both awaiting the answer to our questions. His question was much heavier than mine had been. From the look on his face, it almost appeared as if he brushed my question off completely. I hadn't noticed if he flinched when I asked my question.

That boy.

Bishop.

Fuck.

I frowned, recalling the stories I had been told of Bishop. None of which ended up being remotely true. I remembered how he had been treated at Northside, forced into confessions for simply carrying a different belief.

Devil. Bishop was the Devil to Dad. The boy who cried into my chest, shaking with guilt and grief. Bishop was far from the Devil, though no words would ever convince Dad of that.

Even if I were to tell Dad he was the best thing that has ever happened to me. I'd be shunned.

"Hm?" I hummed, tilting my chin downward. I had my mouth stuffed with salad, but I had stopped chewing. How was I going to talk my way out of this? If Bishop were here, he would be able to talk himself and me out of this.

What would Bishop do?

We had to have made it obvious. Thinking back on it, we made it so obvious. I walked into that bathroom, and Bishop followed. Twice. He was never going to forgive me for this. I felt like he was in the bathroom, watching what Bishop did with his tongue between my legs. I could feel him shaming me for it all.

Dad smiled, cutting another slice of bloody meat. He pulled it between his teeth, blood oozing between his pearls. His smile met his eyes this time. The sight was horrifying. What was the sight of my dad smiling so horrifying?

He used the bloody knife to gesture toward my dress. Directly where my cleavage was. "You still have him on you."

It felt like someone had wrapped their fingers into my neck, and squeezed until my eyes bulged from my skull. I looked down at my dress, toward the precum that had stained the fabric. I looked back to Dad. He didn't look ashamed, or even disappointed. He looked as if he were a void, chewing on his steak, while staring at the stain on my dress.

Dad looked like Baylen. Emotionless.

I wasn't going to lie to him. I wasn't him.

"He is not what you think." Something had changed between me and Dad. A year ago, I would have killed Bishop if he so much as looked at Dad the wrong way. But, I was defending him now. Did I change? Am I a horrible person for defending Bishop, and standing up against my dad?

Dad laughed, wiping his mouth with the corner of a napkin. "Am I such a terrible father that you choose him over me?"

"I'm not making a choice."

He grunted at this, drinking his water in one gulp. "You do think I'm a terrible father. You have looked at me differently. Ever since that bitch of a woman came into town. I should have never let her come near you."

Grandma. That bitch of a woman.

Bile rose in my throat.

"No," I snapped. "I look at you differently because you lie to me. About everything. You go out late, and you lie about where you are going. Obviously, I am going to look at you differently." My voice was a seethe. I wondered if Bishop would be proud of me.

I saw the first emotion fall across his face. The first one I had seen in quite some time. Anger. It slid down his face like a veil; his nails sunk into the side of the table, holding him in place. His body trembled and his eyes narrowed on me.

Why was Dad so angry?

I dipped my head down to my lap. I fiddled with the black ring that sat where my purity ring once did. Bishop had slipped it on my finger during the night, as a reminder of him. I twirled it, imagining him here to ease the tension.

"What happened to you? You used to be so good. You used to respect my privacy. If you don't respect mine, I see no reason I should respect yours," Dad threatened.

I blinked, staring up at him. What did he mean by that? His voice was threatening, dipping low so close ears would not hear what he was saying. Whatever he meant, was not in good intention.

"You're lying to me." My voice started to tremble, along with my jaw. If Bishop were here, he would tell me to grow a pair and keep my voice steady.

Dad changed faces. The anger dissipated, and his face softened. He reached for my hand, grazing his thumb against my knuckles.

I flinched.

"I'm not, sweet girl. I just don't want to speak about this part of my life. I haven't lied to you once. I just need time before I open up about this." The name Father Rowans echoed in my head. Lies. Lies. Lies.

Dad was a liar.

"Bishop and I are together." There was no official title, but as of right now, there was. His face between my legs came into my mind, as my tongue went sharp. "Is that going to be an issue?"

Dad shook his head. "No issue. You live your life, as foolishly as you want. I will live mine. Just like we always have. You lied to me. I don't know why you keep trying to pin me on the lying," Dad muttered, beneath his breath.

I pulled my hand away. "Okay," was all I said. I wanted to run out of this restaurant; I was nauseous at the sight of him. How could he be using a dead man's name to lie?

"I have somewhere I need to be. Are you okay with that?" The words weren't harsh, but whatever he had laced them with was. I flinched, taken aback by his tone.

"Father Rowans?" I asked, matching my tone with his. His head jerked upward, and his eyes narrowed.

"Yes," he bit out. "Would you like me to drop you off or can you wal—."

I didn't even let him finish. "I will walk. Now." I pushed the chair backward, standing from the table. I was starving, but I couldn't eat another bite in front of my lying father.

His hand wrapped tight around my wrist before I could leave. "I know you won't stop seeing him. Sluts will be sluts. But, you do not bring that boy into my home. Unless you wish to live on the streets."

Sluts will be sluts.

I gaped down at him.

Who was sitting down across from me? This wasn't my dad. This was not the man who used to tuck me in at night, and check under my bed for "monsters." We had always had our fights, but never had he been cruel. Harsh. Demeaning.

"Dad—" My jaw trembled. His eyes moved down to the hem of my dress, and then back to my face. It felt like my soul was being inspected, ripped apart. Vulnerable. I had always feared it for this reason alone. Dad was judging every taint in my aura. Had he just determined I would be damned?

He let go of my wrist and cut into his steak. He acted as if I weren't standing two feet from him.

I hoped whatever he was doing was worth it.

VERSE THIRTY-EIGHT

My back slid against the tiles of my shower. I brought my knees into my chest, squeezing my arms tight around my legs. I squeezed hard, trying to ease my trembling body. My fingertips gently traced along the soft skin of my arms.

Slut.

I felt dirty. So, so dirty.

It was strange. A single word, which slid out of people's mouths with no cruel intentions. When Briar had groomed me before we attended the club, the word slut had left her mouth at least a hundred times. But, once it came out of my dad's mouth, it had a new meaning entirely.

A sob slipped out. I buried my face into my kneecaps, hiding in shame from the ghosts of my bathroom.

I sat in the shower for hours, awaiting the front door to slam shut. But, Dad never came home. What in God's name was he doing? For this amount of time?

I slipped out of the shower and back into my bedroom. I threw on a baggy pair of sweatpants and a loose tee shirt. I sat on the edge of my bed, grabbing my phone from beside me.

I frowned, looking down at my phone. Bishop had texted once, asking if I was okay. It was nearly three in the afternoon. By this point, we'd be on the phone bickering about something; however, it would end with him whispering dirty words through the phone.

I scrolled past the message and checked for any text from Dad. I searched for an apology, an explanation. Anything. But, I found none.

My finger hovered above a contact. I stared at the gray icon, debating if calling her was the best thing to do.

Grandma.

I sucked in a breath and rang the line. What was I even going to say? Oh, your son just called me a slut, and he spends most of his time hanging out with a dead man. Hope Florida is nice!

The line went to voicemail.

"Shit," I cursed.

I quickly typed out a message before I convinced myself otherwise. Grandma was wise. She would know how to help me.

ME: call me when you can, please.

I still hadn't the slightest clue what I was going to say to her. I needed some form of family with me. Dad wasn't here. He was standing before me, in the flesh, but after Mom's death, something had disappeared in him. The joy.

I looked back at Bishop's message.

BITCHOP: you good?

I ran a hand through my wet locks. Would Bishop retaliate if he knew Dad had been so harsh?

ME: my dad and i got into a fight.

ME: he knows we are

I stopped, not knowing what word to put at the end of that sentence. Fucking? Dating? Talking? It felt more than fucking, but neither Bishop nor I had been in a relationship. Would we ever be in one? Or, would we continue to cling to each other for release and a set of ears? It felt more than that, too.

ME: speaking with each other.

I didn't think I could have worded it any worse. If Bishop noticed, he did not speak on it.

BITCHOP: bet that went well. are you okay?

My stomach fluttered as I read the words.

I didn't feel the need to call Grandma anymore. To talk to someone. Bishop would listen. Sure, he might throw around some depraved words when I spoke of my dad, but he would listen.

ME: yeah. can i come over?

BITCHOP: obviously.

I let out a breathy laugh as I scanned the last word. I could hear it, in his sassy tone. I smiled, running a hand down my face.

I pushed myself from the bed and made my way toward Dad's room.

Privacy. The word rang through my head as I reached for his door handle. He had respected mine. I wondered if he had heard the thumps in the night when Bishop ungracefully rolled through my window.

He hadn't asked.

Dad had noticed the hickeys on my neck, but he never pried about who they came from.

Was I the issue?

I twisted the door handle, preparing to break the trust between us. Forgive me, I thought, pushing into his bedroom.

My lips parted as his bedroom came into view. It had been years since I last stepped foot in his sacred space. I would never dare enter his room without knocking, but even then, I always stayed at the doorframe.

The room was dull, a muted shade of beige. A queen-sized bed sat in the center of the room. Mom had been the decorator of the two, Dad was never into decorations or color themes. His version of their bedroom was simple. There was a nightstand beside his bed, and a television quietly playing the news.

This felt wrong.

I took a step toward the bed. He had made it to a crisp; the corners were tucked in, not a wrinkle daring to show on his blanket. I wouldn't be surprised if he ironed his sheets. He had always been neat like that.

A bible was open atop his bed. He had been highlighting a passage. From today's sermon, most likely. On his nightstand was a devotional, and a rosary draped over its center.

My mother's rosary.

I frowned seeing the necklace. I missed her. Terribly. I only had Dad now, though I had just severed any tie of trust by stepping foot into this room.

"You're stupid," I said to myself. I should not have done this. I was foolish for believing something was off, for coming in here. He was mourning as I was; whatever was going on was none of my business.

I winced, practically running toward the bedroom door. Shame started to tighten its fingers around my heart, digging hard enough to make my throat swell. I invaded his privacy. He was his own man, I should have not stepped foot in here.

When I walked toward the door, my foot dipped into the rug.

I did not fall, but it creaked loudly and gave way. I knitted my eyebrows together and stared down at the rug that was currently concave into a floorboard.

There was a floorboard out of place.

I kicked the rug aside, reaching for it. The floorboard easily slid out. Did he know about this? The rug that covered it did not have a single footprint on it. Did he know to walk around it? I fiddled with the wood, attempting to fix it for him; it was the least I could do after barging into his room so selfishly.

A rusty box caught my eye, tucked beneath the floorboard that had been out of place.

I hesitated, looking back to the rosary. Would Mom open the box hidden in the floor?

I reached for the dirty box. The latch was already open, making it easy to open the box.

A stench seeped from the box whenever it came ajar.

I didn't examine much of its contents. I had to run toward the toilet at the sight of the first Polaroid.

VERSE THIRTY-NINE

I arrived at the large house atop the hill an hour later. I caught a glimpse of my reflection in one of the cars outside Bishop's home; their home. I looked disastrous. My face was red and puffy, my cheeks slick, and my eyes bloodshot.

I held the small box in my trembling hands.

I couldn't look at anything else. I had seen the first Polaroid but vomited up the nerves and panic within a second. It was too much. I couldn't look at this alone. I needed a second pair of eyes, to ensure that I had not gone insane.

I knocked on the door. I sniffed, looking at my feet. What if I was going insane? There was no way Dad could have had those pictures—

The door swung open. Thankfully, it was Bishop who opened the door. I was not going to be murdered by the maniac tonight.

"Hello, church girl—." Bishop stopped. His eyes moved across my face, touching my cheeks. My condition cut him off mid-sentence. He winced, looking at the box I held in my trembling hands.

"Ethel," he breathed. I stopped his words by burying my face into his chest. I wrapped my arms around his waist, holding him as tight as I could. The box was still in my hand; I wanted to throw it far away. Burn it. "What happened?"

Dad would be home soon.

I needed to show Bishop this and run home before he realized it to be missing. Oh God, what would he do to me if he knew it was missing? What was done to that girl in the photo? I couldn't go back there; I wouldn't be able to step into that house without thinking of what I had seen.

I forced my arms away from him. I looked up at him; his hands lingered over my shoulders, caressing the nape of my neck. I wanted to go back, inside his embrace. Disappear into the safety of him. The comfort.

Bishop grabbed my hand, pulling me inside the home.

The lights were dim, and it was eerily silent throughout the home. From the looks of it, it did not appear that anyone else was home. If they were, they had no intention of making themselves known. I could only hear my shuddered breathing and his combat boots hitting against the heavy floor.

Bishop pulled me onto the couch, beside him. A sleek black coffee table sat in front of us. I place the box down on the table, wrapping my arms around my waist. I wanted to be held; anytime something bad happened, I always wanted to be held. I blame it on the lack of embrace growing up.

"I went into my dad's room," I began. My voice was a croak. I looked away; I couldn't even look at the sinful box. "I found that."

Bishop reached for the box. I stared at the carpet, zoning out on a little hair. I flinched when the latch creaked open.

The first Polaroid flashed into my mind. The Polaroid Bishop would be seeing as soon as he finished opening it.

It was a girl. She was young; she looked my age, maybe younger. She had been tied to a chair by black bindings. Her neck was slumped over, mouth hung ajar. She was dead. Beneath the blood, I bet she had been pale, bruised, and beaten.

I shuddered, closing my eyes.

A dark blindfold was covering her eyes in the photo. I did not need to see her eyes to know the light was gone. She had enough blood running from her throat, and down her bare torso to prove that.

Her ankles had been tied to the legs of the chair in a way to spread and display what was between her legs. Between her thighs, blood was coating the sight of what once was there. The blood from her neck did not reach her legs, though.

Bile rose up my throat.

There were two wounds. One on her throat; one between her legs.

I wrapped my arms tighter around my stomach and shuddered. I kept my gaze on the floor as he opened the box. He pulled out the first po-laroid, setting it on the table. I did not want to see how they progressed. I may be a coward for it, but one was enough. Whatever was in that box was beyond God.

He didn't utter a word. Once. It was silent. Too silent.

I listened to how many Polaroids he placed on the table. My insides flinched with every slap of the photo on the table. He made it four polaroids in before he muttered a "Jesus."

What could he have possibly seen that was worse than the first?

"Ethel," Bishop began. Twenty-three. I counted twenty-three photos being placed on the table. Were they all as terrible as the first? Why did Dad have such a horrific image beneath his floor? There has to be an explanation. He was my dad. "How many of these did you see?"

His tone reminded me of a father I once heard in the movie theatre, telling his children to turn their heads when a sex scene came on the screen.

"Just the first." I squeezed myself harder. "There has to be a reason he has them."

I sounded so fucking stupid. It sounded stupid in my head, and it sounded just as horrible when it came out of my mouth. I knew I shouldn't be defending him. But, he was my rock for all these years. No matter what. Even if he called me nasty words, or lied to me daily, he would be my rock. He had to be; he was all I had.

"Ethel, look at this."

I shook my head, clamping my eyes shut. "No. I can't look at them."

"It's not the polaroids. I'm not going to show you those."

I trusted him to not traumatize me for an eternity, by showing me the photos. I turned my head to face him. From the corner of my eye, I counted twenty-three polaroids. He had placed the photos face down, hiding the monstrosities from me.

The sight of how many there were made my stomach turn.

The IDs in Bishop's hand nearly made me vomit, again.

"All of these people were in the Polaroids," Bishop began, flipping through the IDs. I stared at the smiling faces on the corners of the IDs. They were all young. My age. I recognized no one. Our town was small, I knew almost everyone here. None of these individuals seemed to be from our town. Some were Arkansas IDs, others were California. It was a mix of states. Towns. Ages.

The last ID was a woman I recognized.

She was an outlier. The eldest of the batch. She was around the age of seventy-three; a widow. I knew this because she once sat in the congregation with me. Janyce Williams. She had brought Dad cookies recently. She brought him cookies after nearly every service.

I shook my head, a silent sob coming from my lips. All I could do was say no, over and over, and shake my head.

Was this where he had been?

Doing something that only God had witnessed?

I shook my head again, and again. I was trembling. I didn't feel Bishop shift, pulling me into his chest. But, at some point, he had. I continued to repeat the lie over and over. "No." He was a good man. He had been a good man. He couldn't have done that to the girl in the first Polaroid. Could he have?

I pulled my gaze to Bishop. My eyes were swollen with tears. His face looked so soft; I never thought I would see Bishop without a smirk, or a tensed jaw. He looked as vulnerable as I felt. "No. There is no way he did that to that girl. Those girls. He's a good man. He wouldn't. He can't."

As much as I wanted to believe it, it sounded like one fat lie coming from my mouth.

The lunch we had earlier came to mind, but I pushed it away. It was only opening my eyes more to what was happening. I couldn't see him like this; it was as if my brain wasn't allowing me. He was the man who once walked fifteen flights of stairs with me because of my fear of elevators. The man who would pick me up when I didn't want to step in the rain.

Bishop reached his hand for mine. I flinched but wrapped my fingers around his own. I held onto him, afraid to let go. "Shit," he cursed, tossing the IDs lazily onto the table. "Ethel, either he really likes to collect people's IDs, or—"

"Don't say it," I snapped, looking at his lap. We both knew what he was going to say. Or he likes to hurt them.

A creak echoed through the quiet home. I jerked my head toward the stairs. Baylen stood stoic at the bottom of the stairs, with an empty bottle of wine in his hands. He looked to Bishop first, and then to me.

He scrunched his nose at the sight of me. Like he could smell something from me, all the way from across the room.

Baylen grunted, walking into the kitchen like nothing was happening in the living room.

Once he was out of sight, and earshot, Bishop spoke in a hushed tone. "Baylen has a collection just like this. For his—." Victims. Toys. Playthings. I shot him a glance, cutting him off before one of the words could come out.

"What does Baylen have?" Baylen asked. His figure was on the bottom step, holding two more bottles of red wine. He was light on his feet. I hadn't even heard him leave the kitchen.

"Uh," Bishop started. He looked to me, the mess in front of us, and then to Baylen. Bishop cringed, looking in my direction. Baylen began to approach the table, curious as to what we had sorted out in front of us.

"Sorry," Bishop muttered, running his thumb over my knuckles.

Baylen reached for one of the polaroids. Unlike me, he smiled when he caught a glimpse of whatever horrific image had been captured. What the fuck was wrong with him? "Who do these vile little things belong to?"

Baylen smiled harder, looking to the next.

Bishop and I remained silent. Baylen looked at the tears trailing down my face, staining my skin. Somehow, with a single tear, Baylen had gathered the entire story in his head; him being this observant may be more terrifying than Dad.

"The preacher." Baylen's dimples deepened. He bit his lip. "Now that is scandalous, isn't it?"

I let out another quiet sob. My face twitched and I looked away from him. Bishop didn't deserve to be around someone like Baylen; he was hell in itself. No one, not even the most sinful man to walk the earth, deserved to endure that type of torture.

I reached for the empty box in the center of the table.

I threw it as hard as I could, toward his face.

He looked down toward his chest as the rusty box bounced from his chest and onto the floor. He didn't flinch, despite how hard I threw it. He looked down at it, as though he couldn't quite figure out if he hallucinated it or not.

When he looked back up, it was Bishop he looked at. "I didn't like your bitch very much. Now I really don't like it."

"Baylen," Bishop cautioned. "Off limits."

Baylen looked at me. "You're going to regret that." The pure lack of nothingness in his eyes caused my stomach to twist. He almost terrified me as much as Dad currently did. Could Dad be the same as him? Something evil?

He left Bishop and me without another word.

I gulped, preparing to deal with the inevitable. My dad.

VERSE FORTY

After a long pass of silence, I spoke up.

Bishop held me, with my back to his chest, caressing the underpart of my jaw. My eyes had been glued to the locked box. With every second that passed, it became more real. Dad hurt them. Dad did something to them. Fuck, even if he didn't do that to them, he had some kind of involvement.

"I need to go back," I croaked, still looking at the box. At some point, Bishop had placed the contents back inside of the box. There were more objects than just polaroids and IDs. There were bracelets. Necklaces. Rings. Pins. Even a few strands of red hair.

I hadn't even seen him pack the box up. I was in a new land, hidden deep in my mind, imagining what had conspired with Dad and the woman in the photo. Within another shadow in my head, I thought of Janyce Williams, and the cookies she would always bake for us; what had happened to her?

There had to be some explanation. Even if it was twisted, vile, and sinful. There had to be a reason Dad would do such a thing.

Bishop laughed, twisting his body to face mine. "Fuck. No."

I looked down at our hands. Our fingers were intertwined; he hadn't let go of me since I grabbed onto him.

"I need to put it back. Before he notices it is gone," I explained.

"Ethel, you are not going back there." Bishop's usual flirty, charming tone was gone. He usually sounded as if he didn't have a care in the world. But, right now, his sounded so authoritative; like, if I dared say something else, I would be tied to this couch until I agreed with him.

I dug my nails into the top of his palm. "I've lived with him for my entire life. I want to hear his explanation. From him." *Sluts will be sluts.* I winced, remembering the harsh words he had uttered at lunch. I left my phone at the house. I wondered if Grandma ever called back. Did she know something was off with Dad? She had to have known. That would explain their fights.

"I adore you, church girl. But, you are being very, very, naive right now. Whatever the case with him and the photos, he had some involvement. You aren't going back." *I adore you.* My tear-stained cheeks heated. This was terrible timing for Bishop to make me flustered, given the circumstances.

"I have to put it back," I repeated.

"No."

"Yes."

"No."

"Yes."

"No."

I looked up at him and ground my teeth together. It may be easier to argue with a wall.

"Okay," I hesitated. My gaze dipped down to a tattoo creeping from under his shirt. It was still dark and the house was silent despite Baylen being here. The moonlight illuminated the side of his face. Fuck, he was beautiful. Not just his body, but what radiated around him as well; I could feel it coming from him, like a force. He felt so raw.

"Will you come with me, then?" I asked once I was able to look back at his face. It was a compromise. I was going back; Bishop was not going to let me go back. Maybe we were both walls in this argument.

Bishop looked to the ceiling, rolling his eyes as he blinked. "Okay." He leaned forward, placing a soft kiss on my cheek. I felt his tongue stripe across where my tears had stained the spot on my skin. I shuddered. "Let me go get my phone."

I nodded, watching him make his way up the stairs.

It was just me, and that God-fearing box. Whatever sins were in that box, had a special place in hell. My jaw started to tremble. All of those people, twenty-three of them, were gone. And, here I was, trying to defend him. Maybe I was as terrible as him; whatever it was that he did to them.

"You okay?"

I jumped, looking up at Bishop.

"Yes." I couldn't bring myself to touch the damned box. I imagined Dad, placing the photos neatly in the box. Did he put them in there after he did it? After someone else did it? Was he a spectator?

I swore Bishop could read my mind at some points. He reached for the box, tucking it between his hand and hip. With his other hand, he intertwined his fingers with mine. "This is stupid," Bishop blurted. "Are you sure you want to go back?"

I nodded. Reluctantly, he pulled us both out of the house and toward my own.

VERSE FORTY-ONE

I t took us twenty minutes before we were back inside my home. Even if we were in a rush, I would not push Bishop to drive. I knew it made him uncomfortable.

My stomach sank when we arrived at the front door. Home. I was terrified to step inside of my own home. Even if Dad wasn't here, what if something had happened here? What if I was upstairs, asleep, while Dad brought someone here?

I swallowed a sob. Was he taking those photos, when he was "supposedly" with Father Rowen?

"I can put it inside if you don't want to go in. Just tell me where the room is."

I shook my head, twisting the handle open. "No. Just stay with me."

"I will," Bishop promised.

I kept my fingers locked with his as we walked up the stairs. I looked down at the steps we had once made out on. It was odd, only a little bit ago, we were making out on the stairs, drunk from each other's bodies. But, now, we were holding something so dark.

My stomach twisted and turned with every step we took. This felt wrong. So, so wrong. Everything in this house felt wrong. Every picture frame we passed was of Dad smiling beside my young figure. Mom smiled too, oblivious to the man he would become.

I couldn't get the image of the girl out of my head. Splayed. Bloody. Limp. Abused. Every image of my father we passed, I only saw her; I only saw Janyce's smiling photo in her ID, unaware of what was going to come.

I stopped in front of his door. It was still ajar. I left the door wide open, with the rug rolled back, and the floorboard out of place. If he would have come home, only God would have known how it could have ended. I was too shocked to think; I had followed my gut, running to Bishop.

My hands trembled as I placed the box on the floorboard. I recalled the exact position it had been in, the slight tilt of the rug, and the latch being open. Dad always memorized things; the number of steps it took to get to church, the bites it took to eat his steak. What if he realized I had seen the box?

Bishop stood in the doorway, watching every movement I made. His eyes slid from my hands, and then to my side. His gaze burnt my skin.

"How long do you think this has been here?" I asked as I placed the floorboard back over the gap. I rolled the rug over the floorboard, adjusting it to the tilt it was before. I was partially talking to myself, but Bishop responded, nonetheless.

"One of the polaroids was dated."

I swallowed, looking up at him. I was afraid to ask when. How long had this been occurring? How oblivious had I been? I needed to know, for my sanity. "When?"

"Three years ago."

I looked back to the ground, rubbing my hands down my thighs. How did I not realize something was off? How stupid could I have been? He seemed so normal. We had our fights, but nothing ever pointed to this. Violence. Evil.

Bishop leaned down, snaking his arm around my waist to help me from the floor. I had locked up; every muscle in my body went stiff. I couldn't move. Three years ago. What was I doing three years ago? Was that when we were traveling to California? Was the ID from California his victim? Had I eaten across from him after, oblivious to what coated his soul?

I shook my head, letting out a soft whimper as he pulled me to my feet. "There is no way. There has to be a misunderstanding." Denial was so much easier than acceptance.

"Come here." Bishop pulled me into him, wrapping his fingers around the back of my head. I wrapped my arms around him, tight, holding onto his as if he were going to disappear. I dug my nails into his back, losing myself in his feel. His raw energy.

I thought I might fall in love with him if he didn't let go.

"You're going to stay with me, okay?" Bishop ran his fingers down my strands. My stiff, trembling body slowly relaxed into him. The smell of him. He didn't smell of alcohol anymore; it was just cigarettes. I'd grown to love the smell.

"Okay." Even if part of me was still in denial, the thought of sleeping here alone made something crawl beneath my skin. If Bishop was here, maybe. But, alone? I didn't trust him; especially after lunch today. Something was wrong with Dad.

My fingers dipped a little lower down his back. I grazed something beneath his shirt. I traced the outline of the object with my fingertip. It was a handle. Even through a shirt, I could feel the cold metal outline.

I jerked my head backward, looking toward Bishop. "Is that—?" I gaped.

He nodded.

A gun.

Fuck.

"Bishop," I started.

"I'm not going to shoot him unless you tell me to," Bishop said. There was no emotion behind the words. He said it as if he were talking about the weather. Being around Baylen and Cain must have desensitized him.

My heart picked up. The idea of a gun being involved made this all too real. Nerves swam through my stomach. "Shit, you brought a gun." I ran a hand through my hair. The reality was crumbling down on me like raining bricks. Dad could be dangerous. Dad was dangerous. But, he could be, toward me.

Shit. Shit. Shit.

The front door slammed shut before I was able to panic about the gun, any further.

VERSE FORTY-TWO

I pushed Bishop quickly into my bedroom, quietly shutting my door behind me. I shut off my light and double-checked to make sure the door was locked. I mentally retraced my footsteps, reminding myself that I did indeed shut Dad's door.

Bishop stood flush in front of me. His head was slightly tilted to point toward the door, listening for Dad to come upstairs. His eyes were on me as I did the same.

Heavy footsteps hit the bottom of the stairs.

My stomach dropped, and my heart aligned with every step he took. After the third step, I could no longer hear his footsteps; my heartbeat was the only noise echoing in my head.

"Do we just bring it to the police?" I asked, beneath my breath.

Bishop laughed.

The police? This town's system was a joke. I wondered many nights if the police force had once been efficient in our town. They were corrupted by Cain, fast. Even with him gone, they still were. Baylen had been running around this town like a madman on crack, and two years was all he had been sentenced to.

They feared Cain.

Our fucking police feared a single man.

"You won't get any answers. They will slap him on the wrist for being a bad preacher." He said "bad preacher" as if he were referring to a dog. "Or, they will lock him up but—"

Dad's footsteps reached the top of the stairs. We both looked toward the door, listening to his route as he walked. He began to walk toward my room. His bedroom was on the opposite side of the hall. He wasn't going to his room, he was coming to mine.

Shit.

"I will do whatever you say. You want me to kill him, I will kill him. You want to do nothing, I will hold it above you, but do nothing." Bishop's voice was quiet, hidden beneath the heavy footsteps approaching.

A chill ran down my spine. What if Dad wasn't just a bystander? What if he was doing that? I wanted to hear it from him; what he did to them.

A knock came from the wood. I flinched. Bishop narrowed his eyes toward the door. Would he really kill for me? I did not want him to, ever.

I jerked my eyes back to Bishop. He held a finger to his lips, telling me to be quiet. My heart was rattling hard against my ribcage. I hadn't been this terrified in years. And, it certainly wasn't because of Dad. My God was a cruel, cruel God.

"Sweetheart, are you awake?"

I didn't look away from Bishop, and him the same. I felt like I should be more afraid of him. He had a gun in his pants as if it were an accessory, and he just offered to murder for me, like it was some sort of gift. I shouldn't be thinking of how I felt like I was falling in love with him.

This was the gun-wielding, bloody-handed Bishop I had been so afraid of. But, still, I feel like I could even fall in love with this side of him.

"Sweetheart." I looked away from Bishop when the handle started to move. A key was being inserted into the old knob. Was he going to come in here and check on me? Fuck, this can't be happening. My heart was to the ground at this point, convulsing with fear.

I gestured for Bishop to go into the closet. In response, he mouthed a "fuck you, fuck no." I rolled my eyes and pushed him quietly into the closet. Surprisingly, he allowed me to.

He had a gun. Shit. My throat tightened.

If he wanted to kill Dad, he could.

I slid into the bed, pulling the comforter above me. My back was to the door and closet. Luckily, if Dad came in, he would not be able to see me attempting to "sleep". I pulled the comforter high above my mouth. It was helping to conceal the trembling.

Every dust particle and breath in the air went still. The door slowly creaked open. I kept my eyes clamped tightly shut, reminding myself that Bishop was right behind me. With a gun. Shit.

I wanted to defend Dad, badly. But, the way I reacted told me everything I needed to know. My intuition had always been right. And, right now, my intuition was in absolute shambles.

The bed dipped beside me as Dad sat down.

I couldn't feel where Dad looked; however, I could feel every inch of skin that Bishop's eyes caressed, even if it was through closet slits. He was there. If something, anything, were to go wrong, Bishop was there.

"I'm sorry sweetheart. I didn't mean it." Slut. That's right. Our dinner. That was a fucking joke compared to what I had just found. I'd rather him call me a slut every second of my life, than what I found beneath the floorboards be true.

His hands reached for the back of my head, gently caressing my strands. My face twitched when his tips touched me. It was all I could do to prevent from flinching out of my skin. Thankfully, due to the angle, he was unable to see.

His fingers trailed away from my head, down my side, gently caressing my skin. "You know I get in those moods. I'm sorry." My lip trembled against the pillow, but I stayed still. It was as it always had been. Two different men took up my father's body. A terrible, heinous man, in a gentle set of skin.

If Dad noticed the way my muscles were tensing beneath him, he did not say anything. My body was flexing, trying to push him off of me. I was asleep to him. Had he come in here when I slept before? After he committed his sins? I wanted to sob at the thought.

I held my breath as his hand moved from my waist. He stood from the bed, but his hand stayed planted on my side. His touch slipped away from my waist and to my hip. Then to my outer thigh.

Even through the comforter, it felt as if poison was touching me.

"I'm sorry, sweetheart," he repeated, pulling his hand away.

I could feel the intensity radiating from the closet door. It was a force. Had he seen Dad's lingering hands? God, if you are listening, please do not allow Bishop to step out of that closet and shoot Dad. No matter what he had done, death was immoral. Even if he had caused so much. It wasn't justice.

The moment Dad shut and locked the door, Bishop stumbled from the closet. I moved my head around to face him; I let out the breath I had been holding.

Bishop smiled. Smiled, ear to ear. He did not look happy, rather insane. "Ethel," Bishop warned. "I don't want to kill people. But, right now, I really want to rip his head off."

I sat on the edge of the bed, throwing the comforter to the floor. "No. No. Not death. No—." I was a rambling mess. I leaned over, holding my temples. What the fuck was I supposed to do? The police? Baylen murdered people; recorded it, and everything. He was given a slap on the ass as he walked out of that station.

Something was wrong with this town.

Cursed.

Bishop ran a hand through his hair, sitting on the bed beside me. "What do you want me to do, Ethel?"

I hesitated, looking up at him. He reached for my fingers, intertwining his digits with mine. My stomach fluttered at the feeling. We fit together. Not just in our hands, but in most aspects. And, the parts we didn't, he made fit.

"You were right. I don't want to be here," I croaked.

"Wasn't up for discussion, but okay."

I rolled my eyes. "I want to talk to him first. About it. And, if he doesn't explain what happened," I hesitated, unable to let the words register.

The police would do nothing, I reminded myself. Absolutely. Nothing.

"I want to hear him admit it. And, if he doesn't admit it to me, then—" I stopped again. This time, Bishop was able to finish it for me.

"You talk to him. Then, we make him talk, if worse comes to worse."

I shuddered. Make him talk. "He's my dad. I don't want to hurt him."

"Like those girls in the Polaroids?"

Hypocrite. I felt like a hypocrite. Dad could have killed twenty-three girls, yet the idea of Bishop ending it with one seemed completely immoral.

Something hit inside of my stomach. Hard. Like those girls in the Polaroids. His words repeated in my head, over and over. I wanted to vomit, again, remembering the splayed girl. Dad wouldn't speak to me about it. If I did confront him. Maybe, but doubtfully. Dad had always been stubborn, especially when it came to what he did out of my view.

Bishop could make him less stubborn.

I thought of Janyce and the bloody girl. "Okay. But you can't kill him. Promise me."

God forgive me. What have I gotten myself into? Having to ensure murder was not on the table.

"I promise."

I nodded, looking back at our hands. "Tomorrow, I will bring him to lunch. I will ask him about it. Confront him. If that doesn't work—"

"I will be sitting behind you," Bishop finished. I wanted to throw up. What if he didn't admit it to me? What if he did? I needed to know if other people were involved, or if he was the one who had done that to them.

I frowned, looking at my thighs. What if Bishop wasn't able to make him talk? I knew for a fact that one boy could make a wall weep. Baylen.

For the rest of the night, we stayed tucked in bed. We discussed other topics to avoid the inevitable. I couldn't stop thinking of him. Dad. I sobbed through the night, so quiet Bishop was unable to hear it. He held me through the entire night, nonetheless.

VERSE
FORTY-THREE

"I really do apologize for yesterday. I get into those moods, you know."

I stared down at my untouched Caesar salad. I couldn't eat. I couldn't look at him. All I saw was the young girl from the Polaroid. The ID of Janyce.

A wave of nausea passed. I remembered the countless other girls, to whom he only knew what happened.

I hummed in response, continuing to fiddle with my lettuce. How was I going to bring this up? This wasn't exactly an over-lunch topic to be discussing.

My phone buzzed.

I looked down, seeing Bishop's name illuminating my phone.

BITCHOP: r u okay?

ME: yeah. are you here?

BITCHOP: me and coen are sitting in the booth behind you.

Coen. Bishop had briefly explained what would happen if Dad refused to talk to me. Coen's club offered many, many empty rooms, which Bishop explained Dad would be brought to. After that, he would simply "rough him up" a little.

God, I prayed that Dad talked to me. Some part of good had to be in him, guilty of what he had done.

"You texting someone?" Dad asked, cutting into his steak. I looked down at his hands. It was like looking at Baylen's hands, wondering what they had done in the past. How much blood had been on them?

"Yeah," I replied, my voice dry. I rubbed at my temple; it hadn't stopped throbbing since I discovered the out-of-place floorboard. Grandma had responded, asking me to call her, but I couldn't bring myself to do it. I felt like I would break down.

ME: how do i even start with this?

BITCHOP: doesn't matter. nothing he can do in a crowded restaurant. plus, i'd stab him.

The pounding in my head intensified. I ran a hand down my face. How could he say that so casually?

I locked my phone and placed it beside my thigh. I reminded myself that Bishop and Coen were behind me. If anything were to happen, it would not be here. It was rush hour; he couldn't do anything.

I was scared Dad was going to hurt me.

"Where have you been going the past few nights?" I asked.

Dad's eyes darkened. He narrowed his gaze before responding. "I told you, I've been with Father Rowan." His voice was snappy and tight. He sipped his beer to loosen the tone.

I sucked in a breath. I needed to make him talk to me. If I didn't Bishop would find a way for him to talk; for my sake. Last night, Bishop had told me that if he were given the choice, he would have already killed Dad. Castrated him. Guilty, or not.

"Father Rowans is dead." Once it was out of my mouth, a weight lifted from my shoulders. There was no going back now. "He has been for quite a while now."

Dad's head snapped up toward me. Surprise washed over his darkened face. He sucked in a breath, and just like that, his soft side returned. Two different men were fighting in his body. I didn't think this one would stay for much longer.

He bit into his steak, not looking away from me. "Okay. I've been seeing a woman. I just didn't think I needed to tell you everything."

I knew he was going to use a woman as an excuse. I fucking knew it. And, it was an absolute lie; he told me everything about his dating life. Every date he went on. Every woman.

Even if in some universe, it was a woman, it did not explain the Polaroids. Nothing would justify what was occurring in that first photo. Nothing would justify the horrendous sights I refused to look at.

"You are irritating me with this, Ethel. Drop it. I don't know what happened to you." Dad chewed into his steak, drinking his beer. His knuckles were white around the glass. "I mean, what happened to privacy? You used to be so good. Is it that boy?"

'That boy' shifted in the booth behind me. I could feel him now, his back separated by the cushion behind me. Dad wouldn't recognize Coen; he rarely left his club. Was Coen watching Dad, for Bishop?

"Speaking of, do you not realize how terrible you are to be with him? Do you not remember—?"

"Dad." I cut him off. We were not turning this conversation around on me. I thought of what Bishop would do in this situation. He would be doing better than I currently was, that was for sure. He wouldn't be beating around the bush like some fucking coward.

He wouldn't bite his tongue.

I cleared my throat, taking a sip of water. My throat was tightening; I didn't think I could get the words out. "Did you hurt those girls in the Polaroids?"

VERSE FORTY-FOUR

It felt as though everything in the restaurant went silent.

Beneath his gaze, it was just Dad and me. Though, this wasn't Dad in front of me. I didn't know who the man sitting across from me was.

Chatter hummed through the restaurant, oblivious to the question I had just asked.

He was behind me, I reminded myself. Bishop was there. Coen was there. This place was crowded; I was safe.

Dad started to chew. I hadn't realized he had stopped. He looked down at his steak, cutting into the meat. He smiled like the question didn't even leave my mouth.

"You know, Gianno's is going to go out of business soon. Because of this place. You see how busy it is at eleven in the morning?" Dad gestured around the restaurant with his knife, toward the people sitting around us. He looked back at me, taking a sharp bite into his strip of steak.

Were we supposed to pretend I hadn't asked the question?

I intertwined my hands in my lap, looking down at my phone.

Dad's reaction was worse than his touchy hands last night. He was avoiding the question. He didn't deny it.

Any innocent man would deny it.

Worst of all, he was smiling.

Oh, God, he hurt them. It took every cell in my brain to accept it. He didn't just have something to do with it, he had hurt them too. He would have denied it. Instead, he started talking about this stupid restaurant.

I was going to throw up.

"Dad—" I started, but he cut me off.

"Is your salad not good?" He pointed toward the bowl of lettuce in front of me. "You always liked the salad at Gianno's more. You've always had a thing for salad, even when you were young."

He was making this so, so much worse. He reminded me of how well he knew me. Dad knew almost everything about me. But, I knew nothing of him.

This was going to go nowhere.

Dad was a wall. Even in arguments, there was never a way to get him to bend. In some alternate world, where the police were to interrogate him, he would just sit there. Expressionless. If he did not want to talk, he would not talk. And, right now, he did not want to talk.

"Dad." He tried to interrupt me again, but I kept speaking. "Janyce was one of those IDs. Did you hurt Janyce?"

Dad's jaw became so tight, I believed his teeth were going to shatter. He dipped his chin down and finished the last of his beer. "Not to mention the wine at Gianno's. Maybe on your twenty-first, we can buy a bottle there. It's divine."

I felt Bishop shift behind me. I also shifted in the seat, wrapping my arms around my stomach.

If Dad hurt those people and was not serving in some way by that time, I had no one to blame but myself.

I swallowed the lump in my throat. He needed to talk. Now. Or, they were going to make him. And, I wasn't going to stop him. He hurt them. Please just talk, Dad.

"You know." Slice. Slice. Slice. I watched him cut into his steak. I wasn't able to look at the blood seeping from the meat; I'd never be able to see blood again, after seeing how broken the girl's middle was. "I wish you could have stayed young forever. Back when you respected me. When it was all you cared about."

Slice. Slice. Slice.

He cut so hard into the steak it scraped against his place.

Dad smiled at me, eating his last strip of steak. His last bite of food.

I should have let Bishop decide what to do. This was once his job. When Cain needed someone to be "taken care of", it was Bishop or Baylen he sent. Most of the time, Baylen, but when he was incarcerated, it had been Bishop.

Bishop would know what to do, without killing him. He would know how to get an answer out of him. A confession. It would be another notch on his bedpost.

"Please, Dad. Talk to me," I said.

Dad stared at me as he wiped his mouth clean with the corner of his napkin. His lips were in a tight smile, one that reached his eyes.

I looked away and toward my phone.

ME: it's not going to work.

BITCHOP: clearly.

BITCHOP: what do you want me to do?

What did I want him to do?

Letting Dad walk away, without uttering what had happened, was not justice. Something had happened to them. To Janyce. To the girl in the chair. No one would ever know what had happened to them. Only Dad.

They deserved more than that.

As for the smiling man in front of me? I didn't feel remorse for whatever was about to happen to him. He wasn't my dad anymore.

ME: just don't let him die.

Bishop stayed in his booth until Dad had paid. We walked out of the restaurant, directly beside their booth. I locked eyes with Coen first, then with Bishop across from him. Dad was oblivious to the boys.

I gulped.

Once we made it outside, everything happened in a blur.

VERSE FORTY-FIVE

Just like that, Dad was tied to a chair, with blood running down his forehead.

I stood far across the room. My back was glued to the soundproof wall, and my eyes locked with Dad. His eyes were beginning to twitch open. He had been unconscious through the entire drive to Coen's club.

The second we stepped out of the restaurant, Bishop and Coen followed close behind us. They followed us to the alley street before knocking him unconscious with the handle of Bishop's gun. Throughout the series of events, Coen appeared to be bored.

Solomon had been waiting in a car nearby, to transport us to the club.

The rest was a blur. I was too stunned to even think.

"I can't do blood," Solomon warned. He stood beside me, though he hadn't said a word to me. "If there is blood, I'm out."

I looked up at Solomon. His light brown skin had turned a shade of green. His natural curls were falling into his face, covering his eyes. He did indeed look as though he was on the verge of vomiting.

My gaze moved back to Dad as Coen finished tying him up. We were in one of the rooms on the second floor of his club. I didn't even remember walking up the stairs to get here. It was like I passed out. The place was illuminated by a low, red light. Besides that, I remember nothing.

The room looked as though it was made for torture. There were ropes, whips, clamps, and other items I couldn't even begin to fathom their use.

Coen kneeled, tying the last knot.

"Jesus, Coen," Bishop muttered under his breath. Bishop stood close beside me, but closer to Dad. Dad looked as if a pig would be tied up. Ropes restrained useless areas of his body. The bindings were intricately tied around his body, pinning him to the chair.

I wrapped my arms around my stomach, looking up at Coen. He was staring down at Dad, and the way he had tied him up. "What?" Coen began. "Baylen usually does this stuff. This is the only way I know how to tie someone up. Sorry."

He emphasized the last word, cocking his head as he muttered it.

Beside me, Solomon grabbed the bridge of his nose.

"I don't want Baylen to come. Unless it is the last scenario." Bishop and Coen jerked their head backward to face me. Did they forget I was in the room?

"Yeah," Coen drew out. He ran his fingers through his toffee-colored hair. "I'd rather not spend the evening cleaning up after Baylen."

Cleaning up. Reality twisted my stomach. They were going to hurt Dad. Why wasn't I stopping them? What the fuck was wrong with me?

Our focus shifted to Dad as he stirred awake. He let out a soft groan before jerking his head upward. A line of blood dripped from his temple to his cheek; Bishop had instantly knocked him out cold, with a single hit.

Dad looked around for a moment. Once he took in his surroundings, his eyes met mine.

"Sweetheart," Dad hummed. He smiled. "What is going on?" He tugged at his ropes, but Coen's rigger skills ensured that the bindings tightened around his body. Every movement made the ropes grow tight.

I looked up at Bishop. He looked down at me. "Ethel." Bishop uttered my name slowly as if he were afraid I was going to break at any second. "You should wait outside. If you want."

Solomon spoke before I could.

"You know, I'd love to wait outside."

Coen shot him a glance. Solomon sighed, slumping closer to me against the wall. He crossed his arms over his tense chest.

I shook my head. If Dad was going to be "roughed up", I was going to endure it, just as he was. "No," I croaked. Please just talk, I wanted to tell Dad. Maybe if he was tied up, surrounded by three other men, and the damning evidence in front of him, he would speak.

When Dad and I were eating, Bishop had at some point gone back to the house and retrieved the God-forsaken box. It was now sitting at Dad's feet, a few inches away from Coen's.

Dad looked down at the box. His face hardened the moment his eyes hit the rusty container. He looked to Bishop's first; I couldn't read the expression either of them wore. Next, he looked to Coen, who was distractedly looking around his sexual room. Solomon tensed when Dad met his figure.

Lastly, he looked at me. "Ethel, this is ridiculous. Let's just go home. Talk about this. Alone."

I shook my head. "You did something, Dad. I don't want to be alone with you."

Dad didn't respond. He dipped his chin downward, looking up at me through his eyelashes. It reminded me of how Bishop looked at me. Though, when Bishop did it, I wasn't trembling out of my skin.

Coen crouched down at Dad's feet, unlocking the box. Bishop moved to his side, jutting a gun into Dad's ribcage. Dad looked away from me to focus on what Coen was doing. He pulled out a few Polaroids. His tan face tightened the further he found himself within the stack of polaroids.

Dad flinched in his seat. His foot bucked, attempting to kick Coen's hands, but the ropes only tightened.

"Did you do this, Mr. Fields?" Coen asked, too casually. He slowly placed the polaroids back into the box. He reached for the IDs next. Coen nodded his head, muttering names beneath his breath.

Dad remained silent. As silent as he had been in the restaurant.

"Please answer, Dad." My voice was trembling. I meant to sound threatening, but I sounded terrified. I was terrified. "They're going to hurt you if you don't."

Bishop kept his gun lodged into Dad's ribcage. I forgot it was there. He pushed it every so often, to remind Dad it was still there. It reminded me of how serious our circumstances were; there was a gun.

"You'd let them hurt me?" Dad asked. He wouldn't look away from me.

My jaw trembled as I thought of Janyce. He deserved to be castrated if he did what I think he did to her. Father, or not, Dad deserved this. Bishop was right. "Yes."

Dad blinked. He stared up at me, his lips perking up into a smile. Coen tensed at the sight of him smiling. Solomon and I both stood still, breathing heavily against the wall. Even if he was restrained, it appeared as if he were about to launch himself from the chair and strangle me.

Bishop decided he had been staring for too long. He brought the gun down on the other side of his temple. Hard.

I flinched looking at my feet. Dad's head slumped downward, though he was still conscious. He smiled harder. Dad looked possessed.

"What the fuck," Solomon cursed, beneath his breath.

"Do you regret it?" I asked. I felt like I was going to throw up. Why was he smiling? "Whatever you did to them?"

Silence.

Bishop and Coen took turns hitting his head with the handle of the gun. It wasn't hard enough to cause serious damage, but it would be hard enough to get someone to talk. Someone sane. But, Dad said nothing. He merely smiled and stayed silent.

"Yeah, maybe we need to call Baylen," Coen admitted after the fifth hit. He tossed his hair backward, running his fingers through his hair. I winced seeing blood on his fingers. Dad's blood.

"Oh, God. I can't stomach Baylen," Solomon gaped.

Bishop and Coen both ignored Solomon's comments. Bishop looked at me, awaiting my permission.

I reminded myself of Janyce. The peppy woman who once brought us cookies was now a memory that only Dad knew of. The girl tied in the chair. The various other victims in the IDs. Only Dad knew what happened to them.

I nodded to Bishop.

"I'll call him," Coen informed, after looking between our quiet exchange.

He deserved this. Whatever happened, every drop of blood on his forehead was deserved.

VERSE FORTY-SIX

Bishop stood in front of me. His fingers were intertwined in my hair, pulling my face into his chest. I'd stepped into the hallway to get air, for a moment, and Bishop followed behind.

He hadn't spoken in the past ten minutes. He simply held me as we awaited Baylen's arrival.

"Are you okay?" Bishop asked. He gently caressed my hair with his tips.

"Peachy," I croaked, into his shirt. He felt so warm. So safe. I was melting into the feel of him. How did I feel this safe with the man who caused so much blood to run over Dad's face?

"We can stop at any point. Just say the word."

I shook my head, holding onto him harder. We would never know what happened to them. To Miss Janyce.

"Thank you, Bishop," I said, after a long stretch of silence.

Bishop laughed. "You should not be thanking me for holding your father at gunpoint. That isn't normal." His fingers slipped down to stroke my spine. I shuddered.

"No," I started, my voice lost within the cotton of his shirt. "For being so good. To me."

Bishop tensed. I didn't think he knew how to respond. It didn't matter. He didn't need to. I needed to get the words out, and away from my chest. Bishop wasn't the cruel man I'd envisioned him to be. How had I been so quick to judge? Bishop was a good, good man. To me, at least.

Dad was a bad man.

I pulled my head from his chest. We kept in each other's embrace. He leaned down, planting a soft kiss on my lips. So gentle. My eyes and stomach fluttered to the touch, but my gut twisted as I remembered what was about to happen down the hall.

He wasn't going to die, I reminded myself.

"Look how cute this is," a voice teased from behind me. He bumped hard into my shoulder as he walked past us, uninterested in our affairs.

Bishop and I both pulled away from each other, looking toward Baylen.

I didn't get a glimpse of his face, only the mess of black and red strands.

"Asshole," I seethed, once he slipped inside of the room. There were at least twenty rooms across this hall. How did he know which one Dad was inside?

"You want it to stop," Bishop repeated. "Tell me."

I nodded, and we made our way toward the damned room again.

When we entered, Baylen seemed to be the center of attention. Even Dad was looking at him. He had his fingers intertwined behind his back, a grin spread from one ear to the other. He was the youngest of all of us, yet he had done more than this entire room combined.

I made my way back beside Solomon. Our arms brushed as I took a spot close beside him.

Bishop stalked beside Coen. Both of them watched Baylen as he smiled like a sadistic lunatic.

"You can tell Coen tied him up." Baylen curled his finger beneath the rope restraining Dad. Dad's eyes moved behind Baylen's head, locking with mine. "He tied him up like he was going to fuck 'em."

Baylen clicked his tongue, tilting his head as he looked down at Dad. He slowly followed Dad's gaze. His black eyes dipped down to my feet, and then back to my face. He scowled something under his breath before looking back to Dad.

He crouched down and reached for Dad's calf. His fingers lingered around his limb. He slid his touch down to his ankle.

Baylen bit his lip and looked at Dad as he pulled a knife from his sock. "You are all idiots," Baylen began. He moved to the other ankle. Again, a knife was concealed in his sock. Baylen looked up at Bishop as he threw the knife to the ground. "I know I taught you better than that."

Bishop's jaw flexed. He looked like he wanted to hit Baylen.

The knives were a few inches from Dad's feet. I tensed, shifting against the wall. Was Dad planning on using those on me? Did he know I knew? Why did he bring knives to lunch?

Baylen stood to his feet. He stuffed his hands in his front pockets as he looked down at Dad.

"Coen," Baylen began, slowly. He didn't look away from Dad. He didn't see how tense Coen became beside Bishop. "There is no way your whores actually enjoy being restrained like this."

"Jesus, conversation for a different time," Coen gaped. He ran a hand through his greasy strands.

"There is no way he is talking about sex right now," Solomon mumbled. It was quiet. He had no intention of Baylen hearing him. But, Baylen had heard him.

"What'd you say, princess?" Baylen asked, jerking his head sideways, toward Solomon.

Solomon stayed quiet, tense as a rock beside me. Baylen grinned, the dimples appearing yet again. He looked so strange. He looked young, soft, and innocent; he looked the opposite of his personality. It was like God mixed up bodies when granting Baylen his.

"That's what I thought," Baylen bit out, looking back to Dad.

"Get on with it, Bael." Bishop crossed his arms, taking a step closer toward me. Baylen narrowed his eyes on him.

"Murder makes me horny," Baylen admitted, clicking his tongue.

"Don't kill him," I snapped before I was able to stop myself. Baylen jerked his head toward me. His eyes were full of something.

"Unfortunately," Baylen responded, looking back to Bishop.

Baylen stalked toward me. I watched Bishop tense behind him, taking a step toward Baylen. I thought he was going to reach out and strangle me. His eyes were on me, narrowed, and so angry. But, he reached behind my head, grabbing ahold of something.

It looked like a paddle of sorts.

"This is going to be fun." Baylen smiled, turning his back to me. He walked around the room, grabbing a hold of various items he found hanging on the walls. Baylen continued to pace the walls of the room, clicking his tongue, and muttering about how fascinating these instruments appeared.

"Baylen," Bishop warned. He was having fun with this. How in God's name was he having fun right now?

"Coen," Baylen started, ignoring Bishop's warning. "I'd love for you to show me how your whores enjoy this. Once this cunt is taken care of."

He was referring to Dad, but his eyes landed on me when he said it. I flinched.

"Whatever you say, big man." Big man. Even if he was the smallest, and youngest, his force took up the entire room.

Bishop made his way beside me. He reached down, intertwining his fingers with mine. He leaned into my forehead, planting a kiss on my skin. Dad watched us, but I did not push Bishop away. I squeezed harder.

Baylen reached for Dad's chair. He twisted it a few degrees to the left. It now faced a single-person hammock, hanging from the ceiling by a chain. It appeared to be of leather. Worst of all, Dad was still able to stare at me from the angle; he did just that.

Baylen sat on the hammock, fiddling with one of the knives in his hand.

Bishop wrapped his arm around my shoulder, pulling me hard into him. "Let's get started, yes?"

Baylen propped a leg up on the hammock. He comfortably lounged backward as he stared at Dad. He looked like they were sitting down to have a cup of tea.

"Ethel," Dad began. It was the first time he had spoken in thirty minutes. Maybe Baylen's presence was all that was needed. "You aren't going to let him do this to me."

Bishop held onto me harder, helping my nerves subside.

Baylen's dimples deepened. He looked back at me, flashing a set of white teeth. He hadn't stopped smiling since he entered this room. "Do what?" Baylen began, looking between Dad and I's exchange. "We are just going to have a little conversation."

The sadistic smile on his face and the knife he twirled told a different story.

VERSE
FORTY-SEVEN

"A preacher murdering and raping people. Is that what happened? So fun. So unexpected." Baylen twirled the knife in his hands, kicking his legs beneath the hammock. The swing slowly rocked him back and forth. "I mean, that had to have been what happened. Unless there is more to the story."

Dad stared at me, silent.

"Oh, come on!" Baylen exclaimed, smiling ear to ear. "Spill the details. I'd love to hear all about it."

For a moment, Dad looked ashamed. I saw it, for a brief second. But, it washed away as he smiled.

"Don't look at her. You and I are having a conversation. It's very rude to ignore someone when having a conversation. Isn't it?" Baylen bit the tip of the blade with his teeth. He tilted his head, staring at Dad, and no one but Dad.

Coen made his way to stand beside Bishop. He crossed his arms over his chest. He looked around the room, touching everything but the scene unfolding in front of him. He appeared to be bored.

"He's insane," Bishop said beneath his breath, into my ear. I nodded. I'd agree with that until my death.

"I don't like it when people are rude to me. I also don't like being ignored," Baylen cautioned.

Silence.

"Dad, please," I whispered. Nothing. Not a single word left Dad's curled mouth.

"Okay! You want to play," Baylen exclaimed, running his palms down his pants. Bishop shifted, pulling me closer to his body heat. Safe, I reminded myself. I was safe. Dad, though, wasn't going to be if he didn't start talking.

Dad looked away from me to watch Baylen as he approached. His hands were restrained to the arms of the chair, making it easier for what Baylen was about to do.

He placed the tip of the knife above his fingernail. He traced the outline of his bed for a moment. I didn't see what happened next, but based on Dad's wince and gasp for air, I concluded what occurred.

Baylen tore the fingernail from his skin. Like he would a stray hair.

I buried my face into Bishop's shoulder. He clamped his hand over my open ear. The other was already muffled by his body. I was able to hear it, for a second. Dad cried out in pain. Baylen was hurting Dad, and I let him.

Janyce, I reminded myself.

The girl in the chair.

I twisted my head out of Bishop's grasp. If I was allowing this to happen, I would watch it happen. Even if I had to force myself to.

Baylen was examining the bloody nail in the light, dimples deeper than ever. Blood was dripping from his finger, and into a small pool beneath Dad's hand.

I was going to be sick. Not just from the pain being inflicted on Dad, or the photographs. But, the way they both hadn't stopped smiling. Even after getting his nail ripped out, Dad was smiling.

Baylen grabbed hold of Dad's jaw. He squeezed it so tight that his hands trembled. He forced his mouth open. He placed the nail onto his tongue. The nail had meat and blood still attached. He didn't just cut out the nail, he cut the entire nail bed clean.

He forced his mouth shut. His hand clasped on both his lips and nose, blocking off any airway. "Swallow, preacher," Baylen ordered. His voice dripped with something else entirely. "Swallow."

Dad thrashed and grunted. His noises were muffled by Baylen's hand. But, after a few seconds under his hold, he finally did as he was told. He swallowed his nails and meat.

"Jesus, Baylen," Coen gaped. "You're a little unnecessary sometimes."

Baylen jerked his head back to look at Bishop. He narrowed his gaze; like Bishop had been the one calling him out.

Solomon ran a hand down his face. His eyes had been to the ground since Baylen walked through the door. Coen only looked away when he became distracted by something hanging on the wall. Bishop and I, though, had watched every second.

"I told you I didn't like to be ignored." Baylen made his way back to the hammock. He propped his leg on the edge, as he did before. He bit down on the knife; blood now stained the knife and his teeth.

"Fuck you." Dad spat at his feet. There was blood in his saliva. Baylen laughed, throwing his head backward.

"Now, you know that's no way to talk to a man that just cut your nail off."

"You aren't a man. You're a boy. Untie me, and let's see just how much of a man you are then." Dad spat again. I shuddered, holding tighter onto Bishop. Dad smiled up at Baylen. And, Baylen smiled harder down at him. Their craziness nearly matched each other.

Baylen turned to face Bishop and me. "Bring me his mother."

"For what?" I asked, shaking my head.

Baylen only bit his lip. It spoke more than words could.

"No, Baylen," Bishop snapped.

Baylen rolled his eyes, moving his head to Dad in the motion. "Let's see," Baylen began, continuing his swinging of the hammock. "What would Daddy's perfect little girl want me to ask? Hm. Do you regret whatever it is that you did? What exactly was it that you did?"

Dad winced, looking down at his hand. It didn't appear to hurt nearly as much as one would expect. Dad wasn't gasping in pain anymore; he looked to be more shocked if anything.

"Oh, preacher. I've already told you I don't like to be ignored. Do you need me to prove it again?"

Silence.

Fuck, Dad. Just talk.

Baylen clasped his hands together. He stood from the hammock, moving in front of Dad. His back blocked me from seeing what was happening. I could only hear metal clanking together. Baylen crouched down to grab something from the floor; the paddle.

My stomach twisted and tears blocked my vision. What in God's name was I doing? Allowing?

The paddle came down on top of Dad's hands four times. I heard the loud slap of skin twice, per hand. Every slap, he cried out in pain. He wailed at the last slap. This hurt. Whatever Baylen was doing hurt him badly.

Baylen returned to his hammock.

The first thing I saw was blood.

Blood was dripping down the chair. There was blood everywhere. It coated the nails that stuck out both of his hands, and the skin around it. It looked exactly how I imagined Jesus when he was crucified.

I gasped.

Every person in this room was going to hell. Me included.

"Are you okay? Do you want him to stop?" Bishop asked. Baylen jerked his head around, narrowing his gaze. He acted as if the thought of stopping was as blasphemous as what he just did to Dad's body.

I hesitated, but eventually shook my head.

Dad's eyes darkened. He was panting, wincing, and letting out a cry of pain every few seconds. This was so fucked up. Terrible. I needed to leave this room, but I couldn't bring myself to move. It was happening because of me.

I looked beside me.

Solomon hadn't left, physically. But, he somehow zoned out the entire situation unfolding in front of him.

"Okay, let's have a conversation. That's all this needs to be. Did you just murder? Rape? Indulge? Come on, preacher. Sing for me." Baylen braced his elbows on his knees, looking up at Dad through his eyelashes.

Dad spat at his feet.

"I know you," Dad gasped through heavy breaths. The man was back; the man who possessed Dad's body. When he split, this was the man I feared.

Dad smiled looking at me. "You're all fucking idiots. This entire town. Especially you. Oblivious fucking whore."

Bishop tensed tighter than I did. I held onto him, afraid he was going to lunge at Dad and kill him for calling me a whore.

Dad looked back up at Baylen. "I know you," he repeated. "God, Cheryl was a fun one. Wish he would have made you watch. He made his kids watch."

Baylen wore something besides insanity. Every muscle in his body clenched. He ground his teeth together, and his knuckles went white. He clicked his tongue once. Twice. Thrice.

"Baylen," Coen warned, stepping forward.

No one in the room seemed to understand what Dad meant by 'Cheryl.' Even Bishop, his supposed best friend, was oblivious. Was it someone Baylen knew? How did he know her? What happened to her?

"You should have kept that in. You've officially pissed me off. Which is really, really, not going to end well for you." Baylen relaxed, slightly. But, he still was on the edge of his hammock. He looked one breath away from jumping onto Dad.

Dad laughed, looking back at me. I wasn't crying anymore. I was gaping. A thousand questions ran through my head.

"The only thing I regret is not doing it to you."

"Whoa, whoa," Coen began. He jerked his body away from Baylen, and toward Dad. He held out both of his hands, hoping it would prevent him from speaking anymore. It did not matter. The words were already out.

Baylen and Bishop both lunged toward him. Bishop made it to him first, hitting Dad as hard as he could in the face. Over, and over.

VERSE FORTY-EIGHT

A warm arm wrapped around my head, pulling me into his chest. I didn't stop him. I let out a sob, recalling the words that Dad had just uttered. The only thing I regret is not doing it to you.

Thump. Thump. Thump. The pounding of Bishop's knuckles against Dad's face lined in sync with Solomon's heartbeat.

It was odd. I had barely spoken two words to him in my life, but he comforted me.

"Come on, Bishop," Coen pleaded. The pounding stopped, and within a moment, Bishop's warmth returned beside me.

I pulled away from Solomon. I looked to Bishop first. He was focused on Dad. He breathed heavily through his nostrils. He appeared as if he were going to lunge back on top of the man who was once my dad.

"Bishop," I croaked, beneath my breath. His knuckles were dripping with blood. I could only imagine how terrible Dad currently looked. I didn't care; I didn't spare him a glance. Whatever Baylen was currently doing to him was between them.

Bishop pulled me into his chest. I felt my muscles relax, for a moment. But, Dad's heavy breathing a few feet away reminded me of what currently was going on.

Dad.

I trembled, imagining everything that could have occurred between Dad and me. Good God, almighty, I was living with an actual psychopath. I didn't like to think of people needing to go to hell, but Dad? He needed to rot for an eternity.

I found the courage to look to Dad, though I didn't leave Bishop's arms. His face was covered in blood, from Bishop's fists. But, even then, he was still smiling. Ear to fucking ear. Baylen was standing in front of him, smiling just as hard.

There was no blood on Baylen's fists. It was Bishop who had inflicted the damage on Dad's face.

"He," Baylen spat, with a smile. "Who is he? I want a name."

What was he talking about? Did Bishop know what made Baylen so tense? Of the Cheryl woman Dad had mentioned? I had never heard Dad mention a woman named Cheryl. Who was she? I was afraid to ask because it seemed only Baylen had the answer.

Dad looked at Baylen. Baylen cracked his neck and knuckles, preparing for however Dad chose to answer.

"You know exactly who," Dad replied.

"What is he talking about, Baylen?" Bishop asked. So, he didn't know. None of them seemed to know what the two were speaking of. I doubted

Solomon knew; he only knew the floor at the moment. As for Coen, he was awaiting Baylen's explanation as intently as the rest of us.

Baylen wasn't smiling anymore.

He looked like a mix of too many emotions. "Hm," he hummed. He crouched down toward the box at Dad's feet. He flipped through the polaroids, slowly. He clicked his tongue at the sight of each of them.

"Baylen, use your words," Coen bit out.

He didn't. It was Dad who now smiled so hard, so sadistically. "Familiar?" Dad asked, biting his bloody lip.

This made Baylen smile. He tilted his head sideways, toward me, but he kept his eyes on Dad.

"Ethel, sweetheart," Baylen hummed. My name felt immoral on his tongue. "You should probably leave the room now. Same with you, queasy."

Solomon practically fell out of the room.

I didn't move.

"Baylen," Coen began, taking a step toward the ticking bomb. "You agreed no killing. You are acting like you are about to kill him."

Coen reached for Baylen's bicep. The moment Coen's fingers touched his skin, Baylen jerked his arm backward, elbowing Coen hard in the face. I looked down at Coen in horror; he lay on the ground, holding his now bloody nose.

"Bishop, you should get your cunt out," Baylen mumbled, all too casually.

"Baylen, you swore you weren't going to—" Bishop stopped. The entire room went still. Even Coen, cursing in pain on the floor, went silent as he realized what Baylen was doing.

He was pulling Dad's pants down.

I was only able to see Baylen's back, but I could hear what was oc-curring. Dad's pants and belt hit the ground, pooling at Baylen's knees. Baylen was so angry he was shaking; I could see the trembling in his back.

Dad began to curse, like a chant.

He was going to die.

And, we would never know what happened to them. This was not justice. This was a result of anger, over something none of us knew.

Bishop took a step toward Baylen, slowly. Similar to how one would approach a wild animal. "Baylen, you got to talk, bud."

Baylen grabbed a hold of the knife by his knees, ignoring Bishop. At least he did not hit him as he had done Coen.

A sound echoed through the room. A sound unlike anything I'd heard in my life. It sounded like a crunch. A tear. The noise was similar to how it felt when biting into a piece of fatty meat.

Following the noise was a wail, and a slap as it hit the floor.

It was covered in blood, but there was no mistaking what was making Dad wail so much.

Baylen just castrated him.

"Oh, fuck," Coen cursed, beneath the wails.

A strangled sob came out of my mouth. I pushed my way out of the room, bile rising in my throat. Dad was going to die. I reminded myself that he deserved it. But, this was cruel. Baylen had looked at him like he deserved much worse than his cruelty.

There was a small trash can in the hallway, directly next to where Solomon stood. He was leaning against the wall, playing Candy Crush on his phone; he was completely oblivious to what was going on in the room a few feet away.

I leaned over the trashcan, throwing up into it. The door shut to the damned room, silencing the hall. It was a sex club, of course, the room walls were soundproof. It made sense why Bishop believed this would be the best place to rough him up.

"Shit," Solomon cursed. He reached for my hair, holding it back as I trembled and retched up a month's worth of food. I wouldn't be able to eat thinking of the small piece of bloody flesh that caused Dad to wail in so much pain.

I slumped over the rim of the trashcan once I stopped vomiting. My face was covered in sweat.

"He— He—" I couldn't get the words out through my sobs. Dad was going to die as brutally as those girls in the photos. But, why did it not feel right? It felt horrible.

"Come on." Solomon grabbed my hand, pulling me to my feet. "Let's get air."

I nodded, letting a stranger pull me down the stairs and out the backdoor of the club. I didn't even notice the door the last time I was in this place.

Once outside, I slid down the crimson-colored wall. I pulled my knees to my chest. I was never going to be able to see the color the same again. That horrifying room was red. Baylen's hair had hints of red. Bishop's fists were red. Dad was covered in red, soon to be blue.

I was going to burn every piece of red clothing I owned.

The back door flung open. I flinched, looking up at Bishop's disheveled appearance. His hair was flying in every direction, his knuckles coated in that terrible color, and his shirt splattered with Dad. "Shit," Bishop cursed, coming toward me.

I looked down at the anklet I wore. It had a red heart on it. Red. Blood. Dad. Crimson. Baylen.

He slid down the wall beside me. I crawled into his chest, letting his arm draped around me. The noises coming from my mouth were muffled by the t-shirt he wore.

Dad was dead. If he hadn't died from loss of blood, he was dead from wrath.

"He never said what he did. This was pointless." Death was the easy way out of this. No one would ever know what happened to those girls.

Bishop shook his head, holding me tighter against his chest. "Baylen was off. He knew something."

On cue, the back door swung open. Coen walked out first. His hair was greasy, falling in every way but the center. He held a bloody towel over his nose, stopping the flow of blood that Baylen had inflicted on him. He scowled, looking behind him.

Baylen walked out, a bloody cigarette between his lips, and a bottle of Vodka in his hand.

"What did you do to him?" I spat. I looked up at him with a trembling jaw. He killed him. I did not need to see Dad's lifeless body to prove that. Baylen was covered in blood. He looked like he just walked out of a horror film, alive.

He pulled the cigarette away from his lips, replacing it with the rim of Vodka.

Bishop pulled me tighter into his embrace.

Baylen began to fiddle in his pocket for something. He pulled out a large wad of cash, counting it, before throwing it at Coen's feet. Did they pay him to not kill him?

He spoke, without looking at me, as he did. "I cut off his cock. Forced him to swallow it. And stabbed him thirty-three times." He spoke slowly like one would a child.

A quiet sob hiccupped in my throat.

He looked up at me, smiling. "Don't ask questions if you don't want to hear the answer."

Coen shifted, standing beside Solomon. We all stood flush against one wall, while Baylen was across from us. He squinted up at the sky, oblivious to all of us awaiting him to speak on what he had figured out.

"Jesus Christ, Baylen." Solomon ran a hand down his face. "Did you at least figure something out?"

Baylen took a drag of the cigarette, squinting toward the sky. "Yeah," he drew out.

"Please, do share. You've just murdered someone in my club, I'd like to know if it was worth it," Coen snapped. His tone made Baylen smile harder.

"Pretty boy," Baylen hummed, still looking at the sky. We watched him stare up at the sun, finishing his cigarette. He was silent. I could only hear Bishop's heart against my chest.

"Baylen, use your fucking words, or I swear to God," Bishop warned. Baylen snuffed the cigarette against the wall.

He clicked his tongue, staring down at Bishop. I wondered how they viewed Baylen. Bishop had explained how he had been living with them since he was a teenager. He was practically raised by them. Whatever he witnessed with Cain, this town, and the three boys around me, all developed him into the sadist he was now.

He grunted, looking at Coen. "You got your money back. Couldn't help myself toward the end." He smiled, walking back inside the club without a word of what had happened. When Bishop ran in to get him, he was already gone.

VERSE
FORTY-NINE

I hadn't left my bed in days.

Well, I've left to shower. I attempted to eat as well. But, other than that, I've made myself one with my comforter.

I couldn't move.

I couldn't sleep.

I kept thinking about Dad. The slap of his cock hitting the floor. The wails that radiated throughout the room when Dad was last alive. Baylen's smile. Dad's smile. I regret not doing it to you.

Fuck. Dad was fucking dead.

The girls from the Polaroids were dead.

I trembled, pulling the covers further up my chest. I hid beneath the warmth of my comforter, shutting out the world. We never would know what happened. I knew he was involved, that was confirmed, but only Baylen had figured it out.

My jaw tightened. I wasn't able to cry anymore. After the initial adrenaline washed away, I'd gotten it all out. I was tucked alone in the house he raised me in, grieving through it.

He deserved it, I reminded myself. He was a terrible man. But, it still hurt. Bad. I blamed myself for whatever happened to them. I was, as he put it, an oblivious whore. I had respected his privacy; I hadn't questioned what he possibly could have been doing after hours.

He hadn't deserved my respect.

I opened my phone. Bishop had been texting me daily, asking if I was okay, or ready to move in with him. He was practically pleading with me. I assured him I did, I just needed some time to "pack."

I lied. I hadn't tried to pack once.

I wanted to move in with Bishop, truly; I couldn't concentrate on it right now, though.

All I could think about was him.

He had to have been a bloody mess. Thirty-three stab wounds, according to Baylen. It must have been a horrific sight. How did they not look ill after leaving the room? I wondered what had happened to Dad after he passed on. Was he burnt to a crisp? Were his bones crushed to powder?

A wave of nausea rolled over me again.

I reached for my phone, unlocking it.

Bishop hadn't texted today. Usually, he would have texted by now. Maybe I should text him first; I needed to make sure he knew I was not upset with him.

ME: i'm still packing.

A lie, but I did not want him to think I hesitated about moving in with him. That would help. I think. Being away from this place would help. I needed to get out of bed and this house. But, I couldn't bring myself to move.

Bishop did not respond.

I frowned, throwing my phone face down on the bed. Shortly after, I fell asleep for what felt like the fifth time today.

∞

When I woke, I was not alone.

My eyes rounded as I looked down toward my front. My fingers were lost in a mess of hair, and Bishop's face was stuffed in between my cleavage. I was even pulling him closer to me by the back of his head. How had I not heard him stumble into my room?

Our legs were entangled, and his arms were wrapped around my waist. His fingers lingered at the base of my spine. I had to have woken when we became knotted in this position.

Bishop's breath was steady against my chest. His eyelashes were shut, occasionally fluttering against my skin. Shit, how long had I been asleep? It felt like time ceased to exist right now; hours were blending in with each other.

I looked out the window. It was ajar, moonlight seeping into the room. Fuck, I thought it was noon, not midnight.

I slid away from Bishop, and toward the window; winter was pushing through the open space.

My attire was far from attractive. I wasn't expecting company to climb up a tree and fall into my room like a madman. I was wearing an oversized t-shirt with a pair of cotton panties beneath the shirt.

When I turned back in Bishop's direction, said company was already looking at me.

The side of his face was propped up by the palm of his hand. His hair was a mess, his lips parted, and dark circles formed beneath his eyes. They almost looked as dark as the ones I wore.

He was gorgeous, nonetheless. Beautiful. In the dark, ethereal sort of way.

"You've sure done a lot of packing, I see." The corner of his lip twitched for a split second. His gaze fell to my legs as I walked toward the bed, crawling back into the warmth of it.

I buried myself in his embrace. He didn't question it. Instead, he threaded his fingers against my scalp, caressing the sensitive skin. His other arm wrapped around my waist, pulling me close to him. I felt like I was melting.

"I am not in the mood to pack," I admitted, into his chest. I just wanted to be alone. But, I knew it would help to be out of the house; it was only bringing back the memories of Dad. What Dad once was.

"I know," Bishop muttered, continuing with my hair. "It's been five days. I told myself I'd give you space for five days. After that, well, if you want to rot in this bed, I will as well."

Rot.

That's exactly what I was doing, wasn't it? I was rotting into the sheets of my bed, seeping into my mattress. I'd once read about a girl who never left her bed. Something had happened to her, and she decided she'd never stand again. She pissed, and shit, all over herself day and night.

Eventually, the maggots ate her alive.

That was how I felt. Mentally. Physically, I was taking care of myself.

"Has Baylen said anything?" I asked. I shouldn't talk about it. I should grieve, without the stress of unknown circumstances. But, I needed to. For my sanity.

Bishop shifted, shaking his head.

"No. He is barely home, let alone talking to us."

I pulled my face away from his chest. I looked down at his lips. His breath fanned over my face, heat seeping into my core. His hand came to my face, gently caressing the softness of my cheek with his rough thumb. "God, Ethel." Bishop gaped. Actually gaped. "You're beautiful."

My lips parted. He traced that too.

Beautiful.

I didn't feel beautiful. I never had felt it. But, the way he looked at me made me feel different. He made me feel beautiful.

I reached for his hand, tracing the metal of my purity ring. He wore it; he'd worn it since I gave it to him. "I like you, Bishop. Really. But, I swear, if you break my heart—"

I didn't know what I would do.

Bishop laughed at this, leaning in to plant a kiss on my lips. "You shouldn't be in this house." Kiss. "Can we rot in my bed? It's more comfortable than this stiff shit."

I nodded, kissing him again.

Since my mom's death, and now Dad's, it felt like everything was going wrong. But, now, it felt like something was finally going right. Beneath the ache of everything was a lining of bliss; it was exciting knowing that our souls had found each other in this life.

I think I am in love with him.

VERSE FIFTY

A round two days later, I was back at the house, with Bishop beside me.

Grandma was here.

She planted her suitcases down and went toward the fridge for a beer.

Bishop and I sat at the dining room table, watching her. He sat close beside me. Literally, as close as he could; he had moved a chair next to me to avoid sitting a foot away.

I was surprised that we did not have sex last night. We were all over each other, through the night. I would wake up, and his lips were on mine; I'd fall asleep stroking the length of his torso and wake up doing it.

"Long flight," Grandma began, cracking open a beer with her teeth. "You know, those flight attendants can be real bitches sometimes. Happy sky's this. Happy sky's that." She raised the pitch of her voice, mocking the attendants.

I gulped. She didn't know Dad was dead. She was going to realize. She had to. Her son was to be deemed missing soon. Church was ending, and Dad was not there.

Grandma took a seat across from us. She sipped her beer, looking between Bishop and me. "The boy from the bathroom, I'm assuming." She narrowed her eyes on Bishop.

"The one and only," Bishop replied, grinning at the memory. My face flushed whereas Bishop reclined far in his chair, outstretching an arm over the back of mine.

Grandma grunted, looking back at me. "Where is Eric?"

My stomach dropped, twisted, and contorted in any sick way possible. Where was Eric? That was the question, wasn't it? Was he being eaten by maggots and bugs? Was he a pile of ash in Crimson? Sinking to the bottom of some lake?

I gulped, rubbing my palms up and down my thighs. "Um," I hummed. I looked up to Bishop. He kept his gaze on Grandma, watching her. My leg began to bounce up and down, but his hand snaked around my thigh to calm it.

I looked at the clock behind Grandma's head. A trail of sweat was forming down my back. This was the time that Dad would be getting out of church. So, if anyone had called the police, it would have happened a few minutes ago.

It was odd. A preacher who showed up early to every service, disappearing without a word. He would have told someone; the congregation. If he had to cancel the service, they would know.

Fuck, they were going to know something was wrong.

Someone was going to call for a wellness check. The police would care enough about Dad to check; he was such a good man in this community, after all.

"Dad is—" I stopped. Dead.

"Not going to be here anymore," Bishop finished. "Ethel tells me you two didn't have the best relationship. So, it shouldn't be an issue. Should it?"

Bishop tilted his head, narrowing his eyes at Grandma. He looked threatening. Shit, I forgot what an ass he was. How different he is with me.

Grandma appeared just as intense. Her eyes turned to slits. "Don't get a tone with me, boy."

Was Grandma more worried about his tone, than what Bishop had just said? Did she not care for her son? She hadn't questioned Bishop's words, once.

Bishop opened his mouth. I had no doubt he was planning some snarky response. But, a knock pounded on the door before he could get it off his tongue.

I flinched, which Grandma noticed. She muttered a prayer under her breath before standing from the table. She made her way to the door beside us; the front door. When she opened it, we were able to have a clear view of the policemen standing in the doorframe.

Grandma shot us a glance, before disappearing outside to speak with them.

VERSE FIFTY-ONE

"Shit. Shit. Shit," I cursed beneath my breath. "We are going to be arrested."

"No." Bishop sunk further into his chair, all too relaxed. His hand tightened around my thigh. "Even if we were, Solomon would find out, and Coen would bail us out. But, we won't."

"Why not?" I lowered my voice, afraid the police would hear from outside. I twisted my head in his direction.

"Because. I've never been arrested, and I don't plan on changing that today."

"That is a terrible mindset to have," I muttered. The back of his skull was resting against the edge of the chair, face directed toward the ceiling. But, his eyes were on me. My breath caught. Shit, it was terrible timing for Bishop to be looking at me like that.

"You know, I never asked you to be my girlfriend."

I choked on my breath. His fingers ran small, light circles around my thighs. For a moment, I forgot the seriousness of our situation; I felt as lax as Bishop currently appeared. The police were not outside, talking to Grandma about something she knew nothing of. It was just Bishop.

"I suppose now you know." Bishop squeezed my thigh, hard. I hissed, leaning forward to relieve the sudden pain.

"Was that your attempt at asking me out?" I asked. I bit my lip and twisted in my seat to face him. The police were out there, I reminded myself. I could be going to jail.

Bishop slowly nodded. His hooded eyes hadn't left mine. "More like telling, but you get the point."

I leaned in toward him. I planted a kiss on his lips; a simple peck. But, he fisted my hair, pulling me deep into his face. His tongue slid into my mouth, and the hand on my thigh moved toward my waist.

He pulled at me, trying to get me to crawl on top of him.

The door opened before we could begin whatever Bishop wished to do.

We both pulled away, looking up at Grandma. I was out of breath, lips throbbing from the fast make out session we had just had.

"You know, the police just told me the most fascinating thing," Grandma began. She made her way toward the fridge, grabbing a new beer. "A church member called. For a wellness check. Something about their preacher not showing up for the first time in years."

I knew they would. They loved Dad. He had acted like a very good man. A good preacher.

"You su—" Bishop was interrupted by Grandma's index finger and a slitted glance.

"I was not done. Don't interrupt me. It's disrespectful," Grandma retorted. Bishop tensed but slid further down the chair. He looked over at me, a grin proud on his face.

Her gaze softened when she looked back at me. "Your father moved back to Florida. To retire young. He had a breakdown, which was the reason I flew up here to visit. To make sure you were okay. Father Jones is going to be called to take over the church. That is what I told the police, and that is what happened from this day forward."

Me and Bishop both gaped.

Bishop had nothing to say. A mouth full of remarks had gone silent.

"Grandma," I started. I didn't know what to say. Thankfully, she held up her hand, stopping me.

"I am not going to ask. You are a good person, Ethel. I would trust you with my life. Whatever happened, happened." She took a large swig of beer.

"What happened between you two? Can you tell me, now? He never let me talk about it," I blurted. If we were on the topic of Dad, I wanted the question answered; the one that had been bugging me for years.

Grandma downed the rest of her beer.

Bishop stood from his chair, making his way toward the fridge. He popped it open with his teeth and slid it to Grandma. She smiled, taking another swig.

"Your dad was a terrible teenager. He had always been off, but we never tried to get him help. That was our fault. I blame myself for that, we should have at least gotten him help. It started small, like your grandpa and I would wake up, and he'd be watching us sleep. Saying he had something to ask. We believed him."

Grandma frowned, looking to her lap. "Then, it escalated. He started messing with animals. We found the dog tied to a tree, beaten. He'd get neighborhood cats. He never killed them, but he kicked them. Beat them. But, once he started dating your mom, it all stopped. We assumed he was just being a boy. Or, something like that."

She stopped. She looked up at me, her face softening. "Once she died, though. I was worried for him to be alone with you. Even though he had grown out of it, she wasn't there. I brought up the idea of him moving closer to us, so we could make sure he was okay, but he flipped out. Said he was perfectly fine. And, that he knew how to raise a child. We tried. I really, really tried to get him to move. Or let us move. But, he kept threatening to get legally involved if we tried further. But, after your graduation, we came up. He seemed fine. I—"

Grandma went quiet, looking at her beer. "Ethel, if he hurt you, I would never forgive myself."

He didn't hurt me, I wanted to say. But, the others? Fuck, we could never tell her about this. She would blame herself, day in, and day out for not getting him the help he needed.

I shook my head. "He didn't hurt me," I reassured. He regretted not. Bishop's hand tightened around my thigh, painted nails digging into the skin.

"He seemed fine after the funeral. He acted like he loved you more than he loved himself. We weren't worried."

I wanted to throw up.

Was that love? That room; the words that spewed from his mouth. The lies. The ease of lying. It all made sense. Something had to be medically wrong with him, in the head. It did not justify what he did, but it confirmed my suspicion.

Grandma smiled, forgetting everything she had just said. She brushed it off as if we were talking about the weather. "I hope you two are being careful." She looked at the nonexistent space between us.

Bishop and I both responded at the same time.

"We are."

"Nothing inside," Bishop lied.

Liar. He definitely had been inside of me, and hopefully, he would be inside of me soon. Sex took up fifty percent of my thoughts now. How good it felt that single time. Now that the worry of being arrested, and Grandma had been lifted, I was beyond ready to be alone with Bishop.

His hand slid up my thigh as if he were thinking the same thing.

"I am going to find the legal documents to own this house. Grandpa will be here in a few days, with a U Haul. From this day forward, don't mention him, or ever think of him."

"Shit, Grandma," Bishop teased. "Have you done this before?"

Grandma ignored him.

"Not this house," I replied. Too many memories. It needed to be burned. "Please."

"Besides, Ethel is going to live with me." Bishop's hold over my thigh tightened. I didn't think I had a choice from the way he was holding me, so possessively.

Grandma looked between the both of us. And, then to the hand tapping impatiently against the table. Specifically, the finger that wore my purity ring; the one she had bought me, to wear until marriage. Whatever she was thinking, she kept it to herself.

"Okay and okay. Grandpa and I will go house shopping. But, I swear to the good God almighty, if she ever comes to me, crying over you—"

Grandma looked like she was going to strangle Bishop, just from the thought.

"Got the point, Granny," Bishop retorted. He narrowed his eyes as tightly as hers. I winced at how hard he was grabbing me. Jesus, he was an ass; when he looked at me, his gaze softened.

"Very well. I suppose you should get packing then," Grandma advised. "I have some calls to make."

EPILOGUE

Weeks later

Weeks had passed, and I still hadn't finished packing. All of my necessities were in Bishop's room, but nothing else.

Baylen had yet to be seen. Dad was growing to be a memory.

The home was large, with many guestrooms that were used to collect dust, but we both agreed that I was going to sleep with him. It resulted in us fucking every second of the night and day. I was exhausted. I couldn't move without him ending up inside of me.

I think I've had more sex in the past week than three people combined in a lifetime.

I was on my way to the front door, to leave, but Bishop had grabbed ahold of me. "Bishop," I groaned. His lips moved down my neck, biting at my skin. My back was pressed flush to the door. "I really need to go. Gwen will be there any second. Plus, I told Grandma—"

His teeth grazed against my neck. My eyes fluttered shut, and his hand splayed against my stomach, pushing me harder into the door.

Okay, maybe five minutes wouldn't hurt.

"Stop talking about your Grandma," Bishop snapped, sucking my neck between his teeth. I gasped at the feeling; I still wasn't used to it. My neck was covered in concealer and foundation, yet he was licking it right off. It had to taste terrible.

Bishop's hand slid down the front of my jeans, dipping into my pussy without warning. I was still wet from the three other times we'd had sex this morning. Bishop's stamina was ruthless.

My head slumped forward, slumping onto his shoulder as he worked inside of me. "Shit. There," I gasped.

Bishop's mouth landed beside my ear. "I know, sweet girl," he whispered, continuing to curl inside of me, hitting the spot in the back of my cunt. I'd read a lot about boys not knowing where a girl's clit was, as well as their G-spot. But, Bishop? He knew exactly how to make me feel good; it was concerning how skilled he was at this.

He credited it to Coen and his fascination with sex. Even from a young age, he had taught all of the boys how to find every spot. As Bishop had put it, the dinner conversations with him always resulted in something of the sexual sort.

I'd yet to have dinner with him.

Me and Bishop barely even ate. We had sex, slept, showered, and had more sex.

"Shit," I cursed, gritting my teeth together. I looked down at his hand; his wrist disappeared into the hem of my jeans. His forehead was pressed against mine, watching me as I watched him. I'd noticed Bishop liked eye contact; a lot.

I reached for his length, looking up at him. I stroked him through his jeans, at the same pace he was finger-fucking me.

"Fuck, Ethel." Bishop pulled himself away from me; I whimpered when his fingers left me. He reached for my jeans, yanking them down to my ankles. I stepped out of them fast, throwing them away from us. I felt like clothes were pointless at this point; I was only in them for a few minutes.

"Someone can come down," I panted, jerking at his pants. He removed his pants as fast, and eagerly, as I had. He hauled me up, holding me in the air between the door, and his waist. I wrapped my legs around his torso, pulling him close.

Bishop gnawed at his lip. He looked down at my parted pussy as he rubbed his tip up and down my slit. This was going to be a fast one; I could already feel his precum mixing with my wetness. "Better make it fast then."

He crowned me, for a split second, before pushing himself to the hilt. I cried out at the fullness; my head hit the back of the door as I threw it backward. I would never get used to this; the stretch.

New check off the "Sex with Bishop" bucket list. Have sex against a door.

Bishop held me against the door, two of his hands grabbing hold of my throat, as his hips kept me in place. He squeezed my throat hard, pulling in, and out of my pussy.

"Fuck, Bishop," I gasped. My back curved, pushing my front closer to him. I groaned with every hard, and snappy thrust. The door behind us made a loud pounding sound with every thrust, but I couldn't stop him. It felt too good. So, fucking good; especially, knowing that someone could walk down the stairs, and catch us at any moment.

"Fuck," he growled. I noticed that being around Bishop had caused me to curse more. It was half of what he said.

His nails dug into my neck, adding to the blackening around my vision. My mouth was forced open, pleas, cries, and moans falling out in some chorus. He felt so, so good.

I let out a shuddered groan. My hand flew upward to hold myself steady. In the process, I knocked over a picture frame beside the door; it was a very detailed painting of a vagina, with a broken hymen. Bishop explained it on my third night here. Coen had been suspended for painting it in his freshman year of high school.

We both laughed, looking down at the glass on the floor.

"Floor," I croaked, looking down at the area without glass. The door was too loud, and it was beginning to hurt my back.

Bishop obliged, kneeling on the floor. His hard cock prodded out in front of him. I lost my footing for a moment from how hard he had been thrusting into me. I joined him on the floor, pushing him onto his back. "I want to ride you." I grinned, straddling his hips.

His head tilted backward, hitting the floor. He was a few inches away from the glass I'd just broken. He wasn't even inside of me yet, but his cock was still twitching like he was, and my pussy was convulsing. "Jesus fucking Christ."

I shook my head at that. "Don't say that."

He opened his mouth to reply. With something snarky, I assumed. But, I was already seating myself over him. When slowly sinking over him, every inhale began a sharp breath, and every exhale became a shuddered moan. The position made me feel so full; I was going to come within seconds.

This truly was going to be a quick fuck.

I dug my fingers into his stomach, adjusting to him. He felt so much thicker and longer than before. It felt so good; I couldn't even move.

"Move, Ethel," Bishop pleaded. He grabbed my hips, moving my body. I rocked myself against him; a mix of groans and moves came from us as I continued to rock and bounce. "Fuck, Ethel, you feel good."

I nodded, whimpering in response. My walls were already tightening around him, holding onto him. I dropped my face down to his chest, bracing my hand beside his head. I was two more strokes from coming; I didn't know why I thought it was a good idea to get on top.

As if reading my thoughts, Bishop pulled me tight to his chest. There was no way I was going to be able to ride him from this angle. But, that did not matter. He bent his knees before thrusting up into me.

Hard and fast.

"Shit. Shit. Shit," I chanted. My nails scraped against the door, the floor, and his chest. Anything I could grab onto as he fucked up into me. The slaps of our skin echoed through the quiet house, especially due to the new position. My head was limp against his chest, moans coming uncontrollably out of my mouth.

I tightened around him just as he was about to come. He was twitching and swelling inside of my throbbing pussy. His speed had become so fast I couldn't breathe; I couldn't feel when he was out, or inside of me. I held my breath, allowing him to fuck me through both of our orgasms.

"Oh, God!" I groaned into his neck. My head was spinning, and it felt like my entire core had grown so tight it burst with pleasure. I shuddered, gasping his name through the shocks of my orgasm. I would let him come in me; risk a child in my belly, if it meant him never stopping how good he was hitting that spot.

Bishop pulled out, coming the second his tip slid out of my folds. My pussy was already coated in precum, and my arousal. He only painted it more, stroking himself until his cum was all over my lips.

"Fuck," he groaned as he came. I panted, still throbbing as if he were fucking me. His body relaxed beneath me, and he held me to his chest. I didn't want to even go anymore; I was exhausted.

We both panted against each other. Our bodies were covered in a thin layer of sweat. "Why can't your friend just unpack your grandma's shit? We can go upstairs for another round."

I debated it, for a moment.

I didn't want to move. It felt so good in his arms; safe. I listened to his fast heartbeat, slowly calming down. If I didn't move, we would end up fucking again. And, truly, I told Grandma I would be there thirty minutes ago.

"No," I replied.

"Can I come with you?" Bishop began to trace the length of my spine. I was going to fall asleep. We needed to get dressed; we needed to put on clothes and leave this very public area we were in.

"I suppose," I teased. I pushed myself upward, planting a single kiss on his lips. And then his cock.

I struggled my way back into my skinny jeans, ignoring Bishop's hungry eyes from behind me. He was putting on his clothes, but he was taking his time with it; he was too busy watching my ass struggling to fit in my jeans.

"Gwen is going to be there," I began, putting my shoes on. "Are you okay with that?"

"Yeah, I've been meaning to meet the girl Coen is fucking."

I shook my head. If that were true, I had heard nothing of it from her. Gwen was always reserved; she never spoke of things besides school. "I still don't believe that." I was happy for her, though, if it were true.

"I'll drive."

I looked back at him, curving my brow. From what I had gathered, he hadn't driven since that night. When he was drunk and killed his family in an accident. "You don't have to. It's fine—"

He grabbed a set of keys before I could stop him. He ignored me, opening the door he had just fucked me hard against. "Let's go, church girl."

SERIES WARNING PT. 2

I am coming to speak on the loose ends one more time. Hehe. I know some of y'all are going to come for my head about not going into Cheryl and Baylen; all of that will be resolved in Baylen's story. But, anyways, here are a few extra scenes:)

EXTRA SCENE ONE

"How could you possibly explain how fucking hot it is in the middle of December?"

I watched Bishop walk across the room, trailing close in Grandma's heels. I could hear the smirk in Bishop's voice. Grandma scowled, tugging at the garland wrapped around her neck. She held a bottle of eggnog tightly in her hand. Behind her, Bishop was grinning ear to ear.

Bishop looked at me for a moment. He winked at me, before continuing behind Grandma as she attempted to decorate.

"Is he always like that?" Gwen asked.

I turned to her. She watched Bishop as I had been. He was indeed always like this. Bishop and Grandma argued and argued. Over the most pointless stuff, too. I knew they did not mean it. I was beginning to believe that Bishop just liked to argue with Grandma as a way of bonding with her.

Tonight, he argued about the validity of climate change.

She'd gotten him a sweater for Christmas; the one he was wearing right now. It was a black sweater with large block lettering across the front of his chest; I'm getting coal written across the fabric.

Despite it all, I believed Grandma liked Bishop. And, Bishop liked her. Arguing was their odd way of accepting each other.

I nodded and took a large gulp of my drink. "You should have seen them last night. Bishop smoked a cigarette in the house and she almost set him on fire."

Gwen dipped her chin and snickered. Her hair fell from the side of her face, blocking her from me. She had been glowing recently. She hadn't spoken of Coen, but we knew. Gwen glowed. Coen glowed. Plus, she constantly had the messy hair of someone in a relationship with a nymphomaniac.

"Good God, boy. Five minutes. Leave me alone for five minutes." Bishop and Grandma walked past again. Grandma practically ran away from Bishop; he was hot in her trail spewing about the state of the ozone layer. I had no doubt he would talk my ear off about this fixation tonight.

Bishop muttered something low and left her to her decorating. He turned toward me, a glint of mischief in his eyes. My spine straightened. I feared whatever deviance he was planning. He looked like he was debating grabbing me and taking me to the bathroom. Again. Or, making me take a shot of whatever horrendous liquor he had made me drink before.

Bishop took a step toward me. I tilted my chin upward to meet his eyes. His hand reached for the side of my face. He stroked the pad of his thumb against my lips.

"She likes you," I said.

"Unfortunate for her."

Bishop leaned down, his lips brushing against mine. I shuddered and reached up to his hair. A single kiss. I needed to remind myself of where we were, and our company. If I didn't, we would end up traumatizing Gwen.

On command, Gwen gagged. Loud. "I'm so sorry." She clamped her hand over her mouth, gagging again. "Affection."

Bishop's eyes turned to slits. He looked behind my head and toward Gwen. "Oh, don't start. You've exhausted Coen with affection." He spat out the word.

"Bishop," I warned. I slapped his stomach. I looked at Gwen. Her face, neck, and ears had become an unhealthy shade of red. She scowled, reaching for the closest thing to her; a plastic shot glass.

She threw it as hard as she could toward him. I did not blame her. Bishop could not bite his tongue.

I couldn't help but smile. It felt good being here, with Bishop, Gwen, and Grandma. He fitted with me, and my life. I didn't know how I possibly had been living without him before. Life felt so much better; so much more fun with him. Shit, I even enjoyed grocery shopping with him. He made everything so fascinating.

Gwen picked up a new shot glass and made her way out of the kitchen, toward where Grandma decorated.

"She liked you too." Gwen had a weird way of showing it.

"Everyone likes me," Bishop replied.

I laughed, shaking my head. I couldn't take him seriously when he wore the sweater. Paired with the I'm getting coal was a grumpy face.

I grabbed his hand, tracing the purity ring he wore. My ring. I wore his ring on the finger that was meant to be reserved for marriage. I didn't care about the traditions of that anymore; I had Bishop to thank for that. He already had whatever was meant to be saved for my future husband. No ring, finger, wedding, or ceremony was needed to prove that. He had it.

Bishop's thumb made its way back to my lip. His fingertips moved to my cheek, and then my jawline. Finally, he reached for the necklace I wore. Bishop. Just as he had claimed I would, I wore his name around my neck.

"You're beautiful, Ethel." My stomach flipped. He leaned forward, planting a kiss against my forehead.

My fingers tightened in his sweater. His lips were against my ear, whispering quiet words of affirmation. My breathing was getting heavy; I didn't know how this was normal for someone to have such an effect on me. "So beautiful," he whispered.

His lips moved to the area beneath my ear. My eyes shut and I tilted my head to help him with his movements against me. "I love you."

I stopped breathing. I looked up at him, my fingers still in the fabric of his sweater. We hadn't said it yet. It had been here, for a while, existing among us. Love. But, we hadn't said the three words aloud. Bishop did not need to say three words to show me that it was with us.

"I love you," I replied. I looked up at him through my lashes. I could look at him for hours. I could stare, and stare, to simply take in the beauty of him. He did the same to me for hours, before we slept. Some nights we didn't sleep. Instead, we touched each other in an attempt to mold our bodies into one.

Bishop's lips perked. "Bathroom."

"Please."

Extra Scene Two

Briar was outstretched beside me, the smell of her tanning oil more overwhelming than the ocean in front of us. I didn't think it was possible for something to smell stronger than the sea.

Bishop was asleep. I think. I wasn't sure. He had gone still against my stomach thirty minutes ago, complaining about how much he hated the beach. I was lying down on the towel, holding Bishop's close to me. I had one of Bishop's larger shirts on and a bathing suit beneath it.

"Your boyfriend is sulking," Briar said. She pushed herself up onto her elbows. She pulled her sunglasses onto the bridge of her nose. She peered over the rim of them and toward some of the passing couples.

I bit my lip, looking down at Bishop. His head was in my lap, and my arms held his skull. His face was flush against my stomach. I felt his voice, a weak vibration, penetrate my lower belly. "It's fucking hot."

"You're wearing all black," I pointed out. He was in black jeans and a black hoodie. It was almost ninety degrees outside. We had all decided to drive toward the coast for a week. Coen and Gwen had to take a separate car from us; the two nearly started fucking every time he looked in her direction. Solomon had sat in the backseat of Bishop's car, along with Briar; she practically dragged Solomon.

Unfortunately, Baylen was here too.

Bishop pulled his head up and his eyes met mine. His lips were chapped, and his cheeks were sun kissed. He squinted through the sunlight. I wanted to laugh. The beach was not Bishop's scenery. He'd been clinging to me since we arrived, begging to sleep this terrible idea away.

Bishop leaned down to my thighs. My eyes widened as he planted a kiss on the inner part of it. And then another.

I threaded my fingers through his hair, caressing his scalp. "The hotel is not far." Bishop's voice sounded like a plea.

I felt him smile against me. "Should we go?"

I looked at Briar. She sighed, throwing her hands in the air. "Go. Leave me." She adjusted against the towel, shutting her eyes behind the lightly-tinted frames. "You guys are so in love it makes me sick."

"I'm not going to leave you."

"A shame," Bishop said, looking at Briar. "I'd really like to leave her and get to that room." He squeezed my thigh.

Bishop yawned, pushing me harder onto the towel. He adjusted his position on top of me. He rested the side of his face into the crook of my neck, and his body was flush against mine. "Where did Coen go?" I asked.

"The car." Briar held her phone above her face, scrolling through a collection of videos. "With Gwen." The corner of her lips perked. "For the third time."

"I didn't see them leave," I said

"Yeah. You are too busy eye-fucking each other." She wasn't wrong. I didn't know half of what was occurring around us. When Bishop slept on me, I slept. When he was awake, we kissed and touched each other, uncaring about the eyes and families around us. Nothing too terrible, but we couldn't stop touching each other. I felt like I needed to.

I traced the tips of my fingers down Bishop's back, and then back up. I couldn't stop smiling. I was so fucking happy. Anything that happened now, or had happened, felt like nothing. Life felt too good to exist with any of the bad. I genuinely could not remember a time I'd felt this happy. This content. I was at peace with life, and I knew it was Bishop.

"What are you smiling about?" Bishop asked. He bit his lip before placing a kiss over my belly button.

"You. You dressed like that to the beach."

"You like it."

"I do."

Briar made a noise beside us. "Are you guys going to become one of those awful couples now? You know, the ones that suck each other's face off in public. It makes me sick. I want to be in love."

Neither Bishop nor I replied. We stared at each other, one second away from doing just that.

"No," I replied after a few seconds passed. I looked away from Bishop and toward Briar. Her eyes were away from her phone and toward the approaching figure. She looked through her eyelashes and up toward the silhouette now a few feet away. I'd learned a lot from Briar; mostly about seduction and being a tease. She had a certain glint in her eye, one that would make any sane man weak. She wore it while looking at Solomon.

Solomon sat beside her without a word. He pulled out his laptop, powering it up. He had some type of box that connected to the side of the computer. Briar's lips parted as she stared at him. "You're joking. You actually brought that stupid shit to the beach," she snapped.

Solomon jerked his head toward her, narrowing his eyes. "What's stupid is that you're willingly opening yourself up to skin cancer when it just makes you uglier. But whatever you say." He gestured toward the bottle of tanning lotion beside her. She scowled at his comment.

Bishop laughed, readjusting his head against me.

"Oh, shut up!" Briar scoffed. She pushed herself off of the towel, now completely angled toward Solomon. He looked at her from the side of his eye. "At least go to the room and do that shit."

Solomon ignored her, looking toward Bishop. He hit his bicep to get his attention, but it just resulted in Bishop groaning and wrapping his arms tighter around me. "Get this. I walk into the room and Baylen is with five fucking girls. Man, I've never seen anything like that." Solomon shook his head and looked out into the distance.

Bishop's face pulled away from my stomach. "You swear?"

Solomon nodded. "I'm traumatized."

Bishop smiled hard. He slowly looked at me. My stomach sank; whatever he was about to say was not going to be good. He looked how he had when we went lingerie shopping. He had given me this exact look, and we both ended up fucking in the fitting room.

"What?" I hesitated, concerned about what he was going to say.

"Coen's fucking. Baylen's fucking. I think it's a sign to go to our room and do the same."

Sex would be good. Shit, it sounded really good.

I looked from Bishop to Briar, and then to Solomon. She rolled onto her stomach, 'accidentally' kicking sand onto Solomon. "Whoops," she teased, batting her eyelashes at Solomon. He looked like he was going to kill her.

"Yeah, sounds good," I grunted, pushing me and Bishop away from the bickering two.

Extra Scene Three

I'd been coughing for ten minutes straight. Bishop was beside me, laughing harder than I'd ever seen him laugh. He had a joint in between his fingers. I had taken a long hit of it. I thought I'd done good; I'd really done good for a moment.

Then the coughing hit.

"Why does it--." I started coughing again. Bishop was clenching his stomach, howling with laughter beside me. His eyes were squinted shut, as bloodshot as mine felt. They felt tingly, and my skin felt like it had no bones beneath it. I'd never felt this way before.

"Feel like that," I continued through my final cough.

"I told you to stick with the edible." Bishop had made an edible a few hours ago, and we'd eaten it. For some reason, I'd gotten hungrier after, and eaten more of the edible. It made me feel like I had no bones.

Bishop drew the weed to his lips. He took a long drag of it, though he did not burst into a fit of coughing like I had.

We were outside of our house. The lawn was a little wet from the rain a few hours ago, and the clouds had vanished to reveal a large display of stars above us. I'd been staring at them for the past hour. We both had. Occasionally, he would speak, but I didn't. It felt so good. Not as good as his cock, but nearly.

"Woah," I hummed. I licked my dry lips and returned to his chest. My head was heavy and I was afraid people were watching us. But, I said nothing. I laid the side of my head down onto him and stared back up at the stars. I wondered what he was thinking about; if he was thinking anything. I hadn't been thinking about anything.

Once the edible weighed down on us we stared at each other giggling and trying to undo each other's pants. But, we became distracted by the stars.

"Yeah," Bishop repeated. The stars were beautiful. I hoped he thought the same. I felt Bishop slowly swallow and smack his dry mouth. "Do you think there's anything else up there? Besides religion, don't get going on all of that."

I laughed. Surprisingly, we did not talk about religion much. I felt like we were too drunk with each other to care about anything that was arguable.

"Maybe. I don't really care."

"Yeah. Me neither."

I pulled my head up so that I looked down at him. I opened my mouth to say something, but I forgot what words had been forming on my tongue. I looked upward, trying so hard to remember whatever I had been thinking. But, nothing.

Bishop's fingers landed on my cheek. He caressed the skin. He stared hard at my skin. I felt his gaze invading my pores, just as I was looking at his skin. Sometimes, I felt like there wasn't enough of him to look at. I wanted to see everything. I had, but it would never be enough. I wanted to see every thought he had and every inch of his soul and mind. And, I wanted him to see me the same.

"I love you," Bishop whispered, his fingers at my lips. I bit down on the tip of his thumb, smiling hard.

"I love you."

I did. I had never, ever, felt this before. I felt so full and content. I felt like I finally had completed what I needed to complete. Everything I did now felt so elegant, so beautiful. I felt like I saw the world differently now; I felt it differently. All because of love.

I never wanted to be a girl who changed once she got into a relationship. But, I had. I'd changed for the better. I was so fucking happy.

"I don't want to marry," Bishop began. I knew he didn't. I had agreed. It was too traditional for him and I loved him enough to stray from my traditions. "But, I love you enough to marry you."

I smiled, leaning my head back against him. The edible felt heavy, the love even heavier. "You can be so romantic, you know that?"

Bishop laughed, his hands returning to my back. "Do you like it?"

"I do." It was true; I did. I loved him. I liked this town. I liked his friends (besides Baylen). And, I liked my life. I was at peace with it all. If I were to die tomorrow, I would be happy. I'd be content. I'd fallen in love, and it felt so, so good. I loved him more than anything. Every part. But, if I told him all that he would call me cliche and try to wrestle with me.

"Good," was all he said. We lay there for the rest of the night.

Extra Scene
Four

Bishop and I were an entangled mess of limbs. We stumbled up the steps of our home. My hands were lost in his hair, and his lips were moving hard against mine. His hand was up my dress, and down the hem of my panties.

I moaned into his mouth as his fingers curled inside of my cunt.

"Shit, Bishop." I couldn't walk. I wished we could blink our way into his bedroom, rather than walking across this absurdly large house. I wanted him now.

"Yeah." Bishop pulled his lips away. His forehead was against mine. Heavy breaths intertwined with mine. "Does it feel good, pretty girl?"

I nodded and whimpered. It felt more than good; it was indescribable.

Bishop's back was to the staircase we were unsuccessful in climbing up. He twirled us around so that it was now me with my back to the stairs. In a swift movement, he pushed me backward but wrapped his arms around my waist so that I did not fall hard.

I smiled into his mouth. "Full circle." Kiss. "Hm?"

He smiled harder against my lips. He fiddled with his belt. I grabbed the loops of his pants, yanking them downward. His cock sprung out of his boxers, grazing my forearm. I grabbed his cock, stroking him to the pace he curled inside of me.

I lifted my hips upward until they hit his. He helped me with the fabric of my panties, yanking them down to my ankles. He grabbed the lace and stuffed it into his back pocket; I think he stole my underwear just so we had an excuse to go shopping for more.

"Do you want me to dry fuck you again?" His lips twitched, and he looked down at my legs. "I love being inside, but we can go back to that if you want."

I shook my head. I rolled my hips against his hand. "No. I want you to fuck me."

Bishop grinned, disappearing between my thighs. I reached behind me, holding onto the stairs for support. My other hand, the one that had been around his cock, went to his hair. It felt like I needed to hold onto him when he went down on me. Like I was going to ascend.

His fingers slid out of me. I gritted my teeth and arched my neck. I needed him back inside of me. He left quick kisses on my inner thigh and the apex of my thigh. Occasionally he would bite, leaving dark marks along my skin. Unfortunately, he kept his mouth on my legs, and away from my pussy.

"Look how wet you are." Bishop slid back inside of me. I shuddered and my head hit the stairs hard. He curled his fingers inside of me, once, before pulling the digits out. His fingers were coated in the need for him. There was a string of arousal connecting his fingers and my cunt. He leaned in, lapping all of it up with my tongue.

Bishop may be the death of me.

My pussy tightened around his fingers. I clenched my eyes shut, shaking my head. "Shit Bishop. Get inside of me before I come."

He did not need to be told twice.

Bishop moved upward until he hovered above me. I kept my hands in his hair as he repositioned between my legs. He stroked his cock, once, twice, thrice. I knew he had a condom in his room, but I did not care. It was too far.

"Ready?"

I nodded. I noticed that Bishop would always ask before we fucked. Even when we were high, or on the rare rare occasion we were drunk, he would still ask. I appreciated him for that.

Bishop looked down at where we were about to be conjoined. I shuddered as the tip of his cock slid up and down my slit. My arousal was mixing with his own on the tip of his cock. Anything that was his was mine. Cum included.

I bit my lip as he slid inside of me. I choked as his length filled and stretched me. Never, ever, would I be used to how full he made me feel. I didn't know how I'd gone so long without feeling this. It felt so good, but I knew it was him that made it feel good. It wouldn't feel like this with anyone; it felt so good because I loved him.

"Shit, you feel good." He let out a shuddered breath. He reminded me of it every time. The chokes and moans I let out reminded him of how good he felt.

"Oh, fuck," I groaned. I threw my head backward against the stairs, clamping my eyes shut.

"Eyes on me," Bishop warned, clicking his tongue. He went still inside of me. I groaned before opening my eyes and looking at him. The eye contact made it all too intense. I was going to come too fast if I watched him.

Bishop pulled out of me, before pushing himself back hard inside of me. "Good girl." My stomach flipped at his words.

His thrusts were slow, and hard. It was much more intense like this. I liked it more than the rough sex we usually had; this was intimate and hard. I matched his thrusts and rolled my hips against his at the same pace.

I was tightening and loosening around him, so close to coming. "Please," I gasped. My eyes were fluttering shut, but I focused on keeping them open. I feared he'd stop.

He didn't stop. He pulled out and pushed harder inside of me. And harder. And harder. I couldn't take it much longer.

"Yeah? Does it feel good?" Bishop grinned when he spoke. One hand landed on my breasts. The side of his thumb brushed against my tight buds. I hadn't even taken off my dress; I couldn't waste any more time without him inside of me.

The other hand landed on the side of my head. He held himself in place as his hard, snappy thrusts picked up. My breasts bounced with every movement, and choked cries slipped out of me, and into his lips.

"Mhm," I whined. I reached for his back, holding onto him. My stomach stopped tightening and releasing. It started to tighten. And tighten. The feeling was about to burst inside of me. I felt myself dip, and the feeling of being unable to stop ensued.

Bishop's cock began to swell inside of me. This was the point he'd usually pull out and paint some part of me. Then finish me with his fingers. But, I didn't want him to pull out; I wanted him to keep hitting right where he was. I wanted him to cum inside of me.

"Bishop," I croaked. He pulled his head upward so that it was hovering above me. His lips brushed against mine with every rock. "Come in me."

His hand stilled against my breasts, but his pace picked up. "Are you sure?"

It was a terrible idea, but we would figure it out. I nodded. "Please."

Bishop nodded against my face. He pulled my lip into his teeth. His thrusts were becoming harder and harder. I couldn't feel him leaking, but I could feel my fullness becoming warmer, and warmer, as if something warm were spilling. I smiled. I'd always wanted him to do this, but I was too afraid.

"Are you sure?" Bishop asked again. His breathing was choppy, and his words were more of a groan.

I nodded again. I appreciated every part of him.

Bishop swelled as my core tightened, and within a few more thrusts it all burst. His swelling became too much and eventually, it peaked inside of me. I felt something warm and thick fill me. It was deep; it felt so terribly good.

I cried out as I came. My arms were around his neck, holding onto him as he fucked me through the orgasm. He continued to fuck me, even after he had filled me. He only stopped when he began to soften.

When he pulled out of me, a string of cum leaked out of me, and onto my thighs. Both Bishop and I looked down toward where the cum was currently seeping out of me. I feared I'd want to do it again. We hadn't spoken of children yet. I needed to get on birth control; that felt too good.

"That was the best feeling in the world," Bishop said. He tucked his slick cock into his pants, and I pulled down my dress. I could still feel him leaking out of me; there was so much cum.

"It was." My lips perked. It felt too good for the danger of children attached to it.

Bishop leaned down toward my thigh. He planted a kiss on my knee, staring up at me with his eyelashes covering his vision. "You are so beautiful." He planted a kiss on my other knee. "And good."

I leaned my head back on the stairs. If he didn't stop talking, we were about to fuck again. I reached my fingers for his neck; it was covered in bruises. Sex was definitely our way of expressing our love. Touch and pleasure. "You are too."

"I love you." Bishop kissed my inner thigh this time. I caught a glimpse of some of his cum on the bottom of his lip. Or it was mine. I wasn't sure.

"I love you." I smiled, pulling him back down onto the stairs with me.

BADDIES CLUB

Thank you so much for reading!!!

There will be more books after this. I have plans upon plans. Keep an eye out on my social media for updates. I appreciate it. The QR code above has all of my socials and will update regularly if I get more. It also has my Spotify which has playlists dedicated to the boys!! This was my debut and I published it to get over my fear of publishing. I am terrified lol. But, thank you and make sure to post TikTok's or pictures with the books and tag me!! See you bad bitches in the next one.

www.ingramcontent.com/pod-product-compliance
Lightning Source LLC
Chambersburg PA
CBHW070610300726
48975CB00006B/1773